T0269741

# Murder in the Ranks

# Murder in the Ranks

A NOVEL

Kristi Jones

NEW YORK

This is a work of fiction. All of the names, characters, organizations, places and events portrayed in this novel are either products of the author's imagination or are used fictitiously. Any resemblance to real or actual events, locales, or persons, living or dead, is entirely coincidental.



Published in the United States by Crooked Lane Books, an imprint of The Quick Brown Fox & Company LLC.

Crooked Lane Books and its logo are trademarks of The Quick Brown Fox & Company LLC.

Library of Congress Catalog-in-Publication data available upon request.

ISBN (hardcover): 978-1-63910-971-5
ISBN (ebook): 978-1-63910-972-2

Cover design by Lynn Andreozzi

Printed in the United States.

www.crookedlanebooks.com

Crooked Lane Books
34 West 27th St., 10th Floor
New York, NY 10001

First Edition: November 2024

10 9 8 7 6 5 4 3 2 1

*This book is dedicated*
*to the brave women who served with*
*the 149th Post Headquarters Company*

# Chapter 1

*U.S. Army Navy Dance*
*Algiers Opera House, Bresson Square*
*12 February 1943*
*1900 Hours*

I stared across the smoke-filled auditorium, searching for each member of my squad. I had two jobs tonight. First, ensure Squad B acted in accordance with Army regulations and returned safely back to barracks at twenty-one hundred hours; and second, dance with sweaty GIs.

Couples crowded the stage of the Algiers Opera House. The Maurice Sarner Band, local to Algiers, played a shrill rendition of "Dancing in the Dark" while I smiled and pretended to have a good time. Soldiers and sailors danced with French girls, American and British nurses, and my fellow WAACs. The Army had requisitioned the opera house for social functions shortly after the Allied invasion of North Africa. Located in the heart of Bresson Square, facing the port and the glittering Mediterranean Sea below, the four-story building was partially concealed by tall palm trees and banana shrubs planted along the wide sidewalks of the Boulevard de la Republique. Like much of downtown Algiers, the area was of French design.

The Army-issue utility bag slung around my neck kept my current dance partner from getting too close, but he was trying, nonetheless. They all tried. Since arriving in Algiers, we spent an inordinate amount of time fending off amorous GIs. Officers, enlisted men, British and Australian men—even local Frenchmen—constantly pestered us for dates. But we weren't stationed at Allied Force Headquarters to snag boyfriends. We were here to release men for combat.

"You're one of the Double D's," Private Tommy Wainwright said.

"I'm with the Twenty-Second Post Headquarters Company, yes." We called ourselves the Double Deuces, but the men had chosen a different nickname. Not for the first time, I wondered if the Army planned our company name to coincide with the largest bra size in America.

"You're the first American girl I've danced with in months. We heard about you gals, but honestly, I didn't think it was real."

"Well, we are the first American women soldiers assigned to a combat theater," I said, proud to be serving and not afraid to let this young man know I was more than a dancing partner.

"Do you work for the general?"

Everyone knew that "the general" was General Dwight D. Eisenhower, Supreme Commander of all Allied forces in North Africa. General Eisenhower was the reason the Women's Army Auxiliary Corps was in Algiers. After the invasion in November, the supreme commander quickly realized he needed more men to fight the Nazis in North Africa. While in England, he'd seen firsthand how British women in service helped the war effort, and decided America's women soldiers could replace men in rear-echelon positions, releasing them for duty at the front.

"No, I work in the Adjutant General's office," I shouted back.

Private Wainwright's hand tightened in mine. "Hey, maybe you could extend my leave for a few days? Or give me a permanent post here in the city?"

I forced a laugh. It was a common joke. I'd heard it more than a dozen times from various soldiers when they found out where I worked. I wished I did have the authority to type up new orders and send him right home. I wished I could send them all home. But the hard truth was that too many boys would never go home. They would fight, die, and be buried in the dry desert sands in small, quickly constructed cemeteries across North Africa. The only way to stop the dying was to win the war. Everything depended on winning the war.

"I'm afraid it doesn't work like that, Private."

"I'm just joshing you." He gave me a sheepish smile. "We all want our chance to kick Rommel across the desert and all the way back to Germany."

Back to Germany. I wanted to get back to Germany myself, although I couldn't admit that to Private Wainwright. Or anybody else in my company.

Across the room, I saw Auxiliary Ruth Wentz dancing with "the Octopus."

The Octopus was one Private Carlos Rivera. He was charismatic and handsome with dark hair, dark eyes, and a glittering smile of white, even teeth. He focused his attentions on Ruth most of the time, which surprised me. Ruth wasn't unattractive, but her oft-pronounced goal in life was to be the Army's best soldier. Some of the other girls enjoyed the social requirements of our job, but Ruth always approached them like just another duty. Private Rivera was barking up the wrong tree, lavishing so much attention on Ruth.

"Did you get that scar on the way over?"

I stumbled, bumping elbows with a nearby couple. People rarely asked outright about the forked scar on my forehead. I resisted the urge to rub the raised flesh. My overseas cap dropped down, pointing at the scar like an arrow on a map. Memories of my husband punching a hole in our bedroom wall flooded my brain. I tightened my grip on Private Wainwright's hand.

I was safe.

I was an auxiliary in the Women's Army Auxiliary Corps.

I was a soldier and I belonged here. "No. Car accident back home." The lie was easy as long as he didn't ask me to elaborate. Luckily, the loud music restricted lengthy conversation.

"That's too bad."

I just smiled and nodded, closing the subject.

The song ended and I extricated myself from the boy's arms. I guessed he was at least ten years my junior. I knew I looked much younger than my twenty-nine years. I had my mother's round face and upturned nose that gave an impression of youth, but inside I felt years older. When I looked in the mirror, I saw haunted green eyes standing out starkly against dark circles and paper-pale skin. If anyone cared to look closely, they'd surely see the hard years etched across my face, but I had learned few people looked closely at anything but themselves. "Thank you for the dance, Private."

"One more?" He ran a hand over his hair and licked his lips, blue eyes hopeful.

He was a nice kid, and it was with some regret that I declined. Across the dance floor, Private Rivera held Ruth indecently close, speaking into her ear. Ruth drew back, eyes narrowed.

"I could get us some battery acid," Private Wainwright said, his voice plaintive. Battery acid was what the boys called Army-issue lemonade. The lemon-juice powder tasted like cleaning fluid, especially when mixed with the chlorinated water we had to drink.

"If it was a Coke, I might just take you up on it." I was only half kidding. I missed my weekly treat of drinking a Coke at the soda shop counter with my daughter. Even with all the deprivations in Algiers, sometimes I missed Coke more than I missed bathing. Or maybe I missed it so much because Sadie always looked forward to the treat each week. Thoughts of Sadie were never far from my mind. I pushed away the image of Sadie's Mary Janes dangling from the stool at the soda fountain in Galveston.

Private Wainwright leaned down close again. I smelled brandy on his breath. Brandy was scarcer than soap. He must have bought some on the black market or from a British officer. "We can spike the lemonade. I've got some hootch."

"I'm sorry, Private, but it's almost curfew. The trucks will be here soon to take us back to barracks."

"Aw, c'mon." He looked at his watch. "It's only twenty after seven."

"Sorry, Private. Duty calls." I didn't have time for a second dance. I wanted to make sure Ruth was all right, and I had five other women to keep track of. I took my job as squad leader seriously. I was grateful for the opportunity and for the trust First Officer Fitzgerald had in my abilities. If Fitzgerald knew my full history, she probably wouldn't trust me with KP duty, much less the care of a squad of six women soldiers stationed in a combat theater. But Fitzgerald knew nothing about my past, and I was determined to keep it that way.

"Oh, c'mon," he said again, wrapping his arms around my waist, doing his best impression of the Octopus. "This might be my last dance. Aren't you here to boost my morale?"

I bit my bottom lip, swallowing back the words I wanted to say. Arguing with drunk soldiers only led to more problems. Instead, I stomped hard on his booted foot. Private Wainwright drew back, startled, and I took the opportunity to step away. My uncomfortable Army-issue Oxford browns were good for something, at least.

The young GI shifted his gaze away, clearly embarrassed. "I guess I can wait until next week. If I'm still here."

"Right. Maybe next time." I instantly regretted the words. I'd only been in Algiers for a few weeks, but I knew I'd probably never see Private Wainwright again. And judging by the sudden seriousness in his young face, he knew it better than I did.

A heavy sadness settled into the pit of my stomach. The situation in Algiers and all of North Africa was fluid. Boys arrived and were ordered to various posts at Allied Force Headquarters and in companies all around the city. Signal, Medical, Chemical Warfare, and countless other departments needed men. But the most pressing demand was for combat troops.

The ranks in Tunisia had been reduced after the recent battles around Longstop Hill. Our office was swamped with cables from the War Department, issuing orders to move men and materials to the front as fast as possible. Men in Algiers, initially assigned to Allied Force Headquarters, were being reassigned to combat positions by the hour. By the time the next dance rolled around, Wainwright could be fighting the enemy in Tunisia. Or he could be dead.

I felt a pang of something like guilt at the thought of Private Wainwright being reassigned to a combat unit. But the brave young soldier smiled at me, as if he were oblivious to the real reason for my presence in this war. As if we really were here simply to boost morale. "I'll come find you next time I'm in town, whenever that is, Miss Lincoln. Don't you think I won't."

I smiled in return, not bothering to correct his use of the word *Miss* instead of *Auxiliary*. Enlisted men rarely treated the WAACs like real soldiers. "Make sure you do, Private."

Across the room, Ruth turned her head away and pushed at Private Rivera's chest, struggling to escape his octopus arms. Ruth was a good soldier and no stranger to roughhousing and rough manners. If it were anyone else, I would have already intervened. But I suspected Ruth would resent the intrusion and the implication that she couldn't handle herself. Still, Rivera was making a scene, and it was my job to ensure the safety of the squad. It was also my job to make sure the women acted in accordance with Army regulations and the WAAC Code of Conduct, which meant the scene playing out across the room had to be stopped before it escalated.

"You can call me Tommy."

"Okay, Tommy. It was nice to meet you."

Tommy looked like he wanted to say more. I leaned close and kissed him briefly on the cheek. I knew what he wanted to ask, and I had to stop him. They always wanted to be pen pals. I hated to say no, but I wasn't a free woman.

The kiss worked as expected. He was momentarily stunned into silence.

I gave him a warm smile. The warmest smile I could muster, anyway. Exhaustion gritted my eyes. I'd had a long day, and these nights were always hard after working an early shift. But I needed to stay alert.

"Abyssinia, Miss Lincoln."

*Abyssinia* was a worn-out joke the soldiers used, all run together to say *"I'll be seeing you."* But I wasn't really listening.

Ruth and Rivera had moved off the stage and into the side aisle of the theater. Private Rivera reached out and touched Ruth's face. She jerked her head aside and turned away from him.

Rivera grabbed Ruth by the arm, yanking her hard. Ruth spun around, her hand raised, ready to strike.

Without a word of goodbye to Private Tommy Wainwright, I pushed my way through the crowd. I should have stepped in sooner instead of making small talk with a lonely soldier and reminiscing about ancient history I couldn't change. *Dammit.* I wasn't here to dance in the dark. I was here to watch over my squad, and it seemed I was failing already.

# CHAPTER 2

I forced my feet forward through the crowd of dancing couples and into the aisle. My heartbeat jumped, and I took several shallow steadying breaths. Private Rivera was *not* my husband, and I was not the frightened housewife I'd been before joining the Army. I was squad leader, and it was my responsibility to protect Ruth.

"I said *no*, and I mean it, Rivera," Ruth said as I walked up to them.

"I'm sorry, Ruthie," Rivera said. "You know I didn't mean it."

Hearing those words, my heartbeat slowed, and I felt a measure of relief. He was sorry. The situation was resolving itself.

"C'mon, Ruth. Let's just dance." He winked at me, but his words were for Ruth.

Ruth glanced at the onlookers. She lifted her chin, doing her best impression of a commanding general. "My feet need a rest, Private."

"Aw, c'mon—you love this song." The first strains of "Only Forever" filled the auditorium. The French-accented singer for the Maurice Sarner Band began the song slightly off-key.

"Wentz!" I said, hoping I sounded firm and not frightened. "It's about time to move out."

Rivera frowned. "It's not time yet. It can't be."

"It's time to get to the assembly area," I insisted, stepping between Ruth and Rivera.

I was so tired of dealing with men. Flirtatious men, drunk men, scared men, shy men. Then there were the brutish, angry men who made it very clear they did not like the WAACs. They frightened me, but I did my best to hide my fear.

I reminded myself that most of the boys just wanted to talk to American girls. To have a moment of normality and familiarity in this strange country. The first week of our arrival, men had come from all over, some of them hiking miles into town from their camps in the deserts of French North Africa, just to hear the sound of an American woman's voice. Demand was so high that our company commander had posted a sign-up sheet in the first orderly's office so we could take turns attending dances. Otherwise, we'd scarcely have time for our jobs. Every WAAC had to do her bit, but I was thankful the social events came to a close at nine o'clock. Only a couple of hours left. Private Rivera was right. It was nowhere near time to line up for the trucks. But he didn't need to know that.

"Find yourself another girl, Private."

"There is no other girl for me." Rivera darted to my left, trying to circle around me to get to Ruth. I stumbled into the couple dancing behind me. I waved my arms, trying to catch my balance, and failed. I hit the ground, landing on my side. Pain shot up through my hip. Embarrassed and shaking from the physical impact, I quickly rolled to a sitting position. Dancers spread out around me. I flushed and planted my palms to get purchase. The sooner I lifted myself to a standing position, the sooner I regained control of the situation. But my hip throbbed and my limbs shook. I rubbed at the scar on my forehead, pushing back images of all the times I'd ended up sprawled on the floor after an argument with my long-gone husband.

*Get up.*

But I couldn't do it. I was afraid my shaking legs wouldn't hold me. I was afraid everyone could see the weak little woman I hated so much. It wasn't fear I felt in that moment, but embarrassment. A bone-deep, pervasive shame at being bested by this slightly drunk, overzealous GI.

Corporal Pinski broke through the crowd. He knelt down beside me, and I felt more ashamed than ever. "Dottie, are you okay?"

All I could do was nod.

He held out a hand and I took it. What choice did I have?

He heaved me to my feet. "What the hell happened?"

"Nothing." I avoided Private Rivera's gaze and forced a laugh. "Guess I tripped over my own feet."

Corporal Pinski squeezed my arm. "It happens."

Corporal Pinski stood over six feet tall. Despite his massive size, he was soft-spoken, pale, and gentle. He'd landed in Algiers with the Center Task Force at Oran on D-Day for Operation Torch back in November. Like most men assigned to the rear echelon, he wanted to be at the front. But unlike his buddies in the Adjutant General's office, who made no secret of their annoyance at having to work with females, Corporal Pinski had been an ally since day one. He was kind instead of condescending, respectful instead of flirtatious. He sent money home to his mother back in Indiana every week. All the girls in the Adjutant General's office liked him.

Private Rivera held his arms out, as if to reach for me. I recoiled. Another flood of shame rained down on me. He was just trying to help, and I was acting like a frightened rabbit about to have its neck wrung. "Hey, I'm really sorry. I didn't mean for that to happen," he said, his eyes meeting mine.

"Auxiliary Wentz," Corporal Pinski said, eyes narrowed, "is this dogface bothering you?"

"I'm okay, Corporal."

"This isn't any of your business, Corporal," Private Rivera said. He reached for Ruth, but Pinski placed a hand squarely on his chest and shoved Rivera back. Private Rivera stumbled, fists clenched.

"Hey, what's the big idea?"

Pinski ignored him. "How about a dance, Ruth?"

Private Rivera scowled at Pinski but didn't move to intervene again. "Pulling rank on me, Corporal?"

Pinski looked amused. "If that's what it takes to get you gone, then sure."

The top of Rivera's head sat about chest high to Corporal Pinski. He was handsy, but he was no fool. Rivera pulled at his uniform shirt. I suspected he was sweating bullets underneath. He might act tough, but Corporal Pinski was his superior in this man's Army. "That's all right," he said with a sneer. "Always wanted to see you dance, Corporal. The Army could sell tickets, don'tcha think, ladies?" He cupped his hands around his mouth, and shouted, "Make way, folks, make way! Elephant on the dance floor!"

But the crowd was too busy dancing to Bing Crosby to pay attention to Private Rivera's childish taunting.

"C'mon, Ruth," Rivera said, holding up his hands like a supplicant. "You know you'd rather dance with me."

I noted the hope in his voice. Did the Octopus have real feelings for Ruth?

"Don't put her on the spot like that, Rivera. She's already accepted a dance with me."

Rivera looked from Ruth to Corporal Pinski. "Fine then. What do I care? Plenty of fish in a foreign sea, right, Corporal?"

Private Rivera looked at Ruth as if expecting some kind of answer. But Ruth avoided his gaze. His shoulders dropped, and with a small shake of his head, he turned and skulked off into the crowd.

It appeared he had a small crush on Ruth. Or maybe he was just annoyed that another man had encroached on his claimed territory.

"What do you say, Ruth?" Corporal Pinski asked again. "One last dance before curfew? I promise to keep my hands to myself."

"I don't know, Corporal. I'm pretty tired."

"We'll make it a quick one. I have to get back to the office anyway." Corporal Pinski glanced at the stage. The band struck up the "Jersey Bounce," and couples had turned away from the altercation and gone back to dancing. "It'll put that scene to bed."

Ruth gave Pinski a tired smile. "Sure. One last dance."

Ruth pulled her utility bag over her head and held it out to me. "Will you hold this for me, Lincoln?"

"Sure thing." I slung the utility bag across my chest, in the opposite direction of my own bag. I was fitted out like a paratrooper with two chutes.

Ruth leaned in close, her breath tickling my ear. "Meet me in the courtyard after lights out. *Please.*"

The request startled me. Ruth was the consummate soldier. She followed the rules. Always. Meeting after lights out was against regulations. Going anywhere after lights out was against regulations, though I knew some of the girls did sneak out occasionally. Sometimes to drink French wine and smoke, sometimes to meet a soldier. But Ruth never joined in. Whatever she wanted to talk about, it must be something important.

I clutched Ruth's bag and watched Corporal Pinski swing Ruth onto the dance floor. I'd never seen any sign that Ruth had any feelings for Corporal Pinski, but handing over the bag could only mean one thing. She wanted to be close to him. Had Ruth and Corporal Pinski struck up a romance while working together in the Adjutant General's office? I scoured my memory for some sign they'd been anything other than work colleagues, and came up empty. Whatever Ruth wanted to talk about, I had a feeling my night was going to be long and difficult.

# CHAPTER 3

I checked my wristwatch. Two hours to go. I scanned the auditorium. Where was the rest of my squad? With all the commotion between Rivera and Ruth, I'd lost track of them.

Jean Kirksey's laugh rang out, loud and brash. I spotted her in the lobby, just outside the auditorium. She had her arms draped across the shoulders of two GIs, one on each side. A third stood in front of her and brushed his thumb across the brass Athena pin on her lapel, his hand resting dangerously close to Kirksey's left breast. That was definitely *not* what our insignia was meant for.

I sighed and rubbed my forehead. The women in my squad weren't making my job easy tonight. I strode into the lobby. "Hey, Kirksey, want to go get some battery acid?"

Kirksey blinked and turned her unfocused gaze my way. "Dottie!" she exclaimed, flashing a crooked smile.

She released the two GIs and threw her arms around my neck. She smelled of chewing gum and sweat. "We're invited to a party." She turned to the three soldiers, each one looking from one to another.

I pulled back from Kirksey's hold. She was short and sweet, with an eager smile full of slightly crooked teeth, and a southern drawl that deepened when she was in her cups. "I think maybe you've partied enough for one night, Jeannie."

"Oh, don't be such an old fusspot, Dottie." Kirksey's Mississippi drawl added an extra syllable to my name. She was most definitely drunk. "Besides," she said, drawing out the word to impossible lengths, "I can be late tomorrow. The general won't—"

"Auxiliary," I snapped, shaking her arm roughly. "Get control of yourself this instant."

Kirksey slapped a hand over her mouth. "Oh gawd."

The GIs stepped back, eyes wide.

Kirksey blinked, licked her lips. She rubbed a hand across her mouth. "I'm sorry, Dottie. I didn't mean—" She glanced at the three GIs, but they were already melting into the crowd.

I steered her toward the outer doors. "Get control of yourself, Jeannie," I said, keeping my voice low. "You'll get sent home if anyone else hears that kind of talk. What would the general think?"

Kirksey was one of General Eisenhower's drivers. She spent her days hanging around the St. George Hotel, waiting to be called on to drive the general or one of his staff around town. She knew the city of Algiers as well as she knew the roads and backroads of her hometown in Jackson, Mississippi. She was also entrusted with General Eisenhower's schedule. If any enemy agents heard her reveal information on his whereabouts, she could be in serious trouble. Auxiliaries weren't regular Army, so we couldn't be court-martialed. But I had no doubt the Army would come up with some kind of awful punishment for such transgressions. The real danger, however, was risking the entire war effort with loose lips.

"I'm sorry, Dottie." Kirksey laid a hand across her chest. "Gawd, I can't believe I said that."

"You could put him in danger, Jeannie. We never know who might be listening."

"I know." Kirksey shook her head and took in a couple of sharp breaths. "I'd die if something happened because of me. No more wine for me, Dottie." She gave a shaky laugh. "Maybe ever."

"Don't forget, you represent the Women's Army Auxiliary Corps, Jeannie. Loose lips sink ships. And running off at the mouth only proves what they're saying about us—that we don't belong here."

"I know. I do. I know better." Kirksey gave her head another little shake. She tucked her curly ink-black hair behind her ears and straightened the sleeves of her uniform shirt. She sucked in a breath and met my gaze. "I'll do better."

Kirksey didn't mean any harm. Like most of the girls, she was still learning her place here. But I needed to keep a closer watch over Kirksey's drinking.

"Good. Did you check your coat?"

Kirksey nodded.

"Let's get it and go outside for some fresh air."

"Do you think Mary needs saving?" Kirksey asked, changing the subject.

I gazed across the lobby at a couple moving into the shadows of the south staircase. "I think our Mary is smitten. She might take your head off if you tried to 'save' her now."

"Hard not to be. Him being a duke and all."

"He's not a duke."

Kirksey shrugged. "Duke. Earl. What's the difference?"

"He certainly seems to have won Mary over," I said, ignoring Kirksey's ignorance of the British peerage. Mary gazed up at Captain Haywynn, a dreamy smile stretching her heart-shaped mouth. Mary was the youngest in our company. Naive, pretty, and overly dramatic, she also gave me the most trouble. She had trouble following Army regulations, for one thing. And she was constantly focused on the men. Most recently, her attentions had landed on a British officer, Captain Haywynn, who also happened to be an aristocrat. The Earl of Rockfell was of medium height. In fact, everything about him looked medium to me. He had unremarkable features and a rather weak chin, and walked as if he had sciatica. But the few times I had spoken to him, he had been courteous and pleasant. And he undoubtedly had a thing for Auxiliary Mary Jordan.

British and American officers acted as chaperones at every dance. Although there were regulations against fraternization, many officers ignored the rules if it meant they could get a date with an American girl, enlisted or not. The enlisted men resented the hell out of the officers poaching in their field, but there wasn't much they could do about it. More than one so-called chaperone was dancing with a WAAC. I suspected the young earl had volunteered to chaperone the dance just to be with Auxiliary Jordan.

"She's gone khaki-wacky like everyone else. Well, everyone but you, that is."

"I think it might be a little more than a crush."

"Really?" Kirksey cocked her head, staring at the couple. "You think they're in love?"

"Who knows? Who cares?" Auxiliary Sue Dunworthy materialized out of the crowd like an unwanted guest. Sue was a dark-haired beauty from Tennessee, with penetrating eyes and a Betty Grable figure, visible despite the boxy, unflattering WAAC uniform. I suspected Sue had done some tailoring on her uniform that did not comply with Army regulations. Some of the girls resented Sue for her looks. Maybe they were jealous of her easy beauty, while the rest of us struggled to stay feminine in olive drab and cold saltwater showers. Add to that a distinct lack of soap. Nobody in Algiers smelled particularly good. Most nights, I dreamed about a hot bath with French milled soap and a good hair rinse. I suspected I wasn't the only one.

"Good evening, ladies!" Sue led a suntanned MP with rheumy eyes and a bulbous nose by the hand. He appeared happy to follow.

Kirksey growled, "Another boyfriend. How do you do it, dung beetle?"

"Shut up, Kirksey," Sue said with a lazy smile. Her full, lush lips were often curved in a knowing smile that unsettled me. "Jealousy dulls the complexion."

"Enjoying the dance, Dunworthy?" I asked, putting a hand on Kirksey's arm. I could feel the young woman's anger emanating like heat from a furnace. Sue was a member of Squad B and worked with me in the Adjutant General's office. For reasons unknown to me, Kirksey and Dunworthy had been at each other's throats since our first week in Algiers.

"Why wouldn't we be?" She leaned closer. "Listen up, girls. Gar's found a woman selling silk handkerchiefs in the Casbah. If you're interested, get with me later tonight."

Kirksey drew back. "The Casbah's off-limits to American soldiers."

Sue threw back her head and laughed. She gave her MP a conspiratorial wink. "*We* don't go to the Casbah, silly girl. Gar here has a contact who meets him on the street outside the Casbah. So, are you interested?"

Kirksey shrugged. "Maybe. How much?"

"It's against regulations to buy black-market items," I reminded them. I didn't trust Sue. She was the type of girl my mother had warned me about: a little too calculating, a bit too sly. No wonder men found her so intriguing.

Sue lifted one shoulder. "Who says they're black market? And anyway, even if they were, what could you possibly do about it?"

I just blinked at her, too stunned to reply.

Sue laughed and slapped my arm playfully. "I'm joshing you, Lincoln. But really, if they are black market, there isn't much you or anyone in the WAAC can do about it. We have no power here, doll."

I frowned. What Sue said was true. As an auxiliary force, WAACs weren't subject to military law. We operated under a strict code of conduct, but any infractions were met with mere reprimands and restrictions.

The civilian population in Algiers didn't have much. The Germans and Vichy government officials had pretty much picked the city clean during their occupation. The newly formed North African Trade Board did its best to regulate the sale and distribution of foodstuffs and supplies to thc civilian population, but there were back-alley deals for all sorts of things, from French perfume and brandy to gold and precious gems. But silk was needed for the war effort. I would have to talk to Fitzgerald about it. I had no power to stop the black market in Algiers. But surely First Officer Fitzgerald had the power to stop the girls from dealing in it.

"If I see a silk handkerchief during inspections, it will be confiscated, and disciplinary action will be taken," I said, trying to sound stern.

Sue sighed, rolled her eyes, then whispered something into Gar's ear. He leaned closer and spun Sue toward the auditorium.

"Be at the assembly area at twenty thirty, Dunworthy," I shouted after them. "We're due back at barracks by twenty-one hundred hours on the dot."

Sue raised a hand but didn't look back. Private Gar slipped an arm around Sue's waist as they disappeared into the auditorium.

Kirksey sighed heavily and swayed on her feet.

"Come on, Jeannie," I said, slipping my arm through Kirksey's. "Let's get you some air."

# CHAPTER 4

The air outside was crisp and cool. Despite the blackout, Bresson Square bustled with activity. A soft quarter moon glowed in the cloudless night sky, highlighting the harbor down below. Algiers hugged the curving coastline, gently embracing the bay. Across the Boulevard de la Republique stretched a wide sidewalk built by the French in the last century, a perfect place to gaze out to sea. Barrage balloons hovered above, and the silhouette of Allied ship rigging signaled a dark reminder of the reason we were all here in Algiers.

I pulled my olive drab overcoat closed, taking comfort in the warmth provided by the heavy wool. The coat was Army issue for the men and fell to my ankles, but it did the job. The Double Deuces had not been issued winter uniforms, and so we'd all been given male uniform coats and jackets, scrounged up from supply. The moon emitted enough light to ease the tension I always felt at night. The faint scent of the sea mixed with diesel fuel and lube oil from the ships bobbing gently in the harbor was oddly reassuring.

"It's like a scene from the movie, isn't it? *Algiers*. Did you ever see it? Sometimes I expect to see Hedy Lamar sashaying down the street." Kirksey pulled her uniform jacket closed, shivering. "Or running for her life."

"We're safe here, Jeannie. We have the entire United States Army to protect us."

Jeannie nodded but she didn't look convinced. She smiled at a group of children darting across the square.

A few French civilians walked arm in arm or in groups, noticeable for their Western dress. Native children wore oversized shoes, probably stolen, and moth-eaten sweaters over patched trousers. They sold tangerines and almonds, wine, and olives. A French policeman in his boxy hat and leather holster patrolled the square, but I had never seen a deal interrupted, whether the exchange was for cigarettes or something seedier. Spahi guards also patrolled the square, bayonets gleaming in the moonlight. Their blood-red capes billowed in the breeze. They walked like specters in the night, relics of a time before mechanized warfare, when pirates raided the Barbary Coast. Algiers was a study in contrasts between the Old World and the New. I sometimes felt as if I'd stepped back in time. But then a jeep would rumble by, or an aircraft would fly overhead, and I'd be jolted back to the very real and dangerous present.

During the day, the square would be filled to bursting with French civilians and Arab women and men, and more children. Despite the war raging in the east, the people of Algiers went about their daily lives much as they had before the war. They went to work. They dined in cafés and restaurants. They rode the trolley down to the beach, to frolic in the warm Mediterranean waters. But underneath the bustle of normality was a tension that came from being an occupied city.

French civilians lived under the administration of the Fascist Vichy government, not much different from the very Nazis we were fighting. French prisons and concentration camps across North Africa were filled with French and Arab victims of the regime. The Arab and indigenous Berber population had been struggling under French rule for centuries. The place was a powder keg of conflicting nations and ethnic groups, all loosely held together by a strained cooperation between the Allies and the Vichy French, who promised to control the region as they had since first arriving on the shores of North Africa in 1830. It was an uneasy alliance and a necessary evil for the Allies.

Civilians had to obey a curfew, and of course the blackout affected everyone, but the children of Algiers seemed to live outside the law. I suspected a few continued to ply their trade to American soldiers, selling black-market items well into the night.

The Algiers Opera House, located on Rue Dumont d'Urville, faced the sea. Planted palm trees rose from the center of the small square, and stately French Colonial buildings surrounded it. The opera house itself was located just south of the Casbah, the old quarter of the city.

"You know, Dottie," Jeannie said, taking my arm and leading me toward an elderly native man standing on the corner with a wicker basket full of wine bottles at his feet, "it wouldn't hurt to have a little fun at these things."

"We're not here to have fun, Kirksey. We're here to win the war. We're supposed to be soldiers."

"And we *are* soldiers. Sort of. And we get our jobs done. But some of these boys won't live to see summer, Dottie. What's the harm in giving them some company and a dance?"

I followed Jeannie's gaze and watched a pair of soldiers escorting Butch down the opera house steps. Her pop owned a gas station somewhere in Florida, and she was the best mechanic in the Army, as far as the girls were concerned. She could fix anything. Trucks, radios . . . hell, she could probably fix a tank if the Army let her near one. She was buck-toothed and stocky. But with a boy on each arm, she might have been the prettiest girl in town. "We're not in the USO, Kirksey. And we have work to do."

Jeannie laughed. "We can't work all the time. Let's get some wine and see if that helps us sleep tonight."

"Didn't you just agree to lay off the wine, Kirksey?"

Jeannie sighed. "I know, I know. But how else am I going to get to sleep?"

I nodded but didn't say anything. I knew why Kirksey struggled to sleep. We all struggled to stay warm in the freezing concrete room back at the convent barracks where the Army put us up. Most of the girls were used to a soft bed and a pillow under their head. In Algiers, we had a thin straw mattress and an Army blanket. Pillows were a luxury enjoyed by officers only. But a pillow was the least of Kirksey's worries. She was always worried about the next bombardment.

Just days after our arrival, a few of the girls gathered in the barracks courtyard to watch antiaircraft fire streak across the night sky, watching the Luftwaffe bombing the city. White tracer fire crisscrossed overhead. Searchlights sought out enemy planes. Booming concussions sounded from the port. To our utter amazement, a shell landed nearby, shaking the convent walls where we were being housed. A second shell hit even closer, rocking the earth beneath our feet. When we got back to our squad room, an unexploded shell lay right next to Kirksey's bunk. The near miss had shaken the company's nerves. Jokes were made. Nervous laughter filled the courtyard while the bomb disposal unit came and took care of the shell. But since then, Kirksey had struggled to sleep.

I reached into my utility bag, shifting Ruth's aside, to find my francs. I asked the street seller for a bottle of white wine.

"Cent cinquante francs, mademoiselle," he said, grinning, his remaining teeth starkly white against his tanned face. *One hundred and fifty francs, miss.*

I frowned but handed over two hundred francs. One hundred fifty francs was the usual cost for a bottle of good champagne, but I knew civilians were struggling with shortages. I suspected the Moslem population was struggling a bit more to get supplies.

The man took the money and dipped his head in thanks.

"Why're you always overpaying, Dottie?" Kirksey asked.

I shrugged. "Consider it a tip."

"A tip for what?"

"For being here, at this particular street corner, providing the wine we need before the Army trucks us back, I guess."

Kirksey shifted her gaze away, but not before meeting my eyes and saying under her breath, "Thanks, Dottie."

I tucked the wine bottle under my arm, wondering how I was going to explain the bottle to the rest of the squad. Seconds later, I felt a tug, and just like that, the bottle was gone.

"Hey, kid!" Kirksey shouted. "Give it back!"

I turned and watched a young French boy tearing across the square, the wine bottle grasped between his small hands.

An MP standing at the corner spun around in time to grab the boy. "Hold on there, buddy."

The boy wore an oversized jacket and a dirty cap pushed down low over his face. He also wore blue leather shoes with a stripe down the side that had probably been white at one time. At least, they'd been white when Sadie wore a similar pair. This boy's shoes were crusted with dried mud from the latest rainstorm, and the white had turned a patchy gray. The sight of those shoes hit me like a punch in the stomach. It happened that way sometimes. One minute, I'd be fine and functioning, and the next, the memory of little Sadie would come bearing down on me like an onrushing train. I felt a tearing pain inside, as if Sadie were being ripped from my womb.

But Sadie wasn't here in Algiers. She was somewhere in Nazi Germany, with her father or someone he'd left her with. The pain of not knowing was excruciating, but I had to bottle it up.

"It's all right, Private," I said to the MP holding the thief by the upper arm. The boy looked up. His frightened eyes tore at my heart. He couldn't have been much older than nine or ten. His clothes were tattered, and his cheeks were sunken. He could probably sell the wine for enough money to feed himself for a week.

"The hell it is," the MP barked. He was short, stocky, and unaccountably furious. "Damn Frenchies steal everything that isn't nailed down."

"He's just a kid," Kirksey put in, giving the boy a wink.

"Tu as faim?" I asked. *Are you hungry?*

The boy blinked, then gave a quick nod, darting another frightened glance at the soldier holding his arm.

"He's a thief," the MP said, "and his number's come up."

"Private, he's a hungry boy."

"Don't need to be drinking wine, then, does he?"

The sputter of a Willys jeep, followed by two quick honks, drew my attention away from the overzealous private. The driver lifted himself out of the jeep and tucked a cigarette behind his ear. He wore captain's bars on his left collar. "What's going on here, Private Venturi?"

Said Private Venturi snapped a quick salute while still holding onto the boy's arm. "Caught this man stealing, Captain. Nothing to worry you about." He grinned. "Nothing to do with your panty bandit case."

I turned to the captain. Even in the dim light cast by the opera house, I could see that he was handsome. He had serious blue eyes and a haggard look, as if the very act of walking over had worn him out completely. But he had a strong cleft chin and solid cheekbones bulging beneath his helmet. Underneath his calm demeanor, I sensed strength and a nervous energy in him.

"Blow it out your barracks bag, Venturi." *There it is,* I thought. There was nothing exhausted about the captain's voice. He spoke with calm, even-handed authority.

"Yes, sir, Captain Devlin," Venturi said, wiping the grin off his face. "Boy stole this lady's bottle of wine, sir—that's all."

The captain leveled his gaze my way. I lifted my chin. "It's Auxiliary Lincoln, sir. And the boy can have the wine, sir."

"Auxiliary Lincoln," the captain said, narrowing his eyes at me, then looking to Kirksey. "And you are . . .?"

Kirksey pulled herself up and snapped a salute. "Kirksey, sir. Auxiliary."

"Right."

I felt a fool. I'd forgotten to salute. I wondered briefly if I should do so now, but decided I'd look even more foolish if I saluted late. I'd never forgotten to salute an officer before. Must be the exhaustion, I decided.

The boy reached out a trembling hand, the wine bottle shaking so much I was afraid he'd drop the thing. Gently, I reached out and pried the bottle from his cold little fingers. I smiled at him to show I only wanted to help, but he was blinking, wide-eyed, at Captain Devlin.

"Arrest him, sir?" Venturi asked, yanking hard on the boy's arm. Luckily, I had secured the wine. "Caught this one red-handed."

"Yes, well, I don't see any evidence the boy has our missing panties, now does he?"

Kirksey barked a laugh. The captain turned his penetrating gaze her way, and she took a step backward. "Sorry, sir. It's just that—missing panties?"

Captain Devlin's shoulders fell, and he rubbed at the bridge of his nose. "Not that it's any of your business, young lady, but yes, we have a case of missing panties to investigate. Welcome to the silly side of the war. Our most pressing case in Algiers right now is the panty bandit case."

Kirksey tucked in her lips and raised her eyebrows at me, but wisely held her tongue.

I had to ask. "Why are missing undergarments the most pressing case in Algiers?"

"Because they're *silk* panties," Private Venturi said with a wink.

That was interesting. Any kind of undergarments were scarce in Algiers. Army-issued stockings, bras, panties, and slips were made of nylon. Before the war, Japan had been the largest supplier of silk to the United States. Now the Army needed it to make parachutes and powder bags.

"No further remarks? Smart girl. Now, I'm sure you've been warned against buying on the black market. And while the panty bandit case is cause for endless amusement to some guys," he said, scowling at Private Venturi, "dealing in the black market is a serious crime. And it has absolutely nothing to do with you or with this young thief, stealer of fine wine."

The captain looked down at the boy. "Stealing from the United States Army is a crime, son. I don't want to have to report you to the authorities." He leaned closer, as if sharing a secret with the boy. "The French authorities."

Though I doubted the boy understood the captain, I watched as his eyes grew even wider.

I explained in French that he should not steal from Americans. The boy rattled off a quick response, his overbright eyes defiant.

"What'd he say?" the captain asked.

"I told him he shouldn't steal from Americans. That he should ask." I smiled down at the boy. "He said he's a student, not a beggar."

"A student of thievery," Venturi said, clearly upset that his arrest was falling apart.

"He's hungry, sir," I said, directing my words at the captain.

The captain sighed. "They're all hungry, Auxiliary Lincoln. Let him go, Venturi."

"But, sir—"

"He's a kid, Venturi. He's starving. If Auxiliary Lincoln is willing to overlook his thievery, I think we should be able to do the same."

"Thank you, sir," I said.

He waved a hand, dismissing my thanks. "Typical woman—having a soft spot for kids."

Anger roared inside me at being categorized, yet again, as a weak woman. At the same time, a suffocating pain surged up my throat. The pain could drown me if I let it. It didn't help that he was right; I did have a soft spot for children. I trusted them. Children lied to get out of trouble, but they were authentic. They couldn't help it. They hadn't yet learned to hide behind a facade.

I pushed aside the memories of Sadie and held the bottle out for the boy, who Private Venturi still held firmly in place.

"Sir?" Venturi said, looking confused.

"It's her bottle, Private. She can do what she wants with it. Let the boy go."

Venturi did as he was told, grumbling under his breath. The boy blinked up at me, his gaze shifting from my face to the bottle. I nodded, and he reached out to take it with trembling hands, his fingernails crusted with grime. I held onto it long enough to be certain he wouldn't drop the thing.

"Typical woman," the captain muttered again, lifting one side of his mouth.

"The French are our allies, sir," I said, "and compassion is not exclusively a female trait."

Devlin raised an eyebrow at these words. "Recently, yes, the French are our allies. But a fair number are still very much Vichy. I'd guess you know that, speaking French and all."

I did know. I also knew he was probably right. In the summer of 1940, Hitler's forces had successfully invaded France and forced an armistice. A new government had been set up in the resort town of Vichy. North Africa was left unoccupied until the Americans landed and wrested control from the Vichy officials. Unfortunately, General Eisenhower and the Allies didn't have the resources to fully occupy and administer all of North Africa, so President Roosevelt struck a deal that left most former Vichy collaborators in positions of power all across North Africa.

"Children are not combatants, Captain. Innocent victims should not be held to account for the misdeeds of their parents."

"Things don't always work out the way they should, Lincoln. Hasn't this war taught you anything yet?"

I opened my mouth to respond despite feeling Kirksey's hand on my arm. Maybe Jeannie wanted to stop me from speaking before I found myself in hot water for disrespecting a superior officer.

Or maybe she saw the body falling from the roof of the opera house.

Behind me, Auxiliary Butch Cornfeld, mechanic extraordinaire, let out a shrill, throaty scream. And in the midst of that scream, I heard something I would never forget: the sound of a body hitting concrete at full velocity.

# Chapter 5

"Well, I'll be jiggered," Private Venturi said, dropping a hand to the gun on his hip.

Captain Devlin's face leached color. He rubbed at his chin, his eyes narrowed, as if he were having trouble discerning what he was seeing.

I barely registered the screams and the soldiers pouring out of the Algiers Opera House. I was dimly aware of the French boy darting off down the Boulevard du Centaure, into the bowels of the old city.

My heart pounded like an ack-ack gun. I didn't want to look, and when I did look, my mind struggled to make sense of the crumpled heap lying at the foot of the concrete steps.

*Ruth?*

God, it was Ruth.

Ruth, the consummate soldier, lying on the sidewalk, her hips twisted at an odd angle.

Without thinking, I sprinted toward the body. I dropped to my knees, barely feeling the pain as they scuffed against the rough asphalt.

Auxiliary Ruth Wentz lay in dark pool of her own blood. Her eyes were open, unseeing, and fixed on some distant point.

Even though I knew in my heart that Ruth was dead, I placed my fingers against her throat.

She was still warm.

I felt an overwhelming urge to weep, as if a grenade were lodged in my throat, about to go off. *I must not cry.* Not in front of everyone. American soldiers did not weep in public.

I felt a gentle touch on my arm.

I looked up to see Captain Devlin's sympathetic blue eyes. "Step back, Lincoln. You can't do anything for her now."

I scanned the faces of the crowd gathering outside the opera house. I saw shock. Surprise. Even disgust. Mary Jordan was there, clutching at the earl's sleeve, her face buried in his chest. Sue Dunworthy stood not far from Mary, her head tilted, as if she were trying to understand what she was seeing. I understood the feeling.

"Get up, Lincoln. That's an order."

"I was supposed to protect her," I said, my voice breaking. "I told Kirksey we were safe here."

"There's nothing you can do for her," the captain repeated. His voice was kind but firm.

I got to my feet, my knees shaking and unsteady.

Captain Devlin took my elbow and steered me away from the body while barking orders at the surrounding MPs who'd been assigned guard duty during the dance.

"Venturi, radio medical and tell them we have a suicide."

That single harsh word jolted me out of my shock. "Suicide?"

"Get some guys over here to establish a perimeter around the body. You canvas the area for witnesses. See if anybody saw her jump."

"She didn't jump."

Devlin kept talking to Private Venturi. "Close down the dance. The party's over for tonight."

"Captain Devlin." I stepped into Captain Devlin's line of sight. "Ruth Wentz did not jump."

"Look, Lincoln, I know you're upset. But these things happen. I need you to get out of the way and let me handle this."

The captain walked me back to where Kirksey stood, her mouth agape.

"God, Dottie, is she . . .?" Kirksey clapped a hand over her open mouth. Silent tears streamed down her cheeks. She folded in on herself, as if she were holding herself together by sheer force of will. We had been through four bombardments since arriving in North Africa three weeks before, but we had not seen any casualties. I thought I'd been prepared for that possibility. We'd known we were serving in a combat area, but could anyone ever really prepare for the sight of a human being robbed of life?

"I can't believe this," Kirksey warbled. "This can't be happening."

I looked up to the third floor of the opera house. A mansard roof covered it, and three French doors with transom windows led out to a small balcony. A waist-high stone balustrade enclosed the balcony. From ground level, it looked too high to fall over accidentally.

Kirksey followed my gaze. "Why would she kill herself, Dottie? She seemed fine."

I reviewed the events of the evening. Ruth had seemed much the same as always. Serious. Steady. Determined to do her duty as the Army saw it, and attend the dance. Most of the girls appreciated the chance to socialize with soldiers and blow off some steam after a hard day's work. Algiers offered few enjoyments. After the initial excitement of landing in Algiers, Army life had turned to long days and weathering all the discomforts of living in a combat theater. We slept on uncomfortable straw mattresses in cold, sometimes frigid conditions. The boys in combat units slept in tents on the hard ground, but that didn't make the WAACs' quarters any more comfortable. We ate tasteless rations, though, being in town, we were lucky to get wine and fresh fruit. The only fruit the boys in the field ate were the canned peaches in their rations.

The WAACs worked varying shifts, depending on our assignment and the needs of our commanding officer, First Officer Fitzgerald. I worked the day shift for now, but things were gearing up in Tunisia, and there was talk of moving some of the men in the communications zone to combat units and having the WAACs filling the night shifts once the men left.

Ruth had already volunteered to work the night shift. So had I. Though our reasons differed, we both wanted to do anything and everything to help win the war. Ruth had two brothers in the Army. The oldest, Daniel, was fighting somewhere in the Pacific. Ruth told me that he couldn't say exactly where he was, and she worried about him facing the enemy. Her younger brother was a paratrooper stationed in England for the moment, but we both knew he would be facing combat sooner rather than later.

Had that been what Ruth wanted to talk about? Was one of her brothers hurt? Had Daniel been killed or listed as missing? I didn't think so. Ruth had been her usual calm, steady self when she'd asked to meet later. Well, she hadn't been exactly *calm*. I had seen the tension around her eyes and the released breath that signaled relief when I had agreed to meet.

While the MPs worked to establish a perimeter, I stared at Ruth's crumpled body and tried to imagine Ruth climbing to the roof and leaping to her death. I tried to imagine Ruth in despair. Hurting. And stepping over the edge.

I shook my head. I just couldn't see it. Ruth Wentz had been a rock ever since I'd met her. Everyone knew Ruth as steady and dependable. Always rational. When young Mary Jordan had panicked during the first bombardment, the second night in Algiers, it was Ruth who had calmed the girl; Ruth who had told her to buck up. Weather through. Be a soldier.

How did a woman go from steady and strong to suicidal in a matter of hours? It wasn't possible.

Venturi and three other MPs were moving through the crowd, notebooks out, grabbing at those soldiers trying to leave. Butch was being led away by her dance partner. Corporal Pinski and Sue Dunworthy still stood together on the steps. Mary Jordan was being drawn off by her earl, Captain Haywynn.

Slowly, Captain Devlin and the MPs managed to clear most of the street. French civilians and Arab street sellers dispersed, giving way to the relentless shouting of the Military Police.

I was done watching Captain Devlin chatting with Private Venturi, waiting around for god knows what. I strode over to them, Kirksey at my heels, trying not to look at Ruth's poor broken body. I caught a glimpse of the blood and the odd angles of Ruth's limbs and turned my eyes to Captain Devlin and Private Venturi.

"This will get the WAACs sent home for sure," Venturi was saying. My heart lurched. Most of the men were happy to have the WAACs in theater, even if they wanted dance partners more than coworkers. But there were some who didn't think women belonged in a combat theater at all, and they could be more vocal than the WAAC supporters. It seemed this Private Venturi was one of the naysayers.

"Could be." Devlin pulled out a cigarette from behind his ear and tapped it against his palm.

"About damn time, sir. They shouldn't have been here in the first place."

Devlin nodded but didn't seem to be paying much attention to Venturi's words.

"What's next, sir?" I interjected. I didn't have the faintest idea how to start a death investigation, but I presumed there was some kind of procedure. The Army had procedures for everything.

Venturi and Devlin exchanged a look that I didn't like. Devlin gave me a sympathetic smile that somehow lacked any visible sympathy. "We're waiting for Medical."

I cleared my throat and spoke in a clear voice. "Ruth had no reason to kill herself, Captain. She was happy here. She felt she was helping to win the war and bring her brothers home. There is no way Ruth Wentz committed suicide."

"Nobody ever wants to believe it," Captain Devlin said, softening his voice, "but we all have our limits. Does Wentz drink?"

I was taken aback by the question. "Yes. Most of the girls do. Just like the men." I didn't bother pointing out the obvious. The water supply in Algiers was unsafe, and American soldiers had two options: we could drink the highly chlorinated water available in Lister bags in the barracks and the many offices around the city, or we could purchase cheap French wine. Most opted for the wine, not because anyone wanted to get drunk, but because it tasted far better than the chlorinated water in the Lister bags.

"All right, so maybe she had a drink or two at the dance? Went up to the roof for some fresh air, stumbled, and fell."

"It's possible," I said, trying to remember if Ruth had seemed at all intoxicated before I'd walked Kirksey outside. I didn't think so. "There's one other thing, though."

"What's that?"

I pointed at the body. "Ruth is missing a shoe."

Devlin rolled the cigarette between his fingers, eyes narrowed at the body. "So it flew off on the way down. Look, I'm sorry for your loss, Lincoln. But war is a man's business. It makes sense to me that the woman cracked under the pressure. Too much work. Bad working conditions. Almost nightly bombardments. I see a lot of reasons for you girls to lose it. I don't see any evidence of foul play here."

I bit my bottom lip, thinking how to respond. I had to tread carefully. He was a superior officer, and I had no business telling him how to do his job. Still. "That's because you're not looking, sir."

I walked closer to the body. I pushed aside the emotions threatening to push me to tears at the crumpled form at my feet, and studied what was left of Ruth. I pointed a shaky finger. "Her stockings are snagged, sir. She's missing a shoe. You can't tell me a suicide took off just one shoe and then jumped. There must be a reason it's missing."

Devlin came up beside me. After a moment's silence, he shifted his feet. "All right, that's a bit unusual. But it doesn't prove anything."

"We should go up to the third floor and check things out. Just to be sure."

"Sure of what?"

I hesitated, then said, "Just to be sure there isn't evidence of foul play, sir. We have a duty to investigate."

"Wait just a damn minute," Devlin said, facing me. "There is no *we*. If there is any investigating to be done, I'll do it. You go back to barracks. Have a drink. Get some rest."

"And pack your bags," Venturi said with some relish. I had forgotten he was still standing there.

"Shut up, Venturi," Devlin barked.

"Respectfully, sir," I said with forced calm, "I'm going up there. Ruth Wentz was a member of my squad. If someone hurt her, I need to know."

Captain Devlin held up a hand and cocked his head. "You hear that?"

I sighed, expecting some smart-ass remark.

Instead, the drone of enemy aircraft sounded overhead, followed by the wail of an air raid siren.

# Chapter 6

Strobes of light flickered across the square. I turned toward the harbor. Antiaircraft fire erupted from the ships bobbing on the sea and from multiple points across the city. I clapped my hands over my ears, the explosions echoing inside my skull. My head pounded with each successive concussion. Pain skittered across the back of my teeth.

Kirksey screamed and ran for the opera house.

"Jeannie, wait!" I shouted, but another series of explosions in the harbor drowned out my words.

"Time to pack this up and get to a shelter, Lincoln."

I looked down at Ruth's body. "I can't leave her, sir."

"We can't stand out here, under fire."

I looked over to the harbor again. Arrows of white light streaked across the night sky. The ground beneath my feet rumbled with every shell burst. I instinctually ducked my head but kept my feet planted. "But if she was killed, Captain, or pushed, there will be evidence. We can't just leave her here alone."

"Dammit, Lincoln, she's dead. We need to find shelter. *Now.*"

The sky lit up with tracers as antiaircraft guns fired up across the city. Civilians pushed past MPs at the opera house doors, undoubtedly hurrying into the basement for shelter. I glanced down at Ruth's crumpled body, vulnerable even in death. My feet wanted to run, but my mind was made up. "I'm not leaving her."

"Don't be a damn fool. We could get killed out here."

"Then go find shelter," I said, gritting my teeth. *"Sir."*

Devlin blinked. "I'll ignore that insubordination because I can see you're upset, but don't be a hero, Lincoln. You're going to get yourself killed."

"With all due respect, sir, a shell doesn't discriminate. I'm just as likely to be hit inside the opera house as I am out here. Ruth Wentz was the finest soldier I've seen in this woman's Army. Somebody killed her, sir. I'm staying right here until Medical arrives and I know the evidence is preserved. Even if you think she killed herself, she doesn't deserve to be left out here like last week's garbage. I won't do it."

Captain Devlin ripped off his Garrison cap and rubbed a hand across his scalp. "Cheese and crackers."

"Cheese and crackers?" I would have laughed, but another explosion hit the docks. A large fireball bloomed in the harbor.

"That was a direct hit," Captain Devlin said, his voice eerily calm.

I moved to stand beside him. "On the ship, sir?"

Captain Devlin nodded, his face grim.

"Is it ours?"

Devlin shook his head. "I don't know. I hope not."

A shiver ran through me. Whether it was an American ship or a British one, there was little doubt that sailors were facing the flames now spreading across the harbor.

A succession of shells landed behind the opera house in the hills just above the Casbah. Instinctively, I crouched down. Captain Devlin remained standing, but when he spoke, his voice warbled. "That was close. Too close."

Captain Devlin looked as cocky as ever, but he was rattled. I took some comfort in that. I wasn't the only one who was afraid.

If a shell fell in Bresson Square, we would most likely be killed. But I couldn't bear the thought of leaving Ruth alone. I would stand guard as long as it took.

When another shell landed, this one between Bresson Square and the docks, we both dropped to the ground. Captain Devlin crouched over me. He put his arm around my shaking shoulders and leaned in close. I felt his breath on my ear. "Follow me," he said.

Captain Devlin ran for the jeep and scurried around behind it. I crouched low and ran after him. We both knew a jeep could be obliterated with one shell, but it was something. It was impossible to be sensible in a bombardment. There was no real sense of direction. No front. No back. No behind. No safe place. There was only up and down. Explosion and death. Silence and safety.

Still, I pressed my body up against the reassuring cold metal of the Willys jeep, pulling my legs to my chest, trying to make myself as small as possible. I did this without conscious thought. My body had taken over and was making life-and-death decisions without my help. Captain Devlin wrapped an arm around me, and I tucked into him. His warmth enveloped me. He was a port in the storm of metal streaming across the city.

We stayed that way, crouched together, for what seemed like an eternity.

There was no more talking. Just the sound of the antiaircraft guns and the drone of fighters overhead.

"Damn, screaming Messers," Devlin muttered.

I clapped my hands over my ears. I closed my eyes against the flashing, streaking white lights of the antiaircraft guns. I appreciated Devlin's arm across my shoulders. I resented it too, because I wanted to be strong. I didn't *want* to need a man. Especially now, under bombardment, with an officer right next to me. But during bombardments, survival instinct kicked in, and there was safety in numbers. Or so it seemed. Ruth had felt safe in the company of the Double Deuces. So had I. But once again, life had taught me that safety was an illusion—a story we told ourselves to get through the day.

Listening to the whine of the planes overhead, I wondered if my husband was flying. Could he be flying above me now, dropping bombs on my friends and fellow soldiers? If he knew I was down here, would he still drop his payload? Of course he would. He'd proven that when he'd left me for the Fatherland. He would do his duty. Besides, he couldn't have loved me, or he wouldn't have stolen my daughter.

With every successive concussion, a rising anger exploded inside me. Anger at my husband, Konrad. Anger at Hitler for turning the man I loved into a cruel stranger. Anger at the German people for letting it happen. Anger at myself for not being stronger, for not paying closer attention, for not seeing the direction he was headed before he took Sadie. Anger at myself for not protecting Sadie. Tears streamed down my face. I ducked my head into my sleeve, letting my uniform absorb the evidence of my anguish. Feeling every concussive explosion in my body, fear clenched my muscles. Anger pulsed through my veins. I might never see Sadie again.

Sadie. Was Sadie hiding under her bed this very moment? Was she quaking with fear as Allied bombers flew overhead? I had looked on a map when I'd received that last letter from Konrad. The one I kept hidden underneath my mattress. They were in a town called Minden, in northern Germany. But that had been in 1941. Who knew where they were now? Konrad was most likely in the Luftwaffe, but where was Sadie? If he'd joined the Luftwaffe, as he'd intended, he couldn't take a child. Where had he left our daughter?

The bombardment lasted for over an hour. I lost track of how many bombs fell over Algiers. I knew there would be casualties, and said a silent prayer for those who had been killed or injured.

I glanced at Ruth. She lay in the same position—*of course she is*—frozen in time. It was a strange feeling, seeing her there, unchanged. Somehow it hammered home to me the unchangeable finality of death. Ruth was gone. She'd never run drills with me again. She'd never see her brothers again. My throat swelled and I let quiet tears fall.

The explosions finally ceased, and the antiaircraft guns quieted.

"I think it might be over," Devlin said, his breath rustling my hair. I looked around for my overseas cap and found it lying beside me. I took in a shaking breath and tucked it into my coat pocket.

Slowly, the captain and I unfurled from each other. I swiped at my face, not wanting the captain to see the tears. He might think I was afraid. My arms and legs ached. I leaned back against the jeep and pointed my toes, stretching the stiff muscles. I tilted my head from one side to the other, trying to release the tension in my neck.

Captain Devlin tapped out a cigarette, then offered me the pack.

"No, thanks. Don't smoke." I leaned my head against the cold metal frame of the jeep, grateful that for the moment all was quiet and I was staring out at the billowing fire on the docks instead of at Ruth's crumpled, broken body.

"I don't either," Devlin said.

"Then why do you have cigarettes?"

He shrugged and tapped a cigarette against his knee, his head leaned back against the jeep's doorframe. "Most men in the Army smoke. Makes me fit in, I guess." He shook his head and sat up straighter. "And anyway, gives my hands something to do. Idle hands are the devil's workshop."

I had nothing to say to that. I'd never really warmed to religion.

"You okay, Lincoln?"

I just nodded, not trusting my voice to work.

"Kraut bombings coming more frequently lately. Word is, Rommel is planning some dustup in the east."

Field Marshal Erwin Rommel, commander of the battle-hardened Afrika Corps, was the most feared general in the German Army. He was so wily on the battlefield, always managing to escape complete defeat, that the British labeled him the Desert Fox. "You don't think they plan to retake Algeria?"

Devlin shook his head. "Naw. They just like reminding us they're a hop, skip, and a jump from here, that's all. Telling us Sicily isn't too far away and not to get too comfortable."

"I hope Kirksey is okay." I opened my mouth to tell him about the shell in our barracks, but he spoke first.

"Opera house is still standing. Bombing raids are just another part of the job."

"Except it's not really our job, is it?" I said when I finally felt calm enough to speak. "That's what you all think, and in a way you're right."

"I'm surprised to hear you say I'm right about anything."

I worked to control my shivering. "We're not Regular Army. We're an auxiliary force. We don't get death benefits. We still pay for our mail, for God's sake."

Captain Devlin winced. "I saw that in the *Stars and Stripes*."

It was such a small thing, paying for our letters home. But it chafed at the WAACs. Servicemen didn't pay for their mail. The government shipped their letters home free of charge. The WAACs weren't fighting soldiers, but we were still soldiers. We had volunteered to serve in a combat theater. It didn't seem fair for the Army to charge us to send mail home to our loved ones. Not that I had any loved ones left, but everyone else did.

"There's a big push to change that, though," Devlin said.

"We knew what we were signing up for when we volunteered," I said brusquely. Before accepting our assignment, Colonel Oveta Culp Hobby, supreme commander of the WAACs, had explained our situation. We were an auxiliary force and therefore not entitled to any death benefits or protections if we were captured. Almost all of the company accepted those conditions and volunteered anyway. Another explosion sounded, this one muffled and distant. I forced a laugh. "Okay, we didn't really know what we were getting into. We were told this area was behind the lines."

"Which it is, for the most part. Who knew the damn Krauts would be so persistent?"

This time I laughed freely. "I think the Germans are pretty well known for their persistence."

Devlin chuckled. "You've got guts, Lincoln. I'll give you that. But I'm still not convinced we should be out here in the square, in the open."

"If a male soldier were laying here, even if he'd committed suicide, would you really have left him here alone?"

Devlin cleared his throat. "I'm ashamed to say it, but I think I would have left him. Probably. I'd probably think he didn't do his duty. I'd think that none of us want to be here, but there's a war to win, and he shouldn't have taken the chickenshit way out."

"So you think Ruth was a coward?"

"I didn't say that. I don't think she should have been here in the first place."

An explosion sounded in the distance, then two more, farther south. Captain Devlin tucked his cigarette behind his ear and got to his feet. "I think the Krauts have hightailed it out of here." He reached for the radio. "I'll call the Medical Corps to bring an ambulance. It might take a while, though."

I nodded. Civil Defense was responsible for emergency response to bombardments, but they often requested help from the Army. "And then we'll go up and try to find Ruth's shoe?"

Devlin pulled his cap from his back pocket and settled it in place. "It's a shoe, Lincoln. Shoes fall off."

I studied my own shoes for a moment, then met his gaze. "Sandals fall off. High heels. Maybe even T-straps. But tightly laced Oxfords? I'd guess they have as much chance of falling off as a combat boot, sir."

# CHAPTER 7

I waited with Captain Devlin for the Medical Corps personnel to arrive. "Where will they take her?"

"To the Church Villa."

I nodded. The Church Villa was a small British station hospital just up the road from the St. George Hotel. Both hospitals in Algiers were administered by the British Army. Allied Force Headquarters was a joint command, led by Supreme Commander Eisenhower, and most sections had both British and American personnel, but the hospitals were primarily British operations, staffed with both Americans and other Allied personnel.

When the truck finally arrived and four GIs jumped down, pulling a stretcher from the back of the truck, I turned away and gazed down at the Mediterranean Sea. I didn't want to see Ruth rolled onto the stretcher. It felt like a small betrayal. I should endure the sight and see my fellow soldier through this final journey, but I feared if I saw Ruth hauled away like so much cargo, the image would be indelibly printed on my mind. I preferred to remember Ruth alive.

I tried to tune out Captain Devlin's orders and focus on the ships bobbing in the bay, on the last of the fires being put out by naval personnel. "Put the stretcher over there. Don't walk around in the blood, you idiot," he said.

After a few minutes, the captain came to stand beside me. "The boys have things in hand, Lincoln. Let me take you back to barracks. You've done enough for tonight."

"We have to investigate the third floor, sir," I said, standing tall, determined to get the chance to go up to the third floor and see what evidence might be waiting there.

His blue eyes bored into mine. A muscle in his jaw twitched. After a heavy sigh, he gave a curt nod. "I suppose you've earned that much. All right, you can come with me. To take notes only." He wagged a finger in my face.

I drew in a steadying breath. I wanted more than anything in the world to slap his hand away. Instead, I gave my own curt nod. "Yes, sir. Thank you, sir."

"Let's get this over with," he said, striding toward the opera house.

The lobby was eerily quiet. I could see through the curtained doorways leading to the auditorium that the band was still taking down their instruments. Soldiers lounged in the red velvet seats, talking in small groups. Cigarette smoke hung in the air like a fog as the soldiers, French women, the remaining WAACs, and a few Arab workers waited to be released.

I had no idea where Squad B was now. I should go find them, make sure everyone had gotten back to barracks safely. But I had to know if the third floor held any clues to Ruth's death. My first responsibility was to the soldier I'd lost. The soldier I'd failed to protect.

An MP stood guard just inside the front doors.

"We need to get up to the third floor."

"Yes, sir. This way." The soldier led the way across the empty lobby, to the staircase tucked behind a red velvet curtain. The same red velvet covered the marble stairs leading to the second and then the third floor.

The third floor of the opera house was small, no bigger than my barracks room, but the high mansard roof gave it a cavernous feel. Three sets of French doors were on the opposite wall. The middle set of doors was open, letting in the cold night air.

"Do you think it's unusual that these doors are open?" I asked.

Captain Devlin shrugged. "I don't know. We can ask management, I guess."

I walked out the open doors and onto the small balcony. The stone balustrade reached my waist. "Ruth is about my height. She couldn't have fallen over that wall. Not without some help."

"Any sign of her shoe?" Devlin asked. I looked over my shoulder. The captain still stood at the top of the staircase.

I turned back to the balcony. It was dark. "I think we'll need the flashlight."

"Be careful. We don't need another WAAC going over the side."

I pursed my lips but said nothing.

"Sorry," he said after a moment. "That was uncalled for."

After a moment, I heard the sound of his boots hitting the wood floor. Captain Devlin unclipped his flashlight from his belt and handed it to me.

I took it and clicked it on, holding my hand over the beam. Even though it was an angle-headed flashlight, I wanted to ensure no passing planes caught the light. Another bombardment was unlikely, but I saw no reason to take unnecessary risks. I scanned the small balcony.

"Anything?" Devlin asked.

"No, nothing." I leaned over to look down at the square below. From this height I could see the two MPs standing guard beside the blood stain left by Ruth's body. I wondered who would be responsible for cleaning it up. Bile burned the back of my throat. I pushed my dark thoughts aside. I needed to keep my mind on the facts at hand.

I tried to envision Ruth standing on the balcony and jumping off. She would have had to lift herself up onto the stone balustrade first. Ruth was certainly capable of lifting herself up. But why? What reason did Ruth have for committing suicide? It didn't square with what I knew about Ruth Wentz.

Could she have stumbled and fallen to her death? I leaned against the balcony, trying to imagine losing my balance and going over.

"Lincoln, what the hell are you doing?" Captain Devlin said, his voice pitched higher than usual.

I stepped back from the balcony. "I don't think she could have accidentally fallen, Captain. It's too high. You'd have to lift yourself up and over."

"Would you mind stepping back, Lincoln? You're making me nervous."

"Even if she were drunk, she'd have to lift herself. Besides which, Ruth was sober as a sphinx when I talked to her, and that was less than an hour before her death."

"Maybe she was sitting on the wall? Having a romantic rendezvous, and then she fell backward?"

I glanced at Captain Devlin. He hung back, brows drawn.

"Ruth wasn't really the romantic type, Captain. And even if she were, wouldn't her romantic partner come forward and tell us what happened?"

"Maybe he's scared? Or didn't have time, with the bombardment and all."

"Maybe."

"Anyway, I don't see that shoe. Must have gone over with her."

I winced at the words, spoken so casually, but said nothing. I scanned the balcony again, but there was no sign of Ruth's shoe.

Holding my hand over the flashlight's beam, I scanned the inner room. A three-paneled painted screen blocked off the end of the room farthest from the staircase. I peeked behind it. I saw paint cans and dusty, paint-splattered tarps.

"This is a waste of time, Lincoln. Let's get out of here."

As I turned back toward the balcony one last time, the beam of the flashlight landed on something, a shape. Just to the right of the French doors, lying against the baseboard, was an object about the size of an Oxford brown. I zeroed in on it. My breath wheezed out in surprise and victory. "It's here. I found it!"

"Don't touch it!"

I froze.

Devlin pulled out his notebook. "It's important to document the scene, Lincoln. You'd be surprised what you can learn from the position of things."

"So you agree Ruth was murdered?"

"Not in the least. I have to write a report for suicides as well as anything else."

I pursed my lips but said nothing while Devlin's pencil scurried across first one page, then another. When he finished, he tucked his notebook back into his front pocket, tapped out a cigarette, and stuck it in his mouth. He didn't light it. He sucked on it, and the action seemed to calm him.

"This proves there was foul play," I said.

Devlin squinted at me. "How do you figure that?"

I paced from the darkened space beside the screen and the balcony doors. I knelt and inspected the area around the balustrade. "Look at this!" I cried, pointing my flashlight at the stone railing.

Devlin moved closer. "I don't see anything."

"Right here," I said, my voice shaking. "I think this might be part of her stocking."

He nodded. "Could be."

Looking at the evidence, a scene began to take shape in my mind. "I think I know what happened."

Captain Devlin rolled his eyes. I ignored him and pushed ahead.

"Ruth was on the balcony, pushed up against the balustrade. She turned, maybe to get away from someone, or maybe fighting off her attacker. The heel of her shoe caught in the stone, and as her body turned, the shoe was wedged. Her knees would then be facing the stone and someone pushed her from behind, over the balustrade, scraping her stockings from the knee to the ankle on her way over." I shivered, but it wasn't the cold North African air that made me feel suddenly chilled to the bone.

"And maybe she had a fight with her boyfriend, Lincoln. Maybe he roughed her up a bit. Maybe she roughed him up, for all we know. You girls aren't exactly known for your ladylike behavior, are you?"

I crossed my arms, resisting the urge to hit a superior officer.

Devlin continued. "Maybe she kicked at the balustrade in frustration after he dumped her. Depressed and homesick, she hefted herself up onto the wall and jumped."

"You don't really believe that," I said, incredulous. "Ruth must have struggled with someone. She lost her shoe in the scuffle before she was thrown over the railing."

"Or," Devlin said, drawing out the word, "she had a romantic rendezvous with someone. He dismisses her—maybe he rejected her or something. He leaves. In a fit of despair, she throws herself over."

I arched an eyebrow. "A fit of despair? Really?"

"What?"

"We're not damsels in distress in some ridiculous fairy tale. If Ruth had a romantic rendezvous, which I highly doubt, and it didn't go well, she wouldn't throw herself over. Despite what you might think, most of the women in our company are not pining for a man. We're here to work. Especially Ruth. She wasn't looking for love. She was looking for promotion."

He pulled a cellophane envelope from his breast pocket. Using the end of his pencil, Devlin lifted the scrap of stocking and dropped it into the envelope. He carefully folded over the top and handed it to me. "Hold on to that for me. Do you have a handkerchief?"

"What for?"

"We need to take that shoe into evidence. I don't have a big enough evidence bag. A handkerchief and your purse will have to do."

"It's not a purse. It's an Army-issue utility bag."

"Do you have the handkerchief, or do we need to use one of your stockings?"

I bit down on my lip, hard, to keep from giving Captain Devlin a piece of my mind. Instead, I reached for my utility bag and pulled out a handkerchief. A silk handkerchief.

I didn't own any silk handkerchiefs. In fact, I'd never owned real silk in my life. I noted the soft grain against my fingertips immediately. Glancing down, I realized I'd reached into Ruth's utility bag and remembered Ruth asking me to hold it while she danced. I had forgotten all about it. What was Ruth doing with a silk handkerchief? Had she purchased one from Sue Dunworthy? I couldn't imagine Ruth Wentz buying off the black market. Silk was a scarce commodity used to sew much-needed parachutes for the Army Air Force. The Ruth I knew would never purchase silk, especially for something as frivolous as a handkerchief. For the first time, I had an uneasy feeling in the pit of my stomach. Was it possible I didn't really know Ruth at all?

I swallowed back the lump forming in my throat. I would have to put it with Ruth's things when I got back to barracks. I stuffed Ruth's silk hankie back in the bag and reached into my own utility bag. I pulled out a clean cotton handkerchief and handed it to the captain.

"You girls come exceedingly well equipped, don't you?" Captain Devlin said, glancing at the two bags slung across my shoulders.

"It's not my bag. I was holding it for Ruth while she danced."

"Oh." He gave me a sympathetic smile. "You'll have to turn that over to your commanding officer."

"First Officer Fitzgerald. We're auxiliaries, Captain. We don't use normal Army ranks. Female officers have different names for equivalent Army ranks. A first officer is a captain."

"Right. First officer. Damned inconvenient. Since you have two bags, can we use one to store this piece of possible evidence?"

"Sure." I poured the contents of my own bag into Ruth's. I could use Ruth's bag for the time being.

Captain Devlin took the bag and dropped the shoe into it, handkerchief and all.

I took one last look around the room. I peeked behind the screen again. I still had the flashlight in my hand, and I clicked it on.

"What are you doing, Lincoln?"

I didn't answer immediately. I scanned the paint cans and a canvas draped over a short scaffolding. "There are two sides to a theater."

"What?" Captain Devlin shoved aside the screen, joining me.

"There," I said, unable to keep the excitement out of my voice.

"I'll be damned."

Hidden behind the canvas sheeting was a doorway. I stepped over the paint cans and lifted my flashlight to reveal a set of stairs. I went down a few steps, Devlin on my heels. The stairs led down to the second floor. A long hallway branched off to the left. I started for the hallway, but Devlin put a hand on my arm, bringing me up short. "Where are you going, Lincoln?"

"Someone could have come up this way and surprised Ruth. We have to see where it leads."

"I'm sure it leads down to the lobby."

"I don't think so. I'm guessing it leads to the back of the theater, to the stage area. That means our killer could have come from the dance floor."

"What killer? We don't know she was murdered."

I turned to him, briefly shining the flashlight in his face. He winced and I lowered my arm. "Captain Devlin, I know Ruth Wentz. She wasn't just in my squad; we trained together at Fort Des Moines. There were absolutely no signs that she was even depressed, much less on the verge of suicide. She lost her shoe in a fight. Someone killed her. I'm sure of it."

Devlin frowned. "Let's get out of here. We'll discuss this downstairs."

I clenched my jaw and forced myself to remain calm. "All right, Captain. This way." It didn't make sense to go back upstairs to the third floor, so I moved down the hallway. As expected, the hallway continued to the right, toward the rear of the theater. At the end of the hallway, we reached another staircase. When we reached the first floor, we were standing backstage. I turned a triumphant eye to Captain Devlin.

"It still doesn't prove she was murdered, Lincoln." But he sounded less certain now.

Who had Ruth met on the third floor? We'd have to ask Corporal Pinski where Ruth went after their dance. Maybe he saw her meet up with another soldier. It could be anybody. The dance, like all these events, was an international affair. There were WAACs, Navy, Army, and any number of British soldiers as well. Most of the boys would only have a one- or two-day pass. Most of them would be back in the desert, back in their camps, by midnight. Which meant that if Ruth had been pushed off, we were going to have a hell of time finding out who did it.

Captain Devlin held my utility bag like a stringer of fish.

"There's something else I should tell you," I said.

"What's that?"

"Ruth asked to talk to me later tonight. She asked me to meet her in the courtyard at midnight." I met Devlin's hard stare. "It's against regulations to leave your bunk after lights out. Lots of girls ignore that rule, but Ruth was strictly GI. She never broke regulations, not on purpose."

"So you think she had something important to tell you." It wasn't a question.

"Now I do. I think she was afraid of something, and she wanted to confide in me."

Captain Devlin tucked the utility bag under his arm and adjusted his service cap. "But at the time, you didn't think she was afraid."

I thought back to those final moments with Ruth. I hadn't thought Ruth was afraid. She'd seemed tired out. A little shaken by the scene with Private Rivera.

"I know you don't want to believe it, Lincoln, but the most likely explanation is that she jumped. You need to at least consider the possibility. That this is exactly what it appears to be, another unfortunate suicide." He said the words softly, as if he were afraid I might cry.

But I didn't feel close to tears now. Irritation and anger poured through me. "If you'd known Ruth, you wouldn't say that."

Devlin sighed and shook his head. "She jumped, Lincoln. I know that's tough to accept, but the truth is, it happens all too often in a combat theater. Boys get lonely. Homesick. Depressed. It's not surprising that it would happen to you girls as well."

"We're not 'girls,' Captain," I said, gritting my teeth. "We are soldiers, just like you."

Devlin's jaw tightened. "Look, I appreciate what you're trying to do here, and God knows, we need good secretaries to run this war. And you've got courage. I'll give you that. But consider for a minute, Lincoln, that this has been an upsetting evening for you. Give yourself some time to grieve before you go off on a one-man murder investigation. Doc Edwards at the Church Villa will review the case tomorrow morning. If there's something suspicious about Wentz's death, we'll know soon enough."

# Chapter 8

Captain Devlin steered the jeep behind the opera house and onto Rue Rovigo, a twisting, winding road skirting the Casbah. The streets were filled with civilians who'd come out to discern the damage done by the bombardment. Devlin honked his way through the crowded boulevard and headed for the trolleybus line and Boulevard Gallieni, toward El Biar.

I held on tight, resisting the urge to argue with the captain. He was wrong about Ruth. I knew that as well as I knew anything. I reminded myself that Captain Devlin hadn't known Ruth. He supposed she was nothing more than a weak-willed woman who couldn't take being a soldier.

Devlin took a left on Avenue Barthelemy Vidal and stopped short. A crowd loitered in the street; some spectators wore only their nightclothes. A shell had landed on a shop. I recognized it as the perfumery. The two-story building yawned like a toothless old man. Metal girders glinted in the scant light given off by French policemen's flashlights.

"Should we stop and help out?"

Devlin honked the horn and wedged his way through the throng. A middle-aged Frenchman put a protective arm about his wife and yelled an obscenity. Devlin was undeterred. "Civil Defense will handle it."

The perfumery was only a couple of kilometers from the WAAC barracks. I worried about Kirksey. She would be up all night with nerves when she saw how close the bombs had come to the convent.

Captain Devlin pulled up outside the convent walls, jerked the jeep to a halt, and killed the engine.

The women of the 22nd Post Headquarters Company were housed in a working convent in El Biar, a suburb of Algiers several kilometers away from the city center. The Monastere du Bon Pasteur convent, home of the Contemplative Sisters of the Sacred Heart, was a large complex enclosed behind a concrete wall on a hillside, with a breathtaking view of Algiers and the Mediterranean Sea below. The original structure had been built in the mid-1800s, but over the years, additions had been made. It had the whitewashed stucco walls typical of Algiers, which had given the city its nickname, Alger la Blanche, or the White City. We were billeted in the east wing of the main building, adjacent to the chapel, with a view of the central courtyard. I estimated the convent was home to approximately thirty nuns, led by Mother Superior Mary Theresa Pelletier.

The Army probably thought a convent would feel safe, but most of the girls found it confining. They wanted to be closer to the city, and more than one WAAC had slipped over the convent walls after curfew to go exploring or to meet GIs in Algiers. There was no real safety in a combat theater anyway. We all knew that now.

I climbed out of the jeep, my hamstrings screaming in protest. I needed to do some stretching before hitting the sack.

"Lincoln, I am sorry about your friend." Captain Devlin's face was hidden in shadow, but his words sounded sincere.

"But you won't investigate her death?"

He sighed as if the weight of an 88mm flak gun sat on his chest. He turned in his seat, and I could see the outline of his jaw, his pale eyes gleaming in the faint light from the moon. "Listen, Lincoln. I've got a black market running wild in this city. We've got Army supply disappearing. And when I'm not trying to stop the grift, I'm trying to keep homesick, drunk, scared men from killing one another instead of focusing on the enemy. Your friend's death is unfortunate, but not entirely unexpected. We had two suicides just last week. I won't say it's common, but it does happen. People crack under the pressure, even at headquarters."

I clenched my hands together behind my back. "Sir, I appreciate that you're trying to be kind, but I know in my gut that Ruth was pushed over that balustrade."

Devlin turned the ignition and grabbed the jeep's gear shift. "If you're right, we'll find out. It's nothing for you to worry your pretty head about." And with those words, he pulled away.

Feeling defeated, I trudged through the convent gate and walked the short distance to the central archway leading into the courtyard.

The courtyard was empty, but laughter spilled out from the upper floors surrounding it. Two gnarled trees stood on either end of the courtyard. The girls had tied twine between them, and on sunny days, garters, stockings and uniform shirts and skirts hung there to dry.

Beyond the courtyard, past the chapel, was a small garden sitting on the hillside overlooking the city. The WAACs had set up wicker chairs scavenged from a bombed-out building nearby, and this is where we went for some privacy. The sisters left us there to smoke, chat, write letters, or take a nap after a long day. Sometimes I sat in the little sanctuary, closed my eyes, and listened to the sound of the children playing. I imagined Sadie there, kicking a ball across the orchard, blond pigtails flying out behind her. I imagined what my daughter might look like now. Did she have my bird legs? Did she still have an upturned nose? Had she inherited my freckles?

The nuns took care of more than fifty French children. I wasn't entirely sure what had happened to their parents, and I did not ask. I knew some families had escaped to North Africa when the Germans invaded France. Perhaps their parents had not survived the trip.

The nuns also kept a vegetable garden, a vineyard, and a small orchard, though the grapes were moldy, the trees bare, and the vegetables limited. Like most residents of Algiers, the nuns received most of their foodstuffs from the United States Army and the North African Trade Board. The nuns also earned extra money by helping the company with kitchen chores and laundry.

Anna Marchand, a hired French maid, scurried across the courtyard, giving me a perfunctory wave.

Sixty-six WAACs lived in the convent, and of those, about a dozen spoke French, including me.

The WAAC wing housed a kitchen, seven barrack rooms, and two company staff offices. The infirmary was in the same part of the building, and sick call was held there every morning. Latrine and shower facilities were located at the end of one of the first-floor dormitories.

The children at Bon Pasteur convent added a homey feel. They were housed in separate dormitories at night, but during the day the sisters kept them together and under tight supervision. Sometimes the boys played soccer in the courtyard or in the back field. On any given morning, I would walk down to the courtyard in my Army-issue, green-flannel robe to find girls and boys of varying ages at the trough next to the well, scooping out pails of water, brushing their teeth, and chattering away in French, and my heart would constrict with both pleasure and pain.

I shivered and pulled my olive drab jacket closed. I took the stairs up to the second floor. The interior walls were made of gray concrete blocks and decorated with brightly colored Moorish tiles. Though it was past curfew, light glowed from beneath almost every squad room door. My Oxford browns echoed on the concrete floor. A couple of girls poked their heads out of their rooms, waved, then went back to what they were doing.

Fitzgerald's secretary, Auxiliary Wanda Wooten, sat at the little desk at the end of the hall. Wooten was a pretty blonde who always wore a pained expression. She gave me a tremulous smile and opened her mouth, but before she could speak, First Officer Fitzgerald walked out of her office.

"Lincoln, you're late."

"Yes, ma'am. Captain Devlin said he would have Private Venturi telephone—"

"I got the call," Fitzgerald interrupted. "Come into my office."

First Officer Anita Fitzgerald was tall, lanky, and preternaturally stern. Kirksey said she looked like General Patton's long-lost daughter, and it always made me laugh. It was true: Fitzgerald had the same suntanned skin, piercing narrow eyes, and pompous swagger. She was also tall. I guessed she was just under the six-foot limit imposed by the Army on women soldiers. Fitzy even walked around with her chest thrust out like General Patton, in the same self-important bluster. "I'm meeting with General Eisenhower in the morning. Did you know she was suicidal?"

"No, ma'am. She was not suicidal."

"Obviously you're wrong." Fitzgerald walked to the open window and closed the shutters. I suspected she'd been watching, waiting for me to get back. "Is it possible she fell?"

"It's unlikely. There's a balcony. It's about waist high. But she could have been pushed."

"Pushed?"

"I think that must be what happened. You know Ruth. She was a dedicated soldier. She was glad to be here, doing her duty. She never would have killed herself."

Fitzgerald twisted her razor-thin lips. "Maybe that's just what she wanted us to see. Anyone can crack under the pressure. People have depths, Lincoln."

Why was everyone so quick to accept that Ruth had jumped? "There's been no indication Ruth felt that pressure, ma'am."

"You know our position here in Algiers is precarious at best. Enlisted men want us here for dates and not much else. Most of the officers don't want us here at all. I'm afraid it won't take much to push the general to change his mind about using WAACs in theater. He might decide we're not worth the risk if we start leaping off buildings."

"Even if Ruth did commit suicide, which I don't believe, we're not all jumping off buildings. It doesn't justify sending us all home."

"Oh c'mon, Dottie—you know better than that. Hysterical women have no business serving in a combat theater—that's what they'll say. That we're too emotional. They'll make jokes about Ruth having her period and that she couldn't take the heat. Or maybe she was a princess who couldn't stand living without hot water and fresh meat. Who the hell knows? They don't need much of an excuse."

"I'll find out what happened," I said with conviction.

"No, you will not," Fitzgerald replied just as emphatically. "You'll do your job. While you still can. I'll do my job while I still have it."

"Yes, ma'am."

"And, Dottie?" Fitzgerald's stern blue eyes bored into mine. "Squad B is still your responsibility. See that they are well taken care of."

I swallowed hard. I felt that sting of tears again and forced them back down my throat. "Yes, ma'am. I'll do better."

Fitzgerald's shoulders relaxed. "It's not your fault, Dottie. Whatever Ruth was going through, she could have confided in you. You can't read minds."

My throat swelled. Unable to speak, I just nodded. I didn't believe Ruth had committed suicide, but there was no doubt I had failed in my duty to protect my squad. Nothing First Officer Fitzgerald said would change that.

Fitzgerald opened her mouth, as if she would say more, then gave a brusque nod. "Now get some rest. Tomorrow is going to be a busy day. I don't know if you've heard, but word is the Germans are gearing up for an offensive. Which makes our job all the more important. The more men we can move to the front, the better prepared our forces will be. I hope the brass will decide to keep us here, even after this unfortunate development. But whatever their decision, while we're still here, we can make ourselves useful."

"Right," I said. "Yes, ma'am." I saluted and turned for the door. My empty stomach clenched. I didn't want to go home. I had nothing to go home to.

# Chapter 9

I found Kirksey pacing the squad room, still in uniform.

Mary Jordan lay facing the wall, apparently already asleep. Sue Dunworthy lounged on her bunk in a satin nightdress, painting her nails bloodred. The rest of the girls wore government-issue pajamas, but Sue always wore her satin. Once a week she took it down to the courtyard and washed it in her helmet, then carefully mended the lace at the neckline. It was something of an obsession, but an innocent one in my opinion. All the girls kept something that reminded them of home.

"She's losing it," Sue said, waving the nail polish wand in Kirksey's general direction.

"Shut up, dung beetle," Kirksey said, hands on hips, eyes on her feet.

Sue rolled her eyes but didn't bother to reply.

"Hey, Kirksey," I said, "how are you holding up?"

"I can't stand being in this room, Dottie."

"Okay. Why don't we go down to the courtyard and get some air."

"But Fitzgerald—"

"I'll explain to Fitzgerald if it comes to that."

Technically, we weren't allowed to leave our squad rooms after curfew. It was well past midnight, but I could see the writing on the wall. Kirksey was not going to be able to sleep if she didn't release some of that energy. "Grab your jacket. It's cold outside."

I slipped Ruth's utility bag over my head and laid it on my bed. Kirksey pulled on her jacket and followed me downstairs.

I decided to use the garden. It was secluded and far enough away from the courtyard that we wouldn't disturb the nuns or the WAACs trying to sleep on the second floor.

"I could really use a drink."

"You're safe now, Kirksey. The Germans have come and gone."

"For now. Sorry, I just don't know what to do with myself. I need to do something."

"Let's do some physical training."

Kirksey laughed. "PT? Don't be ridiculous."

"I'm serious. It's cold. It'll warm us up."

"Dottie, I don't need you to be a squad leader right now. I need you to be my friend."

"I *am* being your friend. Look, we can sit here and freeze, or we can do something and take your mind off it."

"I'd rather be going to the pictures. See a show. I wish I were back home right now, Dottie. I want to be here—of course I do. I want to help win the war. But with Ruth dying like that . . . I just don't know."

Kirksey resumed her pacing, this time bumping into the chairs set out around a small birdbath at the center of the garden. I needed to redirect Kirksey's attention before she clattered one of the chairs to the ground and alerted the antiaircraft unit beyond the garden, sitting just inside the convent wall. "Let's start with some arm circles."

"This is so stupid."

"It's not stupid. It's something to do. It will take your mind off your troubles."

"Troubles!" Kirksey laughed, but she followed my lead and lifted her arms. "I still can't quite believe it, about Ruth. She didn't seem suicidal. She seemed fine."

"Do you know if she was upset about anything lately?"

"No. She seemed like her usual self. Bossy. Annoying. A general pain in the ass."

"Kirksey!"

"What? Don't get me wrong—I loved her. We all loved her. But she did have a way of making things difficult. With her endless rule following."

I couldn't argue with that. Ruth was a stickler for regulations, almost to the point of absurdity.

I followed regulations as best I could, but I also adapted to the situation in front of me. The truth was, the WAACs were only an auxiliary force. We weren't Regular Army and we didn't have the same rules as the men. Most of the girls understood this, but Ruth was different. She expected to be treated as a soldier, no different from the men.

"I mean, she memorized the Code of Conduct, for God's sake. Who does that?"

I smiled. "Ruth."

I moved on to swings and flings, throwing both my arms forward, then sideward. Kirksey followed just as if we were back in basic training.

"It rubbed some of the girls the wrong way," Kirksey went on. "She wasn't an officer, but she was always telling everyone their business. Threatening to report people."

This got my attention. Ruth had apparently made some enemies. "Who was she going to report?"

"Well, you for one," Kirksey said, laughing.

"Me?"

"She thought you were too soft on us. I don't think a day went by when she didn't tell one of us that if she were squad leader, we'd all be doing PT every morning. She was always going on about how she'd whip this squad into shape."

I touched my toes, hiding my face. I didn't want Kirksey to see how much that hurt to hear. Ruth thought I'd done a bad job as squad leader, and she was right. One of my squad members was dead.

I switched to high knees. Now I was the one who needed to release nervous energy. I pumped my legs up and down, trying to push aside the pain and resentment I suddenly felt. It hurt to hear that someone I respected had criticized my performance to the other members of the squad. I needed to change the subject. "How are the other girls taking Ruth's death?"

"Everyone's shocked. I don't think any of us know what to think. Ruth killing herself seems so out of character. I mean, of course everyone's upset. Except for Princess Mary."

I stopped marching in place. "Mary? Really?" Mary was the youngest girl in the company. She'd earned the nickname "Princess Mary" back in Daytona Beach before embarkation. Mary was pretty, young, and inexperienced. Ruth had always seemed to watch out for Mary, from what I'd seen. Maybe I'd been wrong in that assessment.

"Gosh," Kirksey said, breathing heavily, "I haven't done this since basic training. I can't believe you get up every day and do this."

"Keeps you strong."

"I guess so." Kirksey touched her toes twice, then stopped.

"You were saying?" I prodded. "About Mary?"

"Well, if anyone was going to jump off a roof, wouldn't you think it'd be Mary? And Ruth was the opposite of Mary. She wasn't a dramatic kind of girl. She always seemed up to snuff. Solid. Dependable."

"I think she was."

"Obviously not, if she killed herself."

*If* Ruth killed herself. Kirksey didn't really mean it, but she was right. Ruth was not the type of woman to kill herself. What's more, there were no signs that she'd ever contemplated such a thing.

I didn't tell Kirksey about my suspicions. It certainly wouldn't help Kirksey sleep if she thought there was a killer on the loose.

"Did you see Ruth go upstairs? At the dance?"

"No." Kirksey put her hands on her hips and stretched her back. "I don't know if this is important. It's probably not, but . . ."

"What is it?"

"Mary and Ruth weren't getting along very well just lately. I saw them arguing at the dance."

"They were fighting?"

"No, I wouldn't say they were fighting. But they were definitely having an argument about something."

"Do you know what the something was?"

Kirksey shook her head. "It was in the auditorium. I couldn't hear them. But I think it might have had something to do with Captain Haywynn. Do you think Ruth had a thing for Captain Haywynn? Maybe she jumped because Mary got him first?"

"I don't think so. I never saw Ruth so much as speak to Captain Haywynn."

"You're right. I guess we'll probably never know what drove her to do such a thing." Kirksey stretched her hands above her head. She was calmer now. The exercises had done the trick. "She came back from the dance and went to bed. Went right to sleep. Not a care in the world. I guess it doesn't bother her. Funny, huh? That the bombardments bother me and not Princess Mary Jordan."

"How are you feeling now?" I asked, deciding to dial the conversation down.

"Tired," Kirksey admitted.

"C'mon. Let's get cleaned up and try and get some shut-eye."

"Okay, deal. Thanks Dottie. I won't say this helped, but it was better than being boxed in that room."

I slung an arm across Kirksey's shoulders and gave her a quick hug. We went back upstairs to our squad room. I thought about

Mary in her bunk, facing the wall. Had she really been asleep? Or had she been unable to face us after her argument with Ruth? Was she upset her last words with Ruth had been harsh? Or was it possible that argument had somehow escalated to murder?

# Chapter 10

We returned to the squad room to fetch our helmets and the small slivers of soap we'd saved from the ship on our journey to Algiers. Soap was hard to find in-theater and was as precious as Texas oil.

We drew water from the well in the courtyard to wash and brush our teeth under the light of a half-moon, then stopped at the bathroom and used the last of the water to flush the toilets.

Back in the squad room, Sue and Mary were asleep. Kirksey dove under her blanket as if the thin wool would protect her from falling shells.

I opened my footlocker, intending to store Ruth's utility bag, then changed my mind. I sat on my bed with Ruth's bag, trying to remember if I'd ever read any protocol on dealing with a deceased soldier's belongings. I felt a twinge of doubt about trespassing on Ruth's privacy, but decided the Army was going to go through Ruth's things anyway. I opened the bag and spilled its contents onto my wool blanket, still stretched tight across the narrow straw mattress.

There was nothing remarkable about Ruth's belongings. She carried sunglasses, a pack of chewing gum, a few francs, a tube of lipstick that had seen better days, and a military-issue black comb. And the silk hankie.

Why did she have a silk handkerchief in her bag? I couldn't imagine Ruth buying anything on the black market. According to Kirksey, she'd been ready to complain about me because I was too lenient with my squad. Would a woman like that really deal in illegal goods? Supplies were scarce, and I hadn't seen a new handkerchief since leaving the States. It was odd.

The only other thing in Ruth's purse was the letter we'd all been ordered to write. *To be opened in the event of my death.* All WAACs in the 22nd Post Headquarters Company wrote letters home to our families to be read in the event of death while stationed overseas. None of us thought we'd ever need them, and there were a lot of jokes thrown around at the time. Unlike male soldiers, WAACs didn't qualify for death benefits, so we didn't have to fill out insurance forms. I distinctly remembered Kirksey joking around, saying, *"In lieu of flowers, please send ten thousand dollars."*

I ran a hand over the sealed letter. I'd have to give it to First Officer Fitzgerald and see that it was mailed to her family. I wondered how Ruth's brothers would take the news. Or would they even get the news? It would probably take weeks for Ruth's mother to get the letter, and then many more weeks for her to send word to her sons in combat.

There was nothing else in the purse. I placed the items in my own footlocker. Until Captain Devlin returned my utility bag, I'd have to use Ruth's for the time being. I would ask Fitzgerald about the letter to Ruth's family in the morning if I had a chance.

*The letter.*

I glanced around the room. Everyone appeared to be asleep. I knew I should get straight into bed and get to sleep myself. Tomorrow was bound to be an unusually busy day. General Rommel and the Afrika Corps were moving in the east which meant the Adjutant General's office would be a hotbed of activity. And we were short a woman now. Exhaustion weighed down every muscle in my body, and still I could not fall asleep. I always felt restless after a bombardment. The echo of explosions resounded in my head, and I had no pillow to pull over my ears to muffle the sound. Did eardrums have memories? I felt certain that mine did. Each bomb, each rapid-fire seventy-five-millimeter shell felt etched into my very flesh.

After Ruth's death and the bombardment, I needed my family. I wanted to hold my own letter. The one I'd received from Konrad just before Pearl Harbor. I knelt down and looked under my bed. Keeping an eye out for any movement from the girls sleeping quietly in their beds, I ran my hands underneath my mattress.

Nothing.

I lifted the blankets, feeling for paper.

Still nothing.

I moved to my footlocker, still open, and sifted through the contents. Moving through my Hobby hat, enlistment papers, transfer orders to North Africa, and a small stack of cash, I blindly felt for the familiar feel of the worn paper envelope.

Nothing.

I shut the footlocker with care. I'd have to look again when the girls were absent and I could do a more thorough search. I crawled into bed and pulled the wool blanket up over my head. My ears were cold, but mostly I wanted privacy. I imagined the drawing tucked safely inside the letter. Sadie had drawn two stick figures on the beach, a sandcastle between them. She'd drawn from memory, a trip we'd made as a family to Galveston when Sadie was three years old. It was one of the last things we'd done as a family. Konrad was noticeably absent from the drawing.

Was this Sadie's memory of home? Could a three-year-old remember such a thing and draw it years later? I had received the letter after my birthday in September, just a few months before Pearl Harbor. There had been a letter from Konrad, telling me Sadie was happy and that he'd done what he had to do for his country. There was no apology for what he'd done. Only explanation and justification.

Usually before bed, I put the paper to my nose and inhaled deeply. It might have been my imagination, but every time I held it to my nose, I felt like I could smell my daughter, detecting a faint odor of talcum powder and Tootsie Pops, Sadie's favorite Sunday treat.

After Konrad left, there had been nights when I contemplated stepping in front of the train that ran behind our house. I'd been so lost and felt so helpless. And hopeless. Then one morning, after a long sleepless night, I'd seen an advertisement in the newspaper: *Who's needed? You are—as you've never been needed before!* I'd felt the writer was speaking directly to me, calling me to join the fight. Nobody wanted to defeat Hitler more than I did in that moment. I'd dressed and headed straight for the recruiting office. The Army had given me more than a job. It had given me a home. Friends. A purpose in life and the chance to win the war and find Sadie. I would protect the Army and the women in my company with my life if I had to.

Sleep beckoned. I tried to think of where I might have put the letter. Had I left it in my shirt pocket? Or the inside pocket of my jacket? I'd look for it first thing in the morning. I had to find it. The letter held all my secrets.

Lost in thoughts of Sadie and the life the Army had given me, I drifted into that place between the waking world and blissful, haunting sleep, only to jerk awake moments later. The image of Ruth's broken body flashed across my mind. Captain Devlin had said a Dr. Edwards at the Church Villa hospital would determine Ruth's cause of death. If I woke early enough, I could swing by and find out if my suspicions were correct. If Ruth had been murdered, I had a duty to find the killer. I had a duty to protect my squad and the home I'd made with the Double Deuces. Drifting off to sleep, determined to uncover the truth, I kept seeing Ruth's shoe lying on the concrete floor, the laces still tied. It was some time before I found reprieve in a short, dreamless sleep.

# CHAPTER 11

I jolted awake to the sound of women's laughter. I blinked away the sleep in my eyes and wished for a tall glass of water. My mouth was desert dry. I had a vague recollection of the warbling muezzin call at dawn. I glanced at my watch: zero seven thirty.

*Damn.*

I had to hurry if I was going to make it to the office before my shift started at zero eight hundred hours. There was no time to stop by the Church Villa. I was late for work. I washed and dressed quickly, slipped my borrowed utility bag over my head, and hustled out of the squad room, to the courtyard. The mess line was short, but I had no time for food. I said good morning to Mother Superior, who stood beside the well, giving instructions to the maid, Anna. I washed my face, brushed my teeth, and hurried to put my things away in the squad room, cursing myself for oversleeping.

My visit to the Church Villa would have to wait.

Outside the convent walls, the street bustled with activity.

Two deuce-and-a-half trucks went past in both directions. I walked northeast, toward the bay and the Rue de Michelet, where I could turn south and head for my office at the Hotel Alexandra.

A jeep pulled up alongside me. I glanced over, hoping to see Captain Devlin; maybe he'd found out Ruth's cause of death. Or maybe he'd decided to interview the girls. Instead, I saw Mary Jordan's boyfriend, Captain Haywynn. He was dressed in his uniform and wore sunglasses, though the day was a muted cloudy blue that I had come to expect in Algiers at this time of year. By nine o'clock, however, the rising sun would highlight the white buildings and dance across the waves of the Mediterranean below, so the sunglasses weren't a bad idea.

"Good morning, Miss Lincoln," Captain Haywynn called. "Care for a ride?"

"No, thank you, Captain. I can walk."

"Don't be silly, Miss Lincoln. I'll give you a lift."

I stopped and looked at my watch again. "Okay, then. Thank you, sir." I climbed into the passenger seat.

Captain Haywynn pulled into traffic. "Terrible business, what happened last evening. Terrible."

"Yes."

"It's got Mary quite upset, you know. They told me just now she's on sick leave. Wouldn't let me see her."

"I'm sorry to hear that. I didn't know she was ill." I didn't point out that he wasn't supposed to be *seeing* her at all. It was against regulations to fraternize with officers.

"I'm sure it's another one of these frightful African bugs. We've all had them."

"Yes," I agreed. Since arriving in Algiers, almost all the girls had fallen ill. I had been sick the previous week but managed to go to work. Some of the girls had been hit with stomach problems that kept them close to the convent's crude toilets.

"I say, I do wish your lot would ease up on the regulations. It pains me not to see her."

"I'm sure Auxiliary Jordan will be up and around in no time, sir."

"Yes, yes. I'm sure she will."

Captain Haywynn swung around the turn on Avenue Georges Clemenceau, without slowing. I grasped the side of the jeep for balance. He honked the horn and passed a donkey cart at the same speed. I decided I would not accept another ride from the earl if the opportunity presented itself again.

"Your friend certainly made a nuisance of herself last night. Still, I'm sorry for her. She didn't seem suicidal, though, did she? Was she depressed?"

I clutched the side of the jeep again. I should have expected the question, but something about his jocular manner grated on me. "Not that I'm aware of, no."

Listening to Captain Haywynn rattle off one question after another, I was reminded of Mary. It seemed they had a lot in common. Both excitable. Young. And very talkative.

"Forgive me for asking, Captain, but how was Ruth a nuisance to you?"

The captain gave the brakes a tap and stopped with surprising ease, to let a trolley pass. "I'd taken Mary up to the roof. Just for some alone time, you understand? Nothing inappropriate. My intentions are completely honorable, I assure you. But that girl Ruth came up to chaperone."

I thought perhaps his intentions on the roof had been less than honorable, seeing as how he was obviously still annoyed that Ruth had interrupted them. No matter that she died shortly after that interruption.

"Not that I minded it. But she had no need to worry."

"What did she say?"

"She came up all in high dudgeon. Said the roof was off-limits and that WAACs were not allowed to fraternize with officers, British or American. Which is true, of course, but everyone knows how I feel about her."

I smiled, but my mind was working. Mary had been on the roof with the earl. And Ruth had followed them. "That sounds like Ruth," I said. "She's all about rules and regulations."

"She was, yes," Captain Haywynn said. "Funny thing, though. I never thought of her as someone who suffered from melancholy."

"No," I agreed. "She seemed happy here."

"She loved playing the soldier. There's no doubt about that. Mary now, she's not really suited to it, I don't think."

"Auxiliary Wentz was not playing soldier. She *was* a soldier. We are soldiers. And Mary's learning," I said, slightly annoyed at this pronouncement.

"Oh, I meant no disrespect, miss. You girls are doing a bang-up job here. Everybody agrees on that. But Mary is an innocent. She belongs in a more gentle environment. I'm trying to convince her to go back to England and stay with my family."

"Oh." This was a surprise. "I didn't realize things were that serious between you two."

"Oh, they're very serious. I intend to marry her."

"Do you really?"

"I haven't asked her yet, so don't tell her. It will be our little secret, yes?" He winked at me.

I shifted in my seat. Was Captain Haywynn really intending to marry Auxiliary Jordan? Or was he just covering for some bad behavior? I would have to speak to Mary about this new romance. Mary had a duty to her country. She wasn't here to find a husband. But if she loved the earl, then she would have to make some tough decisions.

"I don't think she'll be too keen on going to a strange country alone. She wants to stay with me. If I can get leave anytime soon, I'll take her home myself. But until then, she'll have to make do."

"So you left Ruth and Mary alone together?" I asked.

"Yes. But Mary joined me shortly after that. I waited at the bottom of the stairs. Thought I'd let Ruth scold her roundly and then continue with our evening. I'll tell you, the sooner Mary leaves this wretched city, the better."

"I thought the British were more accepting of women in theaters of combat. Seeing as how England has become a theater of war. Hasn't it?"

The earl inclined his head. "True. Our island is under constant attack and has been long before you Yanks arrived. Everyone to the pump, as they say. But my estate is far away from the Desert Fox and his litter of dirty Boches. Besides, dear Mary is different."

"How so?"

"She's not strong enough."

"Maybe she could be," I replied. "Given time, I think she could be. She's already learned so much. Besides, would she be any safer in England, with bombs falling all over the place?"

"My family has an estate in Warwickshire. The Luftwaffe hasn't made it up there yet. Now that you Yanks are in the show, I don't think they will. She'll be safe there."

"I don't think Mary joined the Army to be safe, Captain Haywynn. We look after one another, but we all knew what we were getting into when we volunteered for overseas duty."

The earl gave me a sideways glance. "Come now, Miss Lincoln. One of your own died last night."

I didn't have an answer for that pronouncement.

"You look tired, Miss Lincoln. How are you holding up with these dreadfully long hours?"

"Fine, thank you."

"Well, I know you Americans like your cup of joe, what? But if you need something stronger, don't go off into the Casbah. That's no place for a woman."

"I'm a soldier in the American Army, Captain Haywynn. I know how to handle myself."

"Of course. I meant no offense." We pulled up outside the Hotel Alexandra. I climbed out of the jeep, feeling an irrational need to distance myself from Captain Haywynn. He seemed to be a man who spoke in riddles. He made me uncomfortable, and I felt the need to defend myself, which was silly because he hadn't attacked me in any way. In fact, he'd kindly given me a ride to work.

"Don't worry about me, Captain." I forced a bright smile, teeth and all. "I'm steady as a bullet in a crisis."

"That's all well and good, Miss Lincoln, but you must be on your guard. Algiers is a very dangerous place to be."

# Chapter 12

On the slopes of the Mustapha Superior, nestled in a garden of palm, orange, and lemon trees, north of the Bois de Boulogne, sat the Alexandra Hotel. Birds of paradise towered over beds of bougainvillea, lilies, and winter roses. The Adjutant General's office was located on the top two floors of the Alexandra Hotel, facing the gardens and a tram stop on the other side of the street. I always wished I could see the ocean from the office. Across the blue Mediterranean, over the coast of southern France, through Luxembourg, waited the hills of the Ruhr and the tiny town of Minden, where Sadie might be living. But the view of the bay was on the north side of the hotel.

I showed my pass to the guard at the gate and headed for the stairs. I climbed upstairs to the hum and clack of teletype machines echoing through the dank hallway. Allied soldiers occupied eleven buildings in the city, housing over three hundred offices, but the core leadership worked out of the two luxury hotels in Upper Mustapha. My office, the Correspondence and Orders Subsection of the Personnel Section, was located at the end of the hall on the left.

The office had once been a high-end hotel room. The white-washed walls were accented with Moorish tiles in soft greens and blues. But the United States military had imposed efficiency and order, tearing out the plush carpet and replacing the bedroom furniture with desks and file cabinets. Supplies had been requisitioned by the newly created Services of Supply. Heavy metal typewriters sat on each desk. Maps of the North African coast hung on the walls. All traces of luxury had been removed.

Corporal Pinski sat at his desk, just inside the door, already hard at work. Our office received lists of assignments from the War Department and from various commanders in theater. Our job was to type up all Special Orders and send them to the office across the hall for distribution, or run them to the St. George Hotel, across the street, for immediate delivery.

Sergeant Norman Gilmore acted as the chief personnel clerk. Corporal Pinski was his assistant and our supervisor. He organized the various lists of assignments. Mary and I were tasked with typing up the numbered Special Orders. Sue Dunworthy operated the mimeograph machine. Ruth filed all copies. We all helped with distribution, depending on who was free to run over to the St. George or one of the other offices around the city. The office ran pretty much seamlessly except for Sergeant Gilmore's frequent frustrations and outbursts over minor mistakes or delays. He was a volatile man on the best of days, but lately his anger had exploded, and his manner was more disrespectful than ever. I wondered if he himself was subject to transfer to a combat unit and resented the WAACs for moving into his territory.

Corporal Pinski stopped typing when I walked in. He looked annoyed at the interruption until he saw it was me, and then gave me a sympathetic smile. He rose from his chair and came over to put a hand on my arm. "Dottie, how are you holding up?"

Sue looked up from her typewriter. She was sitting at Mary's desk. Pinski must have recruited her to type orders. With Mary sick and Ruth gone, the personnel office was woefully short-staffed. Pressure sprung behind my eyes, tears threatening, and for the first time that morning, I felt my control slipping. Of all the times to oversleep, I couldn't think of a worse time. No wonder Corporal Pinski was annoyed. Sergeant Gilmore was probably attending a staff meeting. Mary, our fastest typist, was out on sick leave. Ruth, our file clerk, was dead. And I was late to my post. Good soldiers were at their posts on time and prepared. Shame coursed through me.

Suddenly, I missed Ruth. I missed her no-nonsense attitude and her enthusiasm about our job as soldiers. I hadn't realized it before, but Ruth's commitment to the Army had made me feel safe. I hated feeling that the women of the 22nd Post might be in danger. "I'm fine. Well, not fine exactly," I said in a rush. "I'm so, so sorry for being late. I don't know what happened. I heard the muezzin call, but . . ."

Pinski patted my back, his touch soft and hesitant. "Yesterday was traumatic for all of us. Sometimes the body has a mind of its own. You needed rest."

I nodded. "I still can't quite believe it happened."

"I never suspected she was depressed," Pinski said, shoving his hands in his pockets. "Did you?"

I shook my head. "I don't believe she jumped. She wasn't that kind of girl."

Pinski's eyebrows rose. "You think she fell?"

"Maybe." I met Pinski's gaze. "Maybe she was pushed."

Corporal Pinski blew out a loud breath. "Damn." He shook his head. "What makes you think that?"

I flushed. I shouldn't have said anything. "I don't know. I'm just having a hard time accepting that Ruth was suicidal."

"You think it was Rivera? I should have punched that guy. He was making a pest of himself. Always does."

"I don't know what to think," I said, my voice breaking. I felt close to tears again. I didn't want to cry in front of Corporal Pinski. I certainly didn't want to cry in front of Sue Dunworthy. She'd never let me hear the end of it. Crying was a sign of weakness, and

I needed to project strength like a good squad leader. I needed to *be* strong and *feel* strong if I was going to find out what happened to Ruth and protect the other girls in my squad.

I pushed my feelings down deep and changed the subject. "I'd better get to work. I'm sure we're behind."

"Sergeant Gilmore was burning the midnight oil. I already have a stack of new orders to type up and distribute."

"Right. I'll get to it." I shrugged out of my coat and hung it over the back of my chair, the desk closest to Corporal Pinski's.

Pinski picked up a manila envelope from his desk. "General Sawbridge wanted these orders delivered this morning. Could you run them over?"

"You sure you don't want me to type?"

"There's some urgency on these. Looks like Rommel is on the move again. Scuttlebutt is there was a dust-up last night."

"Of course, Corporal. They'll be moving men and materials to the front as fast as possible, I guess."

"We'll be doing the moving, if not the heavy lifting."

"Right. Anything you need, Corporal," I said, retrieving my jacket from the back of my chair. General Sawbridge was the assistant chief of Staff for G-1. He oversaw all personnel in theater.

Corporal Pinski handed over the manila envelope. I hurried into my coat and out of the office. Stepping back onto Avenue Foureau, I made a right and headed up the hill to the St. George Hotel. The St. George was the hub of Allied Force Headquarters. General Eisenhower's offices were located there, as well as those of most of the senior staff officers. It was a sprawling complex with over two hundred rooms.

It wouldn't take any time at all to drop off the orders. I wondered . . .

Captain Devlin had said that a Dr. Edwards would determine Ruth's cause of death. If I hurried, I could swing by the Church Villa and ask the attending doctor if he'd found anything suspicious in the postmortem. Corporal Pinski needed me at the office. With the Germans on the move, the Army needed WAACs more than ever. I wanted to do whatever I could to save lives and ensure victory. The Army had decided my job was to move men and materials to the front, and I would always do that to the very best of my ability. But my first priority had to be protecting the rest of the women in my squad. If Ruth had been murdered, other WAACs might be in danger. We'd be no use to the war effort if we allowed ourselves to be picked off, one by one, like target practice. Surely it wouldn't take long to find this Dr. Edwards and put my suspicions to bed once and for all.

# CHAPTER 13

I dropped the orders off at General Sawbridge's office and continued down Avenue Foureau, walking along the edge of the Bois de Boulogne, toward the Church Villa Hospital, as fast as my feet would carry me. Not for the first time, I wished I could just hop on the passing trolley. But American servicemen and servicewomen were prohibited from using public transportation in Algiers.

The sun struggled to peek out from behind waves of clouds piled on top of the Atlas Mountains like hats in winter. By noon the clouds would burn off or dump water. The weather in Algiers was as changeable as that of south Texas, where I'd met and married Konrad.

The hospital was a converted villa on Rue Michelet. I walked past the outer concrete wall, stacked with sandbags, and through the front door. An Army nurse stood at the front desk, a sheaf of papers in one hand, a telephone receiver in the other. I waited until the nurse was done putting her call through the switchboard, then cleared my throat. The nurse looked up expectantly. "What d'ya want?" she asked in a southern drawl.

"I'm here to ask about Auxiliary Wentz."

"Who?"

"I need to speak with the doctor overseeing the death of Auxiliary Ruth Wentz." I swallowed back the lump ballooning in my throat. "The WAAC who died last night."

"Oh, the jumper." The nurse shifted the papers under her arm and waved at the hallway branching off the main lobby. "Go down the stairs at the end of the hall."

I followed her directions and took the staircase down to a large, cavernous room with concrete walls and a low ceiling. Portable standing lamps had been placed at intervals, their incandescent bulbs shooting down circles of light like searchlights turned toward hell. Several wooden gurneys were lined up against the wall at the back. On one of them was a sheet-covered body, a lamp above highlighting the dips and curves of the body beneath.

Ruth.

Captain Devlin stood beside the table, talking to a British officer wearing a white coat over his winter uniform.

Captain Devlin glanced over and frowned. "What the hell are you doing here?"

"Captain." I saluted, then stood at attention. The cold was thick, like an invisible fog, and I shivered. "I came to inquire about Ruth's cause of death, sir."

Captain Devlin raised a brow. "Don't you have somewhere to be?"

"I'm on a break," I said. It was a lie. I felt a small stab of guilt for lying. I should be back at the office, typing up letters for Corporal Pinski and helping get the new orders out. But I had to know what had happened to Ruth.

Devlin looked at his watch. "You're on a break at nine in the morning?"

"A short one, yes. What are you doing here? I thought you'd decided Ruth was a suicide."

Devlin frowned, and I hoped I wasn't about to be charged with insubordination. But the captain's next question caught me off guard. "How's your shorthand?"

I tried to hide my surprise at the question. "Great."

"Do you have a notebook?"

"No."

"Come here." I complied, and he handed me a small green notebook. I reached out to take it, but he pulled his hand back. "You'll take notes. We'll wrap this up, and then you go back to work and forget this thing. Deal?"

I nodded, then took the proffered notebook. I flipped it open to the stub of pencil marking a blank page.

"Auxiliary Lincoln, meet Major Edwards. Edwards, Auxiliary Lincoln. All right, Doc," Captain Devlin said, motioning to the doctor, who had watched this exchange with disinterest. "Go ahead."

The doctor pulled back the white sheet. I gasped. Ruth lay naked on the table. Her skin resembled the underbelly of a beached fish. Every blemish, every bruise, stood out in stark relief. The smell hit me like a gas attack. My stomach revolted and I dropped my head, struggling not to vomit.

"One wristwatch," the doctor said, setting it on the table. "One necklace—gold. No other jewelry."

"Lincoln," Devlin barked.

I snapped my head up. "Yes, sir."

"You getting this?"

I scribbled, *One wristwatch, one gold necklace.* "Yes, sir. Got it, sir."

"All right, Doc. Did you test for alcohol?" Captain Devlin rubbed his nose. I wondered if the smell bothered him too.

"Yes, she's clean. No alcohol in her system."

I wrote this information down in the notebook.

"This is interesting," the doctor said, leaning over Ruth's body.

"What's that?"

"She has a contusion on the front of her ankle, so that's a neat parlor trick."

"How do you mean?"

"I'd say sometime shortly before she died, she was either hit in the ankle with some sort of club or rock, or she encountered a boulder on her way down."

I hated the glibness in his voice but knew we were in a theater of combat. Most of the young men I danced with at socials were raw recruits and had never seen a battle. But the officers were a different story. Most of the older officers, like Dr. Edwards, had seen combat before. They'd served in the First World War. They were hardened in a way that the young men weren't. Yet.

I guessed Captain Devlin was no more than thirty-five years old. Too young to have served in 1918. But he had the look of a battle-hardened veteran.

"Did you look at her shoe?" I asked.

Major Edwards pointed to a pair of Oxford browns sitting on an empty stretcher. "Yes. The shoe you brought in and the other, which was securely fastened to her foot."

"It was pulled off in the struggle."

"We don't know that," Captain Devlin snapped. "Anything else, Doc?"

"Yes. Three of her fingernails on her left hand are broken."

"Skin or hair or blood underneath?"

"No, nothing like that. But there is a tiny bit of felt."

"Felt?"

"It's just an educated guess at this point, but yes, I think it's felt. We don't have the equipment to do an analysis, but it looks like green felt."

The doctor picked up a petri dish and handed it to Devlin. I peered over his shoulder.

"Do my eyes deceive me or is that Army green?" Devlin asked, looking resigned.

"That's my guess."

"So she didn't jump," I said.

They both looked at me.

"She was pushed," I said in response to the question neither had asked.

"How do you arrive at that conclusion?" Major Edwards asked. But he didn't sound doubtful. He sounded intrigued.

"She has a contusion on her ankle that she probably got by hitting the balustrade on the third floor of the opera house. When she was pushed, she must have instinctually dragged her foot, trying to stop her forward momentum, hitting it as she toppled over."

"So you're saying she turned and tried to grab the perp's jacket?"

"Maybe. But I'm wondering if that happened before she was pushed? Maybe there was a struggle. And he turned her around as she grappled with him? And then pushed her over the side."

Devlin nodded. "That's plausible. Damn. A WAAC killed in a theater of war. This won't go over well."

"No, it won't," I agreed, triumphant at the confirmation that my suspicions had been confirmed. On the heels of that feeling came a wave of shame. Ruth was still dead, and it was no happy thing that she'd been murdered.

"You think it was a lover's spat?" Captain Devlin asked. "A rendezvous gone wrong?"

"That doesn't seem likely, sir."

"Why not?"

"Ruth was very focused on her work. She didn't seem interested in men, sir. She was here to do a job."

"Well, we're all here to do a job, but there seems to be a lot of romance going on."

"Especially with the WAACs," Major Edwards piped in.

I bit the inside of my lip to keep from telling Major Edwards exactly what I thought of that idea. "We're ordered to go to those dances, sir. We didn't come here to have fun. Yes, some of the girls are young and flattered, and maybe a little bored. But most of us came here to help win the war."

"Are you an investigator, Private?" the doctor asked.

"No, sir. And I'm an auxiliary, sir, not a private. Not yet, anyway."

"Then I suggest you leave the investigating to your senior officer here."

"Yes, sir."

Captain Devlin had watched this exchange, his mouth quirked up at the corners. "Thank you, Major. That's all we need for now."

I followed Captain Devlin up the stairs and out into the forecourt of the Church Villa. Devlin donned his sunglasses. The sun had come out and burned away the last of the cloud cover. It would be a warm day. I needed to get back to work. Corporal Pinski and Sue Dunworthy had piles of orders ready for me to type and deliver. At least I had the truth now. Ruth had been murdered. But why? Who would have had a reason to kill her?

"I suppose I was being insubordinate, sir."

Devlin chuckled. "Serves him right. He's got no business giving orders to an American."

"He didn't want me to be part of the investigation," I said.

Devlin pursed his lips. "I don't think it had anything to do with an investigation."

"We know very well that most of the soldiers don't want us here. Especially the brass. Even the British brass. Except General Eisenhower, of course."

"You're a distraction, Lincoln. Not you specifically, but the WAACs in general. I know there's a manpower shortage and the Army needs you, but there's a lot of guys in the Army think that women belong at home. Seems like even some of the Brits don't want women in a combat theater." For some reason, this last thought seemed to amuse the captain.

"Is that what you think, sir?"

"Honestly, I don't know yet. You gals haven't been here that long. But I will say, this situation with Wentz? It won't bode well for the WAACs."

"Why do you say that?"

"If she committed suicide, then the Army might decide the WAACs aren't up to the task."

"But you just said she was murdered!"

"No, I said she was *killed*. I still think the most likely explanation is she had a fight with a boyfriend. Maybe he broke it off or got too frisky, and she broke it off. Either way, that explains the bruises. Things got out of hand, and there was an accident. A terrible accident. And if it was a lover's spat or the result of jealousy, maybe because she danced with another man, or something of that nature, the brass might decide you WAACs are too much of a distraction to the men and shouldn't be here. These men have to go fight, Lincoln. It's hard, and it's not fair, but the men need to be focused on battle. And if there's a little piece of home right here in the theater of operations, maybe they're not so motivated to fight. And maybe if they're dallying with you young ladies at dances every other night, then they're even less focused on fighting. And if they're in love, or falling in love, then maybe that's all the more reason to find a way to avoid the front lines. And the whole reason the WAACs are here is to release a man for combat, right?"

"Yes."

"For the dogface in the Army, the foot soldier, war is killing. And I think the whole plan with the WAACs might backfire in the end. Your friend's death." Captain Devlin rubbed at this forehead. "Or murder. Might be a murder, dammit. It isn't going to help convince anyone that women belong in a theater of combat."

"The Army thinks we belong here," I reminded him. "We know the dangers we face, Captain Devlin. I like to think we offer some comfort to the soldiers when we give them a dance before they're sent off to the desert. Maybe we give them a fond memory of home. But I've never seen any indication that the men think it's anything but a fleeting reprieve. If the Army thinks we're a distraction by dancing with the men, then they should cancel the dances. We'd rather be working anyway. That's where we can make a real difference in this war. Every WAAC sitting at her typewriter or switchboard releases a man to join the fight. And like you said, fighting—and killing—is how we win the war. We have to make the same kind of sacrifices the British have made. Which is everybody in, sir."

"That's true. But we're not the British. The American public prefers to have their women safe and sound at home. Running war bond drives, yes. Rationing, yes. Organizing scrap metal drives, yes. But wearing a uniform and serving in a theater of combat? Under fire? That's a whole new ballgame."

"Sacrifices have to be made, sir. And the more women who join up, the more women who run communications and type and clerk and wash dishes and run mess halls, the more men can fight, and the sooner we can go home. Which is what we all want, right?"

Captain Devlin didn't answer. He pulled out his pack of cigarettes but didn't open it. "Is it at all possible she got into an argument with a lover? The lover left and she decided to end it all?"

"Ruth definitely didn't have a lover, sir. We have a curfew. Besides, we haven't been here that long. Ruth isn't the kind of girl to go off with a gentleman that way. She cared about two things, as far as I could see: rules and regulations."

"Damn."

"Look, maybe you're right, sir. Maybe we don't have a murder here. Maybe there was some kind of accident. I think you're wrong. But Ruth was a soldier—"

"An auxiliary soldier," Devlin interrupted.

"She was here serving her country, sir. She volunteered for this. I think she deserves an investigation into her death, at the very least."

"And you want to help in that investigation."

"I do. I can help."

"Because you speak French?"

"Yes, and German."

Devlin raised his eyebrows. "That's interesting."

"Not really. My mother was from Alsace-Lorraine. Everyone in Alsace speaks French and German."

"But you're not from there," Devlin pointed out.

"I was born in France, actually. Like a lot of ex-Army kids."

"An Army kid? That explains a lot."

I decided not to respond to this enigmatic statement. "Also, I am an excellent notetaker, sir."

Devlin rubbed at his chin. "All right. If I agree to this, you follow my orders. I notice you don't have much respect for rank."

I didn't say anything to this.

"This is the Army. We're not in a Hollywood picture, okay? Investigating crimes is not glamourous. Most of the time it's pretty boring. You are not an MP."

"I don't want to be. I just want to find out what happened to Ruth."

"We'll probably find out she jumped or had some kind of accident. Or we're not going to find out anything at all."

"What do you mean by that?"

"I mean, maybe she jumped, maybe she didn't. We don't have any definitive proof that she was murdered, and I'm warning you ahead of time, it may stay that way. We may never find out what happened up there. We may not find anything more than what we know right now."

"I don't accept that, Captain Devlin. One way or another, we will find out who killed Ruth."

"I'm just trying to prepare you for the very real possibility that even if your friend was murdered, her killer may never be brought to justice."

"I'm not ready to admit defeat before the battle has even begun, sir."

He shook his head, but a smile crept across his face. "I can probably get you transferred for temporary duty to my office as a secretary. For a couple days anyway."

I frowned. "A secretary?"

"I told you, you're not an investigator. The Army will agree to a secretary, though."

"Understood, sir." I felt a twinge of regret, thinking of Corporal Pinski's desk, piled high with Special Orders needing to go out. Maybe Sergeant Gilmore could recruit a clerk from another section for the time being.

"One more thing. I make the final decision about cause of death, and you go along with it. That's the deal. You don't keep looking around, trying to prove your case."

"Yes, sir."

Captain Devlin blew out a long breath. "All right, I have to go make a report to my CO. I guess you're coming with me."

# Chapter 14

Captain Devlin drove to El Biar. The 577th Military Police Company station was located in what I presumed had once been an office building on the main road, Avenue Georges Clemenceau, not too far from the convent. I hiked up my skirt and climbed out of the jeep with as much modesty as I could muster. Looking up at the building, my heart fluttered. I had no idea what Captain Devlin's colonel would think about a WAAC being assigned to a case, but somehow, I doubted he'd be thrilled with the idea. Of course, I only had my experience with Sergeant Gilmore to go on.

Straightening my skirt, I pushed aside my concern. Perhaps the colonel would be thrilled to have an extra set of hands on board.

We walked into the dark interior, and my eyes adjusted to the gloom. The lobby was nothing more than a rectangular room with whitewashed walls. There were no colorful tiles, no plush Turkish rugs, no Moorish design elements at all. My Oxford browns clicked an echoing cacophony on the polished concrete floor that matched the rhythmic typing happening in a nearby office. A single military policeman stood beside a simple wooden desk that held a telephone, a stapler, and a clipboard bursting with attached papers. He saluted Captain Devlin. After a rapid-fire glance at me, he shifted his gaze away and stood at attention.

Private Venturi emerged from an office down the hall. "Captain Devlin, sir, we have a report of shoes being sold out of a garage on Boulevard Gallieni." He saw me and stopped abruptly. His eyes raked over me, head to toe, before shifting his gaze to Captain Devlin. He handed over a sheaf of onion skin papers.

"Shoes? What kind of shoes?" Devlin looked through the paperwork, scanning each page.

"Don't know yet. Might be Army issue though."

Captain Devlin rubbed his thumb and forefinger across his eyebrows. "All right, stand by. I need to see the colonel."

"Should I send a guy over?"

Devlin shook his head. "Just hold on, Private. One operation at a time."

I followed Captain Devlin down the hall behind the lobby desk to an open door, the first office on the left. Colonel Cantry, the provost marshall, sat behind his desk, his chair turned away from us, studying a large map of Algiers tacked to the wall.

Colonel Cantry's office was an exercise in chaos. His desk contained a telephone; a towering stack of file folders; a large, industrial-sized stapler; a name plate; and a pewter ashtray with a pipe resting in its dented bowl. Bits of tobacco littered the entire mess, like snow sprinkled on a mud hill.

The colonel turned and immediately zeroed in on me. He looked me up and down, much like Private Venturi had moments ago, his fleshy lips pursed. He had a square head, wide-set eyes, chiseled jaw, and an Adolf Hitler mustache. His short, dark hair was parted down the middle, calling to mind a vaudeville actor I'd once seen with my father at the Palace Theatre.

He frowned and got to his feet. For a split second, I thought he might bow. I saw the moment he realized he did not need to stand, for he was not in the presence of a lady, but a lady soldier.

He sat back down in his chair, scowling. "Where the . . .?" He cleared his throat and started again. "Where have you been, Devlin?"

Captain Devlin heaved a sigh, as if he knew the colonel was not going to like what he had to say. "I just came from the Doc's ward. Turns out that WAAC situation might be more complicated than we thought."

I frowned. Without thinking, I said, "She wasn't just some WAAC, Captain. She was Auxiliary Ruth Wentz."

Both men turned their heads to stare at me. Both looked shocked. Only the colonel looked angry.

Captain Devlin dipped his head. "Of course. I meant no disrespect." But his words were laced with irritation.

"God damn," Colonel Cantry muttered, apparently forgetting all about manners and how to act in front of a lady. "I'm sorry about the WAAC who jumped, but we don't have a job to do where suicide is concerned."

"I'm afraid it's a bit more complicated than that, sir."

"Nonsense." Colonel Cantry reached for the pipe propped in his ashtray. "Nothing complicated about jumpers."

I laced my hands behind my back and bit down on my lower lip. The colonel's disregard for Ruth's life sent anger coursing through me, but I wanted to stay on the case. Voicing my frustration would only get me sent away.

"Sir, the evidence we've collected so far indicates that Auxiliary Wentz did not jump off that balcony."

Colonel Cantry put his pipe in his mouth and eyed Devlin, completely ignoring my presence. "Not suicide then? Okay, so she fell. It's as simple as that. Get the engineers to put some gates up. Restrict access to the roof. Problem solved."

"You want me to have the engineers put gates on every roof in Algiers, sir?"

"Don't be a wiseass, Devlin."

"Sorry, sir."

The colonel lit his pipe and looked from Devlin to me. "So what do you want then, Devlin? Out with it."

Captain Devlin relayed Dr. Edwards's findings. "We'll need to do a full investigation."

"A full investigation? Are you insane? For Christ's sake, you know we're in the middle of a war. We can't spare personnel for the death of one WAAC who should have stayed home anyway."

I tightened my hands to fists to keep from addressing that particular assertion. Colonel Cantry was a superior officer. Sparring with him over respect for the WAACs would get me nowhere and likely land me in hot water.

"I just need one guy, Colonel."

"Can't do it. If you can't conduct this investigation by yourself, you can't conduct it at all."

"Then I'll use Auxiliary Lincoln here. She's game."

Colonel Cantry's bulbous eyes went wide. "Are you serious?"

"She's already aware of the crime. She can type and take notes. I can use her. It'll make the investigation go faster."

I wasn't sure how I felt about being referred to as an "it," but held my tongue. All I cared about was finding out who had hurt Ruth.

"Maybe you haven't heard, but we're getting our asses handed to us out east," Colonel Cantry said, slamming his chair forward and pounding his fist on the desk. I involuntarily startled at the sudden burst of anger. "We can't waste time and manpower on a dissatisfied WAAC who jumps to her death at a dance."

"I'm sorry, sir," Captain Devlin said with a shrug, unperturbed by Cantry's outburst, "but this isn't some civilian we can pawn off to the French authorities. The WAACs are Army, even if they are only an auxiliary force. This case falls under our jurisdiction."

Colonel Cantry frowned and tapped the bowl of his pipe against his desk, glancing vaguely in my direction, but not meeting my gaze. "You girls shouldn't be here in the first place."

"That may be, sir, but we need them. We need typists. Clerks." Captain Devlin shrugged as if this were a necessary evil they both had to deal with. "We need them to free up the men to fight, sir. It's a devil's bargain, but that's war, I guess."

My anger rose with every word spoken. I opened my mouth, but Devlin spoke again, heading me off. "We'll work as fast as possible to clear the case. Having Auxiliary Lincoln here on board will move things along. She speaks French, so she'll be an asset when interviewing locals."

Colonel Cantry frowned. "Why do you need to interview locals?"

"The dance happened on French property. There were civilians at the dance. Not to mention the Arabs loitering all over the place."

I bit the inside of my cheek to keep a check on my emotions. Maybe it was because I'd lived in Germany as part of the American occupation forces as a kid, but I felt some sympathy for the native population of Algeria. The French had occupied their country for over a hundred years. When the Americans first landed, the population of Berbers and Arabs had been starved to the point of emaciation. They were respected by neither the French nor the Allies.

"Roger that, Captain." Cantry heaved a self-suffering sigh. "All right then. She can serve as your clerk for the duration of your investigation. Which will last three days."

"I need a week."

"Three days, Devlin. And make sure this little lady knows how we run things. Investigations are top secret. This is eyes only. She's not to discuss details of the investigation with anyone. Pound that into her head, Captain. Women talk."

I cleared my throat and steeled my courage. "I know my duty, sir. Of course I'll follow regulations regarding confidential information."

Colonel Cantry spat out his pipe and thrust it at me with each word. "Another word of insubordination from you, and you will be on the next ship home. Do you understand *that*, little lady?"

"Yes, sir," I said a little too loudly. I was a private. He was a colonel. He had no need to speak directly to me. I was his subordinate in this man's Army, and I chided myself for letting my emotions get the better of me. It didn't matter if the colonel thought I was a nuisance. It didn't matter if he thought I didn't belong at AFHQ. All that mattered was that he approved the investigation into Ruth's death.

Captain Devlin frowned. "She's a soldier in this man's Army, sir. She'll do as she's told."

The colonel shook his head. "You're a fool if you believe that. All right, then. Have Venturi draw up temporary orders. Three days, Devlin. That's all you get."

"Thank you, sir."

"And Devlin, just so you know, if she talks, it'll be on your head."

"Yes, sir."

"One more thing," Colonel Cantry said. "Take care of it quietly. If the press gets wind of this, there will be hell to pay."

"Agreed, sir."

"And I need someone on the panty bandit case."

"Why don't you put Venturi on that for now? He's eager."

Colonel Cantry heaved a beleaguered sigh. "I suppose it can wait. Bigger issues blowing up all over the place. Wrap this thing up quick. We're about to have much bigger problems. Things aren't going well at the front. Ike's in a mood. And I want Venturi reporting to you if he finds any new info on the panty bandit."

"Of course, sir."

"All right then. Dismissed." The colonel's phone rang, and he picked up the receiver, shooing them out the door.

Private Venturi still stood in the foyer with his sheaf of papers. Captain Devlin directed Venturi to type up and send a temporary duty request to Sergeant Gilmore at the Adjutant General's office.

I felt a twinge of regret at leaving Corporal Pinski in the lurch with the current offensive underway and so much work to be done. But I also felt a flush of triumph. For the first time since joining the Army, I felt like I'd made a real difference. Maybe Captain Devlin would have pushed for an investigation into Ruth's death if I hadn't stopped by the Church Villa, but I doubted it. Ruth's killer had to be found. Colonel Cantry's outright hostility toward the WAACs was a good reminder of how many American soldiers in Algiers harbored conflicted feelings about women soldiers in their midst. I needed to find out what happened to Ruth and make sure it didn't put any other WAACs in danger.

Outside, the air was heavy. I suspected a storm was coming. The rain would fall, and the streets of Algiers would turn to mud.

Devlin looked at his watch. "Remind me what company Private Rivera's in?"

"It's the Eight-Oh-Five, sir."

"Right. First thing's first. Let's talk to the man who picked a fight with our victim."

# Chapter 15

On our way to the offices of the 805th Signal Company, a light drizzle fell in full daylight. I pulled my overseas cap down low. My hair would end up limp and plastered to my neck. I made a mental note to wash my hair when I got back to barracks. The challenge of personal hygiene was a side of the war the press didn't cover. Nobody back home knew how hard it was to wash your hair using water from a helmet and a sliver of GI-issue soap.

Pushing aside memories of lounging in a deep tub and working shampoo into my hair, I turned my thoughts to the investigation ahead. Despite Captain Devlin's assertion that I would be nothing more than his typist and notetaker, I intended to be an active participant in this investigation. I knew the WAACs. I knew Ruth. Hopefully I'd be able to help find out what had happened on that balcony, despite Captain Devlin's doubts about our possible success in solving the mystery of Ruth's death.

Captain Devlin shifted to a lower gear as we descended the terraced hill. "Do you think Private Rivera wanted a sexual relationship with Auxiliary Wentz? That she rejected him, they struggled, and he threw her off the roof?"

I planted one hand on the dash to keep upright, contemplating the scenario. If he'd asked me the same question before the dance, I'd have insisted Private Rivera was a nice guy. A flirt, yes, but good-natured. However, last night he'd grabbed Ruth's arm, hard. Not to mention that he'd shoved me to the ground. The memory of that moment sent heat rushing up the back of my neck. Maybe Private Rivera was hiding a malevolent nature beneath his easygoing charm. "I suppose it's possible, sir. But I'm not sure I believe he's capable of such a thing."

"Why not?"

"I've never really seen him angry. He's pushy, yes. And flirtatious. But I never saw any indication he was violent. Not on purpose, at least."

"Not on purpose?"

"He accidentally knocked me down last night," I admitted.

Devlin stomped on the brake and pulled the jeep over to the side of the road. He flung an arm across the back of my seat and turned to face me. "I think you'd better tell me more, don't you?"

I detailed the events from the previous evening and my awkward encounter with Private Rivera. "But," I insisted, "it was an accident. He's not a violent man."

"You think you know him well enough to say that?"

"I guess not. But he was pushy with all the girls. He tried it with me. And Kirksey. He asks for a dance, gets a little handsy. Wants to make a date. He gets turned down and then he makes a joke. He never seemed angry. And I'm certain pushing me down was an accident. If anything, it calmed him down. I think it embarrassed him. He left pretty quickly after that."

"Maybe he was just good at hiding his emotions. Maybe he was tired of getting rejected."

"Maybe."

"Every man has his breaking point, Lincoln." Captain Devlin pulled back onto the road. "The boys, they may joke around and flirt and act like any other man stateside. But the truth is, these boys are desperate. Even the ones in the rear echelon. They're lonely. Homesick. And not to be indelicate, but they want to get laid. You girls are like low-hanging fruit, tempting them with dances and kisses."

"Are you saying a man won't take no for an answer?"

"No. I'm saying soldiers are not men. At least not the men you knew back home. They're soldiers. And every soldier has his breaking point."

"That's a bit unsettling."

"Yes, it is."

"The thing is, sir, there wasn't that much time between Private Rivera leaving the dance floor and Ruth's death. They'd already had an altercation. If Ruth went upstairs and Rivera followed her, he would have had to build up that anger quickly. From the little I know about him; he just doesn't seem the type to fly off the handle like that."

"Maybe he didn't fly off the handle. Maybe he followed her upstairs with a plan to kill her."

I spent the rest of the ride trying to envision Private Rivera climbing up to the third floor, intending to kill Ruth. I pictured Rivera's easy smile and gentle teasing. I tried to imagine that smile turned to a murdering sneer.

The streets were crowded with military vehicles, a couple of sedans that were most likely being driven by American civilians working for the State Department, streetcars, and several Arab-driven donkey carts.

We found ourselves stuck behind a donkey cart. The back wagon was filled with burlap sacks, probably fruit and vegetables headed to the market at Bresson Square. "It's a simpler way of life that these Arabs have, isn't it?" Devlin mused.

"Looks like a life of poverty to me. I don't know how simple that is, sir."

"Have you ever been without money, Lincoln?"

"Not like this." When Konrad left, I'd had a few frightening months. I'd quit my job at Baker Hughes to marry Konrad. When he left, I hadn't been able to get my old position back and took a lower-paying job at the telephone company. But I'd managed to make ends meet.

Unfortunately, I hadn't had near enough money for a ticket to sail to Germany and find Sadie. Still, I'd always had more than the kids running around the streets of Algiers. I wondered if the boy who'd stolen the wine the night of Ruth's death had been able to sell the bottle. I hoped so.

"Makes you wonder if they'd all have been better off if the French had never come here."

"I'm sure they'd agree, sir."

The donkey cart stopped to allow a streetcar to pass and Devlin slammed on the brakes. A group of street children swarmed the jeep. My throat constricted, and I resisted the urge to pull some money from my utility bag.

I thought of Sadie. Where was she this very moment? Was she safe? Was someone feeding her well? If Konrad hadn't volunteered for military service as soon as he returned to Germany, I had no doubt he'd have been drafted by now. Maybe even killed. Who was taking care of Sadie now? It was a question that haunted me daily.

"You have to watch that bleeding heart, Lincoln."

I flushed, embarrassed to be caught out, even if Captain Devlin had the wrong idea about my sudden melancholy. "I don't think there's anything wrong with caring about children, sir."

"There's not. But we can't save them."

"We shouldn't ignore them either."

"I started out as a beat cop in Salinas. We had swarms of people on the streets, starving, looking for food. There were so many kids and families in trouble. We had abusive husbands, dead husbands, and absent husbands looking for work. Kids so poor they stole to survive. I learned pretty quick, you can't save them. The world is a grinder, Lincoln. It just mashes people up and you're lucky if you come out of it whole."

"Did you come out whole?"

Devlin gave me a sideways glance but didn't answer. The donkey cart jerked into motion, and Devlin shifted the jeep into gear.

"Where is Salinas anyway?" I asked, trying to lighten the sudden tension.

"California. You ever been?"

"No."

"You should go sometime. It's a swell place, if you can get out of Salinas."

We pulled up to a modern French Colonial apartment building on Boulevard Baudin, next door to the American Red Cross Club. Like every other office at AFHQ, the signal office was a barrage of activity. The clack of teletype machines was rhythmic, loud, and pounding. Not for the first time, I thanked God I hadn't been assigned to Signal. I would have left work with a daily migraine.

Captain Devlin grabbed the nearest GI. "Hey, hold up, Private. We're looking for Private Rivera with the Eight-Oh-Five."

The private didn't stop to salute, but kept walking and said over his shoulder, "Eight-Oh-Five is on the second floor, sir."

I followed Captain Devlin up the side staircase to the second floor, where things were a bit quieter. Again, Devlin asked the first GI he saw. He was efficient, if nothing else. His easy going manner seemed to take people off guard. "We're looking for Private Rivera."

This soldier saluted. "Yes, sir. He's not here, sir."

The young soldier looked about sixteen years old. His uniform hung on him like an oversized burlap sack. He had a thin face and ears the size of war tubas.

"You know him?"

"I do, sir."

"And he's not here?"

"No, sir. He's out on a job."

"Out on a job where?"

The kid frowned. "Sorry, sir. That's top secret."

"For the love of god," Devlin muttered. "All right. Who's his CO?"

"Major Horton."

"He here?"

"No, sir, he's out on a job too."

"Let me guess. Top secret?"

"Yes, sir."

"What's your name, Private?"

The boy glanced at me and then quickly away. "Private Eddie Shottler, sir."

"Private, were you at the dance last night?" I asked.

"No, ma'am," he said. "But I was sorry to hear about what happened."

"Thank you, Private," I said, surprised by his compassion.

"Is Rivera in trouble?"

"Why would you ask that, Private?" I asked, watching him carefully.

Shottler shrugged. "Don't know. All these questions, I guess."

"Has Private Rivera ever been in trouble before?" Captain Devlin asked.

"No. Rivera is a good guy. Maybe he's a little wild. There have been a few problems, but nothing major."

"What kinds of problems?" Captain Devlin asked, jerking his chin up.

"Nothing, sir." Private Shottler turned the color of an overripe tomato. "He gets drunk sometimes, but don't we all?"

"Sure we do," Devlin agreed. "And that's a problem?"

"He gets a little pushy with the girls maybe," Private Shottler said, his voice pitching higher. I didn't think Private Shottler could be a day over seventeen, if that. I'd heard rumors that the Army had its fair share of underage soldiers, but Shottler was the first one I'd met that was unquestionably under eighteen. His voice was still breaking.

"What girls?"

"The French girls." He blushed, his eyes downcast. "Some of the WAACs too."

"Any rape accusations?"

Private Shottler's head snapped up. "No, no. Nothing like that, sir. We don't need to rape anybody. We can just pay." He looked at me and flushed again. I forced a tight smile but was pretty sure he could read the disapproval on my face. He looked back to Captain Devlin. "You know what I mean."

"Why don't you explain it to me?" There was a warning note in Captain Devlin's voice.

"Well, we just pay. You can get a girl on the cheap here. You don't need to force anyone, do you?" he asked, sounding eager, like a young child looking for approval. I remembered Captain Haywynn saying that Mary didn't belong here. That she was too young. The same could be said for Private Shottler.

"Did you and Private Rivera partake of this particular pleasure last night?"

Private Shottler's face reddened. "I didn't, sir. I was on guard duty last night."

"Do you know if Private Rivera visited any establishments?"

Shottler cleared his throat, avoiding my direct gaze. "I wouldn't know, sir."

"Did he have a favorite?"

Shottler glanced at me, his expression pained. I felt sorry for the young man but also had a very strong feeling of disgust. "Le Sphinx."

"All right, Private. When you see Rivera, tell him we're looking for him. Tell him to report to the Five Hundred and Seventy-Seventh MP headquarters ASAP."

"Yes, sir." With visible relief, Private Shottler turned and scurried down the hall.

Devlin made for the stairs, and I hurried after him. "Do you think he'll give Rivera that message?"

"Oh yeah. Doesn't mean Rivera will come looking for me, though. Especially if he's guilty."

"Right."

"You want to keep your perps guessing, Lincoln. Let him think we'll wait around for him to come to us."

"But we won't?"

"Hell, no. I'll tell the colonel to talk to Rivera's CO. We'll find out where he is. It'll take a little bit of time, but he's not going anywhere. He's not going AWOL. If he did push Wentz off that roof, he doesn't think we have any proof. Probably thinks he's sitting clear and pretty."

Outside, the sun beat down, warming my skin. Devlin put his sunglasses on. The rain had cleared, and the sun was shining on the bustling white city like icing on a cake.

"Where to now, sir?"

"Well, I guess we should swing by your barracks and let your commanding officer know about your temporary duty. Maybe talk to a couple of the WAACs who were at the dance and might have seen something."

"They'll all be at work, sir. Except Mary, that is."

"Mary?"

"Auxiliary Jordan. She went to sick call this morning. She'll be there."

"This is the one dating the Tommy?"

"Yes, sir."

"Good. Good plan, Lincoln."

I climbed into the jeep, thinking that this job was a lot more interesting than typing up orders for the Adjutant General's office. Immediately after that thought, I felt a dagger of guilt. I wouldn't be here if Ruth hadn't been killed.

# Chapter 16

"Lincoln, what are you doing here?"

First Officer Fitzgerald stood in the courtyard, speaking to Mother Superior. I knew the two women clashed on multiple occasions, each struggling to get her way, neither speaking the other's language. Mother Superior wanted to ensure that the sisters of the convent were left alone to do God's work in prayer and take care of the orphans under their care. First Officer Fitzgerald wanted order, and access to the kitchens, the latrines, and the grounds. The two women were in a constant battle for control over their two separate domains housed under one large, sprawling roof.

I greeted Mother Superior in French. I had exchanged pleasantries with Sister Mary Theresa a handful of times. The woman was not pleased to have this invasion of young women descend onto the peace and routine of her convent, but she had little choice in the matter. The Army was paying her, and though the French still maintained administrative control of North Africa, everyone knew it was at the pleasure of the United States Government.

"Officer Fitzgerald?"

"Yes?"

"I'm Captain Devlin. It may come as some surprise, but Auxiliary Lincoln here has been assigned to the Five Hundred and Seventy-Seventh Military Police Company on temporary duty."

Fitzgerald frowned. "Why?"

First Officer Fitzgerald was always direct and to the point. Captain Devlin blinked but answered evenly enough. "I'm investigating the death of Auxiliary Wentz. We're short-staffed, and Lincoln volunteered."

"But Auxiliary Lincoln has other duties. She's assigned to the Adjutant General's office."

"Yes," Devlin said with an even calm, "but this investigation takes precedent for the time being."

Fitzgerald twisted her lips, obviously frustrated by this bit of news but reluctant to challenge a male officer. Technically, Fitzgerald was an officer in her own right, but only under the auxiliary status. WAACs, even officers, were prohibited from giving orders to men. Fitzgerald had no choice but to follow his orders and go along with the plan. I had not anticipated that my first officer would wish to do anything else.

Fitzgerald lifted her chin. "And you came up here to tell me this personally? For what reason?"

Captain Devlin's lips twitched. He gave a small shake of his head. "I'm here to interview a witness."

"Auxiliary Jordan was seen with Ruth shortly before she died," I explained.

"She called in at sick bay and has been confined to barracks for the day," Fitzgerald said.

"I still need to speak with her," Devlin insisted.

"This is highly irregular, Captain. I can't let you into her quarters. You're a man," Fitzgerald said, stating the obvious. I suppressed a smile. Fitzy was obviously disconcerted to have a man intruding into her domain, and for the first time she reminded me of Mother Superior.

"I do have an auxiliary with me, First Officer."

Fitzgerald turned a disapproving eye my way. "Yes, I'm aware of that. There's not much I can do about your requisitioning Auxiliary Lincoln, but I am not aware of any Army regulation that requires me to allow a male officer into an enlisted woman's private quarters while she is ill."

Devlin heaved a sigh. "You're right, of course," the captain said, his voice low, conspiratorial. "But one of your auxiliaries has been killed, and it's my job to find the culprit. Auxiliary Jordan is known to have associated with the victim, and I need a word with her. I will not overtax her. I will wait while you prepare her for my interview. But to refuse me an interview will impede this investigation. And that *is* against Army regulations, First Officer. Are you willing to accept that responsibility?"

First Officer Fitzgerald sucked a breath in through her nose and breathed it out. "Auxiliary Wentz was murdered?"

"Yes," I said, knowing this information would shock Fitzie.

"My god. Are you sure?"

"Unfortunately, it looks that way, yes," Captain Devlin replied.

Fitzgerald swayed slightly on her feet. I wanted to go to her, to give her some support, but I knew such attention in front of another officer would not be welcomed.

"I can't believe it. One of our girls was murdered? Why?"

"That's what we're trying to find out."

"And you think poor Mary knows something about this?" Fitzgerald had recovered herself. She licked her lips, her expression thoughtful. "They were close, Ruth and Mary. Ruth took the girl under her wing from the start. She watched out for Mary."

Devlin nodded. "That's what I've been told."

Fitzgerald looked at me. "Of course, Lincoln would have mentioned that. And you think Mary was mixed up in this somehow?"

"We just need to interview everyone who was at the dance last night and was seen with the victim. Purely routine."

Fitzgerald frowned. "It is highly irregular, but I guess I need to make an exception in this case."

Officer Fitzgerald sent her secretary, Auxiliary Wooten, to notify Jordan that she would be interviewed. When we entered sick bay ten minutes later, Mary Jordan was sitting upright in bed, her green felt robe cinched tightly around her waist and her hair tied up in a flowered head scarf with a neat bow on top. Someone, Auxiliary Wooten I presumed, had placed two wooden chairs beside Mary's bed. She looked tired, but her face brightened when she saw Captain Devlin.

"Auxiliary Jordan, I'm Captain Devlin. You know Auxiliary Lincoln." Mary Jordan smiled at the captain, lifting her shoulders in a coquettish display of vulnerability.

I didn't believe it for a moment. Mary was young and immature, but she wasn't the damsel in distress Captain Haywynn saw when he looked at her.

Devlin asked, "I understand you were friends with Auxiliary Wentz?"

I took this first question as my cue to pull out the green notebook.

Mary's eyes flicked to the pencil, and her alabaster brow crinkled. "I don't know if I would say we were *friends*, sir. I mean, I'm friendly with all the girls. We're all friends."

Devlin gave her a patient smile. "Of course you are. I've been told that Auxiliary Wentz was very kind to you when you first met in Daytona Beach?"

Mary blinked back tears. "I thought so at the time."

"You didn't think so later?"

"Ruth was . . ." Mary hesitated. "She isn't as nice as everyone thinks she is."

Mary used the present tense when talking about Ruth. That was interesting and a little sad.

"Why do you say that?" Devlin asked, keeping his voice soft, conciliatory.

"I don't know. She just . . ." Mary stopped. She twisted her pretty mouth in thought. "She was only nice to you if she could get something from you."

Captain Devlin rubbed his chin. "That's quite an accusation."

"I don't want to talk about this anymore," Mary said, pouting. "I really don't feel well." She turned her head away and coughed gently. It was quite obviously a fake cough. "Could you get me a glass of water, Dottie?"

Captain Devlin stood up. "I'll go. You stay with her, Lincoln. Make sure she's all right." He gave Mary a big smile. It was a handsome smile.

Mary smiled back, lowering her eyelids. "Thank you, Captain."

I leaned forward and gave Mary what I hoped was a reassuring smile. "Captain Devlin didn't mean to upset you, Mary. And no one is accusing you of anything."

"I know that!" Mary exclaimed, pushing herself up to a full sitting position. "I didn't do anything."

"Captain Devlin is just trying to figure out Ruth's movements from last night. We're talking to everybody at the dance. Who she might have been with before she . . ." I didn't know how to finish that sentence.

Mary's eyes filled with tears suddenly. "I didn't see her. I mean, I was with her on the ride over."

I nodded. I knew that already. I also knew Mary had been on the third floor with Captain Haywynn, but decided to keep that information to myself for the moment. I tried to remember what we'd talked about on the ride to the dance. Ruth had been asking about Captain Haywynn. Looking back, Mary had acted annoyed with Ruth's questions. "I remember Ruth was asking about the earl—about Captain Haywynn, I mean."

"I think she was jealous."

"Jealous?"

"Because she couldn't—" Mary broke off and waved a hand. "Nobody likes *her.* It's not my fault that men like me."

I felt a chill creep up my spine. There was something sickening about Mary speaking ill of Ruth. "We all seem to be getting a lot of attention from the opposite sex. I'm sure Ruth was happy for you, Mary."

"She wasn't," Mary spat with some venom. "It's not just me. I didn't mean she was jealous because she's not getting her own boys. I think she's jealous because Charlie's an earl."

"You think she wanted to date someone from the aristocracy?" I asked, trying to gentle my tone, even as I felt a rising tide of incredulity. Ruth was as grounded as they came. I couldn't imagine Ruth caring one whit for a soldier's upbringing or heritage. The very idea was ludicrous.

"I don't know. It just seemed like it bothered her."

I suspected that much was true. Ruth undoubtedly disapproved of Mary getting involved with an officer. Any officer. It was against regulations.

"Maybe she just wanted to look out for you? Maybe she was worried that his attentions weren't honorable?" I felt a little silly using such old-fashioned language, but didn't know how else to ask. And I didn't want to accuse Mary of having sexual relations with the earl, but I suspected Ruth's real concern was pregnancy.

"Well," Mary said, crossing her arms over her robe, "it's none of her business, is it?"

I chose my next words carefully. "Ruth cared about you, Mary. She cared about all the girls. She probably thought she was protecting you."

Mary barked a laugh. "Protecting me? From Charlie? He's the sweetest man I've ever met!"

"He's handsome too."

Mary blushed. "Isn't he though? Your captain is a dish too. He looks like Dana Andrews, doesn't he?"

It was such a childish thing to say that I had to bite my lip to keep from laughing. Maybe Captain Devlin and the earl were right. Maybe Mary had no business being in the Army. I didn't bother to explain that romance was the furthest thing from my mind. Mary probably wouldn't believe me anyway. I decided to attack from a different angle.

"You know, *your* captain gave me a ride to work this morning."

Mary blinked.

"Captain Haywynn. He told me what happened last night."

"Well," Mary said, looking away. "I told you she was jealous."

"Mary, when you left Ruth, was she alone?" I didn't want to accuse Mary outright of throwing Ruth off the roof of a building. Could this young woman really do such a thing? I couldn't picture it. She was selfish. She was childish. And she was petty. But she wasn't murderous. Still, I watched Mary's reaction carefully.

The girl paled. Her eyes welled with tears. I didn't see guilt on Mary's heart-shaped face. I saw fear.

"I didn't see anyone else," Mary sniffed, "but someone else must have been there."

"Why do you say that?"

"Because when I went back downstairs, nobody was coming up. So if someone pushed her, they must have been on the roof already."

I pictured the third-floor layout. It was a small space. Someone could have been hiding in the opposite stairwell. Had the killer come from the other side of the theater? I remembered the doorway behind the canvas curtain, leading to the staircase and the second floor. If the killer came up that way, would he have been seen?

The third floor would have been dark as pitch anywhere away from the balcony and the scant moonlight shining through the tall windows. If he came upstairs via the back stage area, he could have waited, hidden in the shadows, until Ruth was alone. But that didn't make sense. Nobody could have known Ruth would go upstairs, could he?

"It could have been me," Mary said in a small voice. "If I hadn't left, it could have been me."

In that moment, Mary looked like the child she was. Captain Haywynn was right: she wasn't a soldier. She was a frightened young girl who'd signed up for an adventure. If I saw the earl again, I made a mental note to offer him some encouragement in his pursuit. Mary could do worse than a kindly earl with an overprotective side.

"You'll find out who did this, won't you? Because if someone killed her, then I could be next. Any one of us could be next."

I reached for her hand. "We're going to do everything we can to find out what happened. But in the meantime, don't go anywhere alone. Follow regulations. Get home by curfew. And no more sneaking around with your handsome fella, okay?"

"But Dottie, Ruth always followed regulations. Why wasn't she safe?"

Captain Devlin returned with a canteen and saved me from having to answer that question, to which I had no answer. Yet.

"Here you go, Auxiliary Jordan. Fresh from the Lister bag."

Mary made a face. "It's disgusting stuff, isn't it? Funny the things you miss here. What kind of a place doesn't even have decent water?"

Devlin handed over the canteen. Mary held it loosely in her hands.

"I'm sorry to have disturbed you, Auxiliary Jordan. I hope you're feeling better soon."

"Thank you, Captain." She was back to batting her eyelashes.

"I'm sure we'll see you on the dance floor, fit as a fiddle, in no time."

She laughed. A sweet, tinkling sound. "I hope so."

"Lincoln, let's leave this young lady to her rest," Devlin said, smiling down at Mary.

Mary smiled back, her cupid bow mouth curled, her face flushed. She looked young and beautiful and all innocence. *It's quite a show,* I thought.

At the door, he turned back. "Oh, one more thing, Jordan," Devlin said in his usual gruff tone of voice.

"Yes?" Mary asked, the wariness creeping back into her pretty face.

"You saw Auxiliary Wentz with Private Rivera last night?"

"Yes. Carlos is very flirty. He tried it with me, but I set him straight."

Captain Devlin cleared his throat and glanced at me, raising one eyebrow. "Did you, by any chance, see Rivera leave the stage? Or leave the auditorium at any time?"

Mary bit her bottom lip, thinking about it for a minute. I had the distinct impression that she was mulling something over. "You know what? I did see him leave. After Dottie intervened, Ruth was talking to Pesky, and then I think I saw Carlos dancing on stage."

"You saw him onstage *after* dancing with Ruth?"

"Yes," she said, nodding. "Yes, I did."

"While Auxiliary Wentz was talking to Pesky? Who is Pesky?"

Mary gave a trilling laugh and covered her mouth with her hand. "Oh, we call Corporal Pinski that sometimes. Not to be mean. And not to his face. He gets a little bossy, always telling us what to do."

"Corporal Pinski *is* our boss, Mary. It's his job to tell us what to do."

"Don't be such an old fusspot, Dottie. I don't mean anything by it."

"So Wentz was talking to Corporal Pinski," Captain Devlin said. "And Private Rivera was dancing onstage. Do you know who he was dancing with?"

Mary shook her head, her blond curls bouncing. "No, I'm sorry. It was so crowded up there, it might not even be him I saw."

"But at the time, you thought it was Private Rivera."

"I did. I mean, it was just a blur really. But that's what I remember."

"All right, then, thank you, Auxiliary Jordan. Take care of yourself and get back to fighting fit."

"Thank you, Captain," Mary sang out cheerfully, as if they were talking about anything but murder. I felt that same chill creep up my spine. The girl was either completely self-absorbed or unashamedly heartless. I couldn't decide which.

"Well, that was as clear as mud," Devlin muttered. Once we were in the hallway, Devlin stopped and pulled at his collar. "That girl has absolutely no business being here."

I didn't want to agree that any woman in the 22nd Post Headquarters Company shouldn't be in theater, but Devlin was right. Mary Jordan had no business being assigned overseas. She was still a child in many ways. A child with a woman's body and a woman's attractions. "I guess I see what you mean about distractions," I conceded. "In this one instance, anyway."

Devlin raised an eyebrow. "I take it she's unusual in your group."

"Oh yes. Like I said, she's the youngest."

"And Wentz was protective of her," Devlin mused.

"She was." I relayed the rest of the conversation I'd had with Mary Jordan while he was out getting water from the Lister bag.

"And yet, little miss priss said Wentz was a nuisance more than a help."

"I noticed that too. It surprises me."

"So something changed between them?"

"Apparently."

"Did you ever see them argue or anything like that? Did Wentz mention any problems or altercations with Jordan?"

"No. I think Mary's right, though. I don't think Ruth approved of her relationship with Captain Haywynn. But it didn't have anything to do with jealousy. She didn't approve of breaking regulations and dating officers."

"Well, nobody would approve of that."

"What do you mean?"

Devlin shrugged. "Boys get jealous when the girls go off with the Brits or the Australians. Or the French, though I haven't seen much of that, thank God. They were our enemies a month ago."

"By girls, you mean the WAACs."

"The boys think American girls should date American men. And enlisted men should have first dibs on enlisted women."

"Dibs? We're not items at an auction."

"You know what I mean. Anyway, it's not all that important, I guess, because there's no way that girl"—Devlin flashed his thumb toward the sick bay— "killed anyone."

"Well, at least in that we are entirely in agreement, sir."

"One more thing. Did you notice she called Private Rivera 'Carlos'?"

I had noticed. "I think she and Private Rivera might have dated when we first arrived. There were a couple of dances when they were palling around together."

"Interesting."

I waited for Captain Devlin to elaborate, but he said nothing more about it. Sunglasses in hand, he headed back to the courtyard.

Auxiliary Wooten was waiting for us. "Dottie, Officer Fitzgerald wants to see you in her office."

This brought me up short. I looked at Captain Devlin. I couldn't refuse to go, but I was under orders from Captain Devlin.

"You go ahead. I'll meet you in the jeep."

# Chapter 17

First Officer Fitzgerald stood at the window of her office, looking down at the courtyard. I stood at attention and waited for her to acknowledge me. When she turned, I noted the shadows under her blue eyes. "Lincoln."

I snapped a salute.

"At ease." Fitzgerald gestured to the single chair sitting opposite her desk. I sat down on the hard wooden chair, spine straight, wondering what was coming next.

Fitzgerald took her own seat and gestured to a sheaf of paper resting on her desktop. "I received this from the AG's office. It's your order for temporary duty."

"Yes, ma'am."

"I wanted to discuss it with you before I sign it."

"I'm sorry to be abandoning Squad B, but it's only for three days."

Officer Fitzgerald frowned, the faint wrinkles around her eyes deepening. "The squad needs a leader today. Especially after what's happened to Auxiliary Wentz. I can't just wait for you to get back. Assuming you come back at all."

"Of course I'm coming back. Colonel Cantry authorized only these three days for the investigation."

"Be that as it may, you know the demand for WAACs is high. I don't doubt that Captain Devlin will want to keep you on after the investigation is complete. I'm sure he's as inundated with paperwork as the rest of us."

I opened my mouth to argue this point, but hesitated. Fitzgerald might be right. There was a huge demand for secretaries, even from the officers who didn't think women belonged in a combat theater. The war was generating massive amounts of paperwork and Captain Devlin had seemed eager to get me to take notes for him.

"Even if that's true, ma'am, I have no plans to make this a permanent transfer. If Captain Devlin does want a secretary, and the AG's office is willing to let me go, I'd still be free to see to my duties as squad leader. After the investigation is complete, that is. No matter what my assignment is, it shouldn't affect my ability to act as squad leader."

Fitzgerald smiled weakly. "Lincoln, working with military police is a full-time job. You will be at Captain Devlin's beck and call around the clock. Whatever happens with your future assignment, I can't depend on your presence here for the next three days. Squad B will be without a leader. That is not a workable solution."

"But I'll be back, ma'am. My place is here, with my squad."

"Then you should consider refusing the assignment." Fitzgerald leaned back in her chair. "I won't sign this, and you can stay where you are."

"But what about Ruth?"

"Auxiliary Wentz's death is unfortunate. I'm sure Captain Devlin will do his duty and investigate the matter thoroughly."

*But he won't.* Captain Devlin was more interested in his panty bandit case. If I wasn't part of the investigation, Ruth's killer might never be found. Devlin would question a few people and call it an accident. There would be no justice for Ruth. Her killer would be free to kill again. Other women in the company might be at risk.

I debated whether to say any of this to First Officer Fitzgerald. She was notoriously lenient in some areas of Army rules and regulations. But she was still an officer. As a private, asserting my opinion about the crime might be viewed as insubordination. And she wasn't wrong. I was leaving Squad B without a leader. An ache pulsed at the base of my neck. "I'm afraid I can't do that, Officer Fitzgerald."

Fitzgerald gazed at me for a long moment.

"I'm sorry, ma'am. I appreciate the opportunity to lead Squad B, but I have to see this through. Ruth was in my squad and someone killed her. I can't walk away from that responsibility."

Fitzgerald sighed heavily. She picked up a pen. "Very well." She signed the order. Flipping through the typed sheets and carbons, she handed me a copy. "You can take that to the AG's office then. That will be all, Lincoln."

I stood up, hesitated. "Will you assign someone else to the Adjutant General's office while I'm gone?"

"That will be up to the AG's office," she said, pulling a file from the stack on her desk and flipping it open. "If they request a replacement, I'll assign someone. That's all, Lincoln. The captain is waiting. Better get a move on."

Our interview was over.

I'd made my choice. I hoped I wouldn't come to regret it.

# CHAPTER 18

We drove back down the hill toward Mustapha Superior, my mind racing with uncertainty. I'd abandoned my squad. First Officer Fitzgerald had every right to strip me of my leadership position. A position I'd never really wanted. But having it stripped away hurt more than I'd expected. I'd gained some respect from Fitzgerald, and now she'd all but accused me of abandoning my post. Good soldiers did not abandon their posts.

Captain Devlin drove the couple miles down the Rue Michelet to the Hotel Alexandra. He parked right in front of the building. The MP stationed at the gate came out waving his white-gloved hands. "You can't park here, sir."

"Official business, Private. We won't be long." Without waiting for the guard to answer, Captain Devlin walked right past him.

I climbed out of the jeep and followed Devlin. The captain was his superior; there was nothing the poor private could do. I knew from experience if another officer complained about the jeep, the enlisted man would have to take the heat. It wasn't fair but it was the Army.

The Hotel Alexandra was a beehive of activity. WAACs and GIs crisscrossed the lobby, holding sheaves of papers in their arms. The clack of typewriters and teletype machines sounded like a stampede of grinding metal. Voices, raised and agitated, echoed down the stairs.

The Adjutant General's office was always busy, but this was unusual. "Things must be heating up in Tunisia."

Devlin frowned. "Must be."

We climbed the stairs to the top floor. When we walked into the office, I couldn't help but feel the place had a ghostlike quality to it without Ruth and Mary. Sue sat at her typewriter, banging away on the keyboard, surrounded by stacks of papers. She glanced up, almond eyes narrowing when she saw me. "Where the hell have you been?"

Corporal Pinski twisted away from his work, irritation stark on his face. He must be furious with me. He'd expected me back hours ago. Then his gaze landed on Captain Devlin. He stood up and snapped to attention. "Sir."

Captain Devlin nodded and got right to the point. "At ease, Corporal. I'm sure you're aware of the investigation into Auxiliary Wentz's death. I know you're busy, but I need to ask you and Auxiliary Dunworthy here a few questions."

"Oh." Pinski looked from Devlin to Sue, and back again. "Yes, sir. We're a little busy. I hope it won't take too long."

"Thank you, Corporal. I'll be quick. I understand you intervened in an altercation between Auxiliary Wentz and a Private Carlos Rivera last night at the dance?"

Corporal Pinski ran a hand across the back of his neck. "I did, sir. Private Rivera was getting fresh, and Auxiliary Wentz looked distressed, so I stepped in. I try to watch out for the women in my section, sir."

"Good man," Devlin said blandly. "And you had words with him?"

Corporal Pinski glanced at me. "I did. After he pushed Dottie—I mean, Auxiliary Lincoln, I told him to get lost."

"I appreciated that, Corporal," I said.

Corporal Pinski shook his head, a self-deprecating smile tugging at his lips. "I should have intervened sooner. Everyone could see he was making a nuisance of himself."

"Did you see where Private Rivera went after this altercation?" Devlin asked.

"I'm afraid not, sir. I was dancing with Ruth after that. Then I went for some lemonade before heading back here. I had the night shift."

Captain Devlin nodded. "All right, Corporal. That's all I need. I hate to tell you this, but I'm requisitioning Auxiliary Lincoln here. She'll be on TD with the Five Hundred and Seventy-Seventh for the next three days."

I pulled out my temporary duty order and handed it to Corporal Pinski. "I'm sorry to be leaving you in a bind, Corporal."

Pinski laid the order on top of his stack of papers. He had a stencil in place and began typing, no doubt adding my name to the Special Order. "Don't worry about it, Dottie. We'll manage." He scanned the order. "Will you be back on Thursday?"

"I will. I'll come in early."

Corporal Pinski's long fingers flew across the typewriter keys. "Good. With Ruth gone, and now you, we'll be behind."

"I know. I'm sorry about this."

Pinski winked at me. "Not your call. Officer's orders."

"Thanks, Corporal." I couldn't very well tell him I'd insisted on an investigation and practically begged for the temporary duty, purposely leaving him in the lurch. The stack of assignment lists on Pinski's desk was higher than I'd ever seen before. I contemplated offering to come in after my shift with Captain Devlin, but the truth was, I didn't know if we'd be working regular shift hours. We might be tracking down Private Rivera well into the night for all I knew.

Captain Devlin motioned to Sue, who had watched this exchange with her usual nonchalance. "Auxiliary Dunworthy, isn't it? I'd like a word."

"Are you serious?" She said, her mouth hanging open in indignation. "I'm kind of in the middle of something here, Captain."

"Auxiliary Dunworthy," Corporal Pinski said, his voice soft but resolute, "a superior officer is requesting an interview. Don't be insubordinate."

"Yes, sir," Sue muttered, knowing Pinski hated being called *sir.* She pulled herself out of her chair, straightened her skirt, and let out a weary sigh. Arching her back, stretching her sore muscles, Sue took her time sauntering over to the office door. "Any chance we can go out into the hall for a smoke? Sergeant Gilmore is allergic to smoke." She rolled her eyes, as if this was most ridiculous thing in the world.

"Where is Sergeant Gilmore?" Captain Devlin asked, heading out into the hallway.

"Weekly staff meeting with the brass," Sue said, flicking open a slim silver lighter. I wondered if she'd brought the lighter from home or purchased it in Algiers. "It's going longer than usual. I imagine they have a lot to talk about, what with the Krauts on the move."

"All right, Dunworthy. We just want to confirm your whereabouts on the night of the murder. Lincoln, take notes."

I nodded and reached into my utility bag for the green notebook.

"What time did you arrive at the dance?"

Sue shrugged. "I don't know. I went on the trucks like everyone else. What time was it, Dottie?"

There was a challenge in Sue's eyes, but I wasn't about to take the bait. "Eighteen hundred hours."

Sue smiled sweetly. "Eighteen hundred hours, then."

"Were you with anyone?"

"Sure. I was with the twenty or so other girls in the truck."

Captain Devlin ignored her insubordinate tone. "I was under the impression you had a date."

"I met Gar at the dance. He's sweet on me."

"And you spoke with the victim? Auxiliary Wentz?"

"Honey, I talked to everybody, I think." She laughed and batted her eyes. "It was a dance, Captain. Lots of socializing going on."

"So you and Private Mitchell are seeing each other?"

"Oh." She waved a well-manicured hand. She wore cherry-red nail polish, which was against regulations. Devlin didn't seem to notice, but then he probably had no idea brightly colored polish was against WAAC regulations. "That's just talk."

"But you were with him last night," Devlin pressed.

"Well." She lifted her delicate shoulders. "I danced with him. He's sweet on me, like I said."

"But you're not sweet on him?"

"I haven't decided yet. I like to keep my options open."

Devlin smiled. "I can see that. So, you saw Wentz on the dance floor?"

"I saw her trying to escape Private Rivera's clutches. We all saw that, didn't we, Dottie?"

I smiled but didn't reply.

"So you were under the impression that Private Rivera's attentions were unwanted."

Sue laughed. "Oh, I would say so. She was pushing him away. Dottie saw."

Again I stayed silent. It wasn't my role to confirm or deny Sue's version of events. This was Captain Devlin's interview.

Sue narrowed her eyes at me, clearly unhappy with my silence.

"When was the last time you saw Auxiliary Wentz that night?"

Sue twisted her painted lips. "Hmm. On the dance floor. Rivera was all over her, and Ruth was trying to get away from him. And then Corporal Pinski very gallantly acted the hero and told Rivera to scram. He really was heroic, wasn't he?"

Sue looked directly at me. This time I had no choice but to answer. "He was, yes." I didn't think Corporal Pinski would appreciate being described as a romantic hero, but he had been very gallant.

"He's very protective of us, our corporal."

"And then?" Captain Devlin prompted.

"After that, we all kind of went our separate ways. After she was rescued, Ruth danced with Corporal Pinski, and I didn't see her again."

"Did she leave the auditorium?"

"Well, she must have, but I didn't see her leave."

"And where were you?"

"All night? I don't know. I was circulating. That's what the Army tells us to do, you know. Boost morale and all that."

"So you were with a lot of soldiers that night?"

Sue's smile withered. "I was with Gar most of the evening, if you must know."

"Just so I have this right: you didn't see Auxiliary Wentz with Rivera again after she was rescued by the corporal?"

"No, but that doesn't mean he didn't find her after she danced with Corporal Pinski. I had the distinct impression Private Rivera wasn't going to take no for an answer."

"What makes you say that?"

"He was very persistent, Captain. It was awkward for all of us."

"All right, then. Thank you, Auxiliary Dunworthy. You can get back to work."

"Thank you, sir," Dunworthy sang, and gave him a saucy smile. She sashayed back into the office and glanced back one more time to smile at Captain Devlin.

"She's awfully chipper," Captain Devlin mused, "considering one of her friends died last night."

"Water off a duck's back."

"What's that, Lincoln?"

"Nothing ever seems to bother Sue. Ever. She just rolls with things."

"Maybe that's the best way to be in the Army."

"Maybe."

We walked down the stairs and out into the sunshine. The guard snapped a salute to Captain Devlin.

"Is that true? What Dunworthy said about things being awkward for all of you? That Rivera was being really aggressive in his pursuit?"

I considered the question, thinking back over the past few dances. "I never thought so, no. It was a little awkward last night, but I'm not sure why. When Corporal Pinski came to her rescue, I got the impression Ruth was annoyed. Like maybe she didn't want to be rescued. I think maybe she wanted to handle it herself."

"Maybe she liked Rivera?"

"But she was pushing him away."

"Maybe she was flirting." Captain Devlin put on his sunglasses.

I laughed. "Ruth wasn't like that. But something was off about Ruth that night. I can't put my finger on it exactly, but I got the feeling there was something else going on."

"Between Wentz and Rivera?"

"Maybe. I'm sorry I can't be more specific. She wanted to talk to me after curfew, which was highly unusual. I can't help but wonder if she knew she was in some kind of danger."

"Maybe she just wanted to chat? Or report some minor issue?"

"Probably," I said, but my mind was elsewhere. My missing letter. Had Ruth found my letter? Was that why she'd wanted to meet after hours? Maybe she planned to turn me in herself and was giving me fair warning. Or had she planned to challenge me about being a bad squad leader? As soon as I got back to barracks, I needed to scour the barracks. If the letter wasn't in my footlocker, I'd look through Ruth's. I had to find it and burn it. The risk was too great. I'd been a fool to keep it at all. If someone else found it, or took it, I could be looking at expulsion. Or worse. Pushing away my morbid thoughts, I focused on Captain Devlin. Squaring my shoulders, I asked, "What do we do now?"

Devlin leaned against the jeep and pulled out a cigarette. Arab kids swarmed the car, and Devlin waved them away.

I resisted the urge to pull out the pack of Dentyne I had in my purse. I felt a tug on my skirt and clutched my utility bag closer. Most of the older kids were practiced in the art of pickpocketing. I didn't blame them for stealing. They were filthy, shoeless, and dirt poor. But I didn't want to lose my meager belongings either.

"Let's have dinner at Chez Pilar."

"What does that have to do with Ruth's murder?"

"Nothing," he admitted. "But we do need to eat. It won't take long."

"But we're supposed to be investigating Ruth's murder. We only have three days."

Captain Devlin climbed into the jeep and started the engine. I remained standing on the sidewalk. "Look, Lincoln, we have to talk to Private Rivera. He's our prime suspect, and he's out on a job. Until then, I can't waste time doing nothing. I have other cases."

"The panty bandit case?"

"Exactly." Devlin looked at his watch. "We'll swing by Henri's, ask some questions, get some vittles."

"Who's Henri?"

"He runs Chez Pilar. We can ask Henri if he's heard anything. He has his ear to the ground in Algiers."

"What kind of things? What would he hear?"

Devlin threw up his hands and twisted in his seat. "I don't know—like, maybe your friend had some contacts with the locals. Maybe she was causing mischief with a Vichy official? Maybe she got into an argument with someone. We won't know until we ask."

"That's ridiculous. Ruth never went anywhere."

"Lincoln, your friend might have been killed. If she was, I guarantee she went somewhere and either saw something or did something to get herself killed. Now are you getting in so we can go ask questions, or are you staying here to type up orders?"

I got into the jeep. I was pretty sure Captain Devlin was lying about the café. He had some other reason to go there and meet this Henri. I would bet my meager life savings, it had nothing to do with Ruth's murder. But orders were orders.

# Chapter 19

Chez Pilar, on the Avenue Foureau Lamy, was a well-known café near the US Consulate. This part of Mustapha Superior was a place of winding streets with shade trees on either side. Villas with extensive grounds hulked behind stone walls.

The whitewashed stucco café squatted between two French colonial apartment buildings. An ornate wooden door, carved with geometric shapes, sat between two horseshoe arched windows. Blue, yellow, and red tiles spelled out the name of the establishment above the door. Flat-topped trees planted in sidewalk beds and greenery spilling out of the arched windows gave the place a homey feel . . . if home happened to be on the Mediterranean coast.

Captain Devlin reached across me and popped open the metal glove compartment. He grabbed a couple packs of cigarettes and thrust them at me. "Here, can you hold these for me?"

"Sure."

"Can't leave anything in the jeep. Light fingers. Anything that's not nailed down, disappears. Kids mostly." Captain Devlin climbed out of the jeep. A convoy of trucks passed by, and he edged his way around the jeep to join me on the sidewalk.

Two young boys, dressed in rags, came up to the jeep, holding out a small basket of tangerines. They were small and shriveled, the last of the spring crop.

"Don't give 'em anything."

I stuffed the cigarettes deep down into my utility bag. "Why not?"

"If you give 'em something now, when we come out, there'll be twenty more. They'll clean you out."

I ignored him and handed over a pack of gum.

"Don't be a stooge, Lincoln," Captain Devlin said, giving her a rueful look.

"Some would call it kindness, sir." I pushed past the boys, now pressing close, tugging at my skirt. Maybe Captain Devlin had been right. I should have waited until we left.

"Some would." Devlin laughed and opened the door of the café. "Shoo, kids. That's all you get."

I hurried into the restaurant, holding my utility bag close, resisting the urge to open my bag and give them the rest of my chewing gum and French francs.

I took in my surroundings, astonished. I'd heard about Chez Pilar. The earl had taken Mary to dinner here the previous week. Mary had gushed about the "high-class" place where Captain Haywynn took her. I thought she'd been exaggerating, but Chez Pilar was lovely.

The walls were painted a rich burgundy. A mahogany bar ran the length of the room. Shining brass beer taps gleamed in the dim light cast by small chandeliers overhead. Round tables covered with crisp white tablecloths were each set with a vase of flowers and tealight candles. We might have been inside any café in Paris, except the carved wood; carefully placed tiles; and rich, jewel-toned chairs added the extra luxury of the East. Rumor had it that they had a real French chef, though the menu was limited.

An eager young man with close-cropped blond hair and a crooked smile came over as soon as we stepped inside. "Captain!" the young man exclaimed, bowing slightly, wringing a dish towel in his hands.

"Hey, kid. Two today."

The kid grinned broadly and led us to a table in the back, next to an ornately carved wainscotting. Above the table hung an oil painting of the Bay of Algiers, old, faded and cracked.

"We'll start with some wine," Devlin said.

"Yes, sir. Very good, sir," the boy said with a heavy French accent. He hurried toward the kitchen.

I looked around at the crowded restaurant.

"Do you see him?" Captain Devlin asked. He didn't need to explain who he meant.

"No."

"Take out your notebook."

I complied, wondering why I needed the notebook for a meal.

A middle-aged man came to the table. He was gaunt, with a large, crooked nose and narrow eyes. His craggy face had seen the rougher side of life, but he had kind eyes. He wore a black suit, complete with waistcoat and white linen.

"Bonjour, Captain Devlin!" he exclaimed. "How are you today?"

The captain got to his feet and shook the man's hand. "Very good, Henri. Allow me to introduce Auxiliary Lincoln, one of our fine female soldiers."

Henri bowed. "Mademoiselle Lincoln, it is a pleasure."

"Enchante."

"You speak French?" he asked in his native tongue.

"Yes, my mother was French."

Henri put a hand to his chest, as if this were shocking information. "Where was she from?"

"A little town. Fougerolles."

"And how did a French girl from Fougerolles end up with an American daughter?" Henri asked in English, glancing at Captain Devlin. "I don't believe the captain speaks French."

"You know damn well I don't, Henri," Devlin said good-naturedly.

"So how is it that a French mademoiselle marries an American?" Henri asked again, switching back to English.

"They met during the war. The last war."

"Ah," he said, a sadness clouding his sparkling eyes.

"My father flew with the Escadrille."

"Did he indeed?" Henri exclaimed, looking intrigued. His face turned serious. He had an uncanny way of switching emotional reactions in a heartbeat. I wondered how much of this display was authentic and how much was an effort to charm Americans, the newest occupying force in Algiers. "We are very grateful to all the Americans who came to fight with us," he said now, sounding genuinely appreciative for my father's service.

"It was his honor."

"And you did not follow in your father's footsteps?" Henri asked, a mischievous glint in his eye.

I grinned. "I did, in fact. I can fly."

"Can you indeed?"

"I flew with my father sometimes, yes." I didn't really want to talk about my flying days. It would only lead to more painful memories, and this wasn't the time or place to stumble into tears.

"And is your father still flying?" Henri asked, saving me from traveling down that particular memory lane.

"He's passed away."

"Oh, I am sorry."

"Thank you."

"So," Henri said, as if closing the subject of death, "today I have for you an omelet."

"That sounds amazing," I said. "I haven't had fresh eggs in months."

"Oh, but they are powdered," Henri explained, regret on his face.

"Oh," I said, trying hard to hide my disappointment.

"But I believe our chef does a very good job with them. And I have some tangerine."

I met Devlin's gaze and knew we were both thinking of the shriveled tangerines the boys outside had tried to sell.

"Sounds delicious, Henri," Devlin said. "Come for a visit after we eat."

"How do they get powdered eggs?" I asked after Henri hurried into the kitchen to turn in our order.

"The North African Trade Board has an agreement with the French government to feed the civilian population, so they get a lot of the same rations we do."

"I didn't know that."

"No reason you should. I take it you don't come to town very often."

"No, never. Too busy."

"Right. You're here to win the war," he said with a smile.

"Why did you ask Henri to visit with us after we eat?" I asked, ignoring the jibe.

"Like I said, Henri has his ear to the ground around here. He knows everything. Just thought I'd ask if he heard anything about what happened last night. It's possible that our killer is not an American. More than possible, I'd say."

I blinked. I'd never considered that a local might have been responsible for Ruth's death. "But why would a Frenchman, or woman, want to kill an American soldier?"

"I doubt they thought they were killing a soldier."

"But Ruth was in uniform."

He put his hands up in surrender. "Fair enough. Could be a million different reasons why someone might murder an American. But what I'm thinking is maybe Wentz had some kind of relationship with one of our local Frenchman. Is that at all possible?"

"I really don't think so. I never saw any evidence of that."

"And you talked to her often?"

"We worked together every day," I reminded him. "And we're bunkmates."

"Who else is in your room?"

"Me. Ruth. Mary Jordan. Sue Dunworthy. Jeannie Kirksey, who you met last night. She was with me when Ruth. . . ."

"Right, the weeper. Anyone else?"

"Butch. Well, we call her that. Her name is Mabel Cornfeld. She works in the motor pool."

"And the rest of you work together in the Adjutant General's office?"

"Except Kirksey. She works for the general."

Captain Devlin whistled. "One of *those* WAACs."

"Yes." *Those* WAACs were the privileged few who worked directly with General Eisenhower, the best assignment a WAAC could get.

"And you don't think Wentz had a boyfriend?"

"No."

Henri arrived with two plates. The omelets were made from powdered eggs, as advertised, but Henri had added some fresh herbs, and it was quite delicious. The wedges of tangerine tasted fresh and sweet. The wine was fruity and refreshingly cool. It was, in fact, the best meal I'd eaten since arriving in North Africa.

"So, tell me more about Ruth. Did she have any trouble with anyone? Any of the girls in the convent or the office have a problem with her?"

"Ruth was a rule follower." I remembered Kirksey saying Ruth planned to lodge a complaint against me. "She wasn't afraid to report people if she thought they were breaking Army regulations."

Devlin whistled. "I'm guessing that didn't make her popular in your unit."

"Most of us brushed it off. A lot of the girls teased her. But there's a lot of that in the WAAC."

"A lot of that in the Army. Lots of bullying and bellyaching."

"Exactly. Nothing that warranted murder."

"Okay," Devlin said, returning to his omelet. He took a few bites, washed it down with a large swallow of wine, and leaned his elbows on the table again. "Who was she close to?"

I swallowed the last bit of powdered eggs. "Ruth wasn't really one to get close. She dedicated her time to her job. She watched out for Mary Jordan as much as possible, but I wouldn't say they were close."

After the plates were cleared and the blond waiter had poured more wine, Henri came out from the kitchens with a wineglass and pulled up a chair.

"So, Captain, you wish to speak," he said, pouring himself a glass of wine. "We will speak in English, yes?"

"That would be good, Henri—thanks," Devlin said, laughing.

Henri put up his hands and winked at me.

"Tell me, Henri, what's the scuttlebutt about the American soldier who was killed last night?"

Henri's bushy black eyebrows rose at least an inch. He had a very mobile, expressive face. "Killed? The girl who fell from the roof was killed?"

Devlin nodded, catching my eye. "It looks that way, yes."

Henri blew out a long breath through pursed lips. "That I did not know. How very sad."

"So you've heard nothing about it?"

"No, nothing. But if I hear anything, I will, of course, let you know."

"Fair enough." Devlin took another sip of wine and closed his notebook. "Anything else going on?"

Henri eyed him for a moment. "There is talk. The families of the Jews in the camps—there is talk they are planning something."

"Planning what?"

Henri shrugged. "That I do not know. Maybe planning to break them out?"

"Good god."

"Oui. It would be bad, no? Some of the Jews are still in hiding, in the town. I give them food when I can. It is bad for them, and they worry the Americans do not know."

Devlin nodded. "Anything more specific than that?"

"No."

"Okay. If you hear anything new, you let me know. I'll be back soon."

"Of course," Henri said, getting to his feet. "Of course."

Devlin stood and I followed suit.

"There is one thing," Henri said, stepping closer and putting a hand on Captain Devlin's shoulder. "There have been some sales going on that I think you might wish to know."

"Sales?"

"Mais oui. Some sales of American goods."

"What kind of goods?"

Henri waved a hand. "Clothing mostly. Things like stockings, shoes, even undergarments."

"Is that so?" Devlin said mildly. I resisted the urge to make eye contact. Henri was speaking of the so-called panty bandit. "Who's selling them?"

Henri waved his hands again. It was like a tick with him. "Different people. But it has increased in the last couple weeks. There has been more and more merchandise available. It is unusual."

Devlin nodded. "Any munitions?"

"Oh no, nothing like that. But there have been C-rations."

"Really?"

"Oui."

"Could they be getting them from the trade board?"

"I do not believe so, no. They are like soldier's rations. When we get ours, they are in a box, you know? For civilians. But these are for the field."

"Make a note of that for me, will you, Lincoln?"

"Yes, sir." I jotted down the information.

"Thanks, Henri. I appreciate the info." He pulled a stack of francs from his pocket and pulled out several bills. "Hey, Lincoln, give me those smokes."

I stuffed the notebook into my bag and handed over the cigarettes. Devlin passed them on to Henri, along with the francs. "Keep your ears to the ground. I'll be back."

Henri nodded, then turned to me and made a little bow. He held out his hand. I took it intending to shake goodbye, but Henri had other ideas. He kissed the back of my hand lightly. "Mademoiselle, it was a pleasure."

"Likewise, Monsieur."

I followed Devlin out the door and back onto the sidewalk.

Once outside, I asked, "You pay for information?"

"I consider it a kindness," Devlin said, cracking a smile.

"It's a payoff," I said, with raised eyebrows.

"Look, Lincoln." Devlin stopped in front of the jeep. "This is how things are done here, all right? Algiers is a piss pot. You've got ex-Vichy fascists running the government. You've got German sympathizers trying to run sabotage missions. You've got Arabs constantly threatening to rise up in revolt. You've got Jews in concentration camps who should be joining the fight against the Axis. And to top it all off, we've got the biggest hodgepodge at Allied Force Headquarters, who can't agree what to have for dinner. Brits, Americans, Aussies, Scots, Irish—not to the mention the damn Free French. Algiers is the melting pot from hell. Everyone wants a piece of the pie, and nobody wants to share. Henri is useful to me. He listens. He pays attention. And he's not stingy with information, no matter what I give him. So I'm happy to pay him for his efforts."

"How do you know he's not passing information to the other side?"

"I don't. But what he didn't tell you is that he himself fought in France for four years, in the trenches. He loves Americans. He thinks Americans saved France then, and he believes Americans will save France now and liberate his home country. That's why he was so jazzed, hearing about your father. I couldn't have made that up. It's perfect. He'll want to help us now more than ever. He's a patriot, Lincoln. He's one of the good guys. And he has four grandchildren here in Algiers, with very little food. The Germans practically starved them all out. And we're not doing much better. He's serving powdered eggs in his own goddamned restaurant—you can imagine what they eat at home. The cigarettes will buy food for a week, hopefully. And if I had any more, I'd give them to him."

I felt justifiably chastised. "Point taken, sir. Sorry. I didn't know."

"Don't be sorry. This is Algiers. Most of us live isolated in our barracks and in our offices and never have to think about these things. Why should you be any different?"

"I'm sorry, sir. I just want to find out who hurt Ruth." I rubbed at the scar under my cap, feeling exasperated. "I'm missing work, important work, to do this. I'm eating in restaurants, and Ruth's killer is running around free. There has to be something else we can do."

Captain Devlin leaned against the jeep, one hand in his pocket, squinting at me in the late afternoon sun setting over the Atlas Mountains. "Investigations take time, Lincoln. We put in a full day's work. Let's get some shut-eye and start early tomorrow. I'll pick you up at zero six hundred hours. We'll hunt Rivera down, no matter how top secret his position."

# Chapter 20

Captain Devlin dropped me off at the convent. Mess leader Auxiliary Lindley was busy directing her staff to clean up after dinner. "We have some leftovers, Dottie, if you're hungry."

"No, thanks, Gertie. I got some food in town."

"Uh-oh."

I smiled. It wasn't uncommon for soldiers eating in town to come back with food poisoning. "Just some powdered eggs and a tangerine. I should be fine."

"Let's hope so," she sang out, then turned back to the well where her team was scouring deep aluminum pots. The well was the only water source in the convent. Twice a day an Arab man and his son hitched up a horse or mule to a pole extending from the center. Blindfolded, the animal walked in circles, bringing up water that spilled into a trough. Each day, the girls brought their helmets down to the well to use as a basin to wash, brush their teeth, and do laundry in the courtyard. And of course, the mess used the well for cooking and cleaning.

I climbed the stairs, my legs and shoulders stiff from bouncing around in Captain Devlin's jeep.

Walking down the hall to my squad room, I realized Fitzgerald might have already assigned a replacement leader. Who would she choose? Kirksey was my first choice. Despite her fears about bombardments, she was well liked, and I thought some extra responsibility might help her focus. But working with General Eisenhower's busy schedule would make it difficult for her to assume any leadership role with the squad. Mary was too young. Mabel was too self-effacing. It was only when I got to the door that dread dropped like a tank. Sue Dunworthy was the most likely choice. *Oh God. Sue Dunworthy as squad leader? What have I done?*

Mary Jordan was propped up on one elbow on her bed, flipping through an old copy of *Yank* magazine. She was alone.

"Hi, Mary. How are you feeling?"

"Better." Mary didn't look up.

"That's good."

"How's your handsome captain?"

I considered correcting Mary, to insist she be professional, to explain that Captain Devlin was our superior officer, and nothing more. But I was too tired to argue and suspected Mary wouldn't understand anyway. "Did you make it to work today?"

Mary looked up, her lips pursed, eyes wounded. "You know I was sick."

"Well, I'm sure Corporal Pinski will be glad to have you back tomorrow."

Mary resumed her perusal of the magazine with a heavy sigh. "Work. It's such a drag."

I decided not to go down that road. When Mary was in a mood, there was no reasoning with her. If Ruth were here, she'd point out the important job Mary was doing, but I couldn't muster the energy. "I think I'll go for a jog before lights out. Wanna come?"

"You're not serious?"

I changed into a pair of men's khaki trousers that I'd bought off a soldier back in Daytona. I threw a sweater vest over my uniform shirt and pulled on my olive drab jacket. It was too cold to wear the light seersucker exercise dress.

"You're going to freeze to death," Mary said drolly.

"Not if I keep moving."

"Why do you bother, Dottie, really?"

"Keeps me focused." That wasn't a complete lie. PT did help me stay focused, but more importantly, it helped me stay strong. Being married to Konrad had left me weak and vulnerable. I didn't want to be weak anymore. I wanted to be strong so when the time came to get Sadie back, I'd have a fighting chance. But Mary Jordan wouldn't understand any of that, so I said nothing.

I walked outside and jogged around the perimeter of the orchard behind the convent. The trees were still leafless, and the rocky ground was tricky to navigate in the dark. I followed a narrow path up the slope of the hill and back down three times, finishing winded, my leg muscles screaming, but my head clear. Sweating now, I pulled off the jacket and headed for the bathroom. The jog would help me sleep. I'd be well rested and ready to find Private Rivera in the morning.

Sue Dunworthy sat in a chair on the patio, the glow of a cigarette in her hand. I lifted a hand, intent on getting to the bathroom and changing for bed.

"Too bad about Ruth," Sue called.

I stopped and faced her. Sue leaned back in her chair, arms crossed over her chest. She wore the standard-issue green felt robe, but she'd embroidered red roses into the lapels.

"Yes," I agreed, "it's a terrible blow for the squad and the company."

"I didn't expect her to be so soft. She didn't strike me as a damsel-in-distress type. I would think if anyone took a header off a building, it would be Mary."

"That's not a very nice thing to say."

Sue shrugged. "I don't think I'm a very nice girl." Her eyes sought out mine in the darkness. "Do you?"

I shook my head. I was too tired for Sue's games. "I'm going to bed."

"So you think maybe someone pushed her off that balcony?"

"Maybe," I said, the cobwebs of exhaustion vanishing.

"Ruth didn't seem like the suicidal type, did she?"

"No. No, she didn't."

"So someone pushed her over. And you got yourself a job with the MPs to investigate?"

I crossed my arms against a sudden chill, feeling as if I were being pushed against a tide. "What are you saying, Sue?"

Sue lifted one shoulder and took a drag off her cigarette. "Just seems strange, that's all."

"Sue, if you know something, you need to tell us."

"Us? Are you an MP now? I thought you were just taking notes."

"I am." I hated the defensiveness in my voice. "You should tell Captain Devlin if you know anything. Did you see something?"

"It was a busy dance. Lots of people." Sue flicked ash off her stub of a cigarette. "Maybe *you* pushed her off that roof?"

Anger pulsed in my temple, sending fire through my scar. Sue liked to push buttons. The trick was to keep a straight face and not let her ruffle your feathers. "Don't be ridiculous."

Sue cocked her head, her eyes roaming my face. I suspected she was looking for a crack in my armor. Some weakness she could exploit.

After a moment and a last suck on her cigarette, Sue tossed the butt and pulled a piece of paper from the pocket of her bathrobe. "I wonder if you're capable of murder. This letter just might suggest that you are."

"What is that?" I was tired and out of patience. I'd witnessed the death of a good soldier, sparred with a belligerent captain, and endured a bombardment out in the open air. I had no time for Sue's little games.

"It's a letter," Sue said, waggling the paper. "I'm pretty sure you're Dorothea."

My heart stuttered. Cold washed over my body. My lips went numb. "Give it back," I managed, reaching for the letter.

Sue pulled the letter out of my reach and laughed. "Not so fast."

"You went through my things," I said, shocked and knowing I shouldn't be. It had been foolish to keep the letter.

"I would never," Sue said, blinking in phony wide-eyed innocence. "I found it on the floor beside your bed."

My mind raced. It was possible. I tried to be careful with the letter, but I returned to the convent each night completely exhausted from a long day's work. Had I dropped it beside my bed while changing?

"So you're working for the Germans." Sue chewed her bottom lip, tapping the letter on her open palm.

"Of course not."

"Really? Because this is a letter with a swastika on it. And it's from Germany."

"I'm not a German," I said with forced calm. Why did I keep the envelope? I didn't need it. I'd long ago memorized the last known address for my daughter. "I do speak German, but I'm not a sympathizer."

"Then why do you have a Nazi letter?" Sue lifted her right hand and waved the faded white envelope.

I sucked in a breath, the clean, cold air bracing. I did not like Sue Dunworthy. The girl was trouble. She'd been trouble since Daytona Beach. But it was a fair question.

"I have family in Germany, okay? They wrote to me before the war, and I keep the letter because it's all I have left."

The words were difficult to say because they were too close to the painful truth.

But I had to give Sue some sort of explanation. The last thing I needed was a disciplinary review over my German relatives.

"You a Jew?" Sue asked, narrowing her beautiful almond-shaped eyes.

I sighed. It would be easier if I just said yes. That would explain the letter expediently. But before I could consider that option, the truth was out of my mouth. "No."

Sue cocked her head, looking me up and down. "Okay, then. So what family do you have in Krautsville?"

"I'm not working for the Germans. Look at the date."

"I can't read this Kraut writing," Sue scoffed.

"It's from before we ever got here, Sue."

Sue shrugged and got to her feet. "So I guess you want this back."

It wasn't a question.

"It's not yours," I said, trying to hide how much I wanted it back, though I heard the wanting in my own voice. I didn't want it back for the reasons Sue assumed, but that didn't matter.

I decided to get aggressive. Sue Dunworthy was a hard girl. Niceties would only dig the hole deeper. "Look, Dunworthy, not that it's any of your business, but they're my mother's family, okay? They're from Alsace-Lorraine, so when the Germans invaded, they lost their chance to get out. Like everyone else in their village, they speak German and French. Like me. Doesn't make us Nazis. Got it?"

Sue put up her hands, giving me a supercilious smile. "All right, all right. Don't get your khaki panties in a bunch, Lincoln. Just seemed strange, that's all. Especially with a killer on the loose."

I should have destroyed the letter. But it contained the drawing. Somehow the drawing was part of the letter. The letter told me where Sadie had been in 1941, and the drawing, done in colored pencil, was my most prized possession.

Sadie had signed the drawing, but I would have recognized her hand anywhere. Two stick figures standing on the beach. My brown hair falling around my shoulders and curling at the ends, a solid helmet of coiffed hair. Sadie's blond ringlets braided and tied off at the ends with red ribbons. I couldn't picture Konrad brushing Sadie's hair and braiding it neatly. Did Konrad have a lover? Or was Sadie living with her grandmother? The postmark on the letter was stamped "Minden."

I couldn't bring myself to destroy it. The last little bit of my former life. Without it, I would be alone. Permanently and irrevocably alone. No, I needed to keep it a little bit longer. But the danger had always been there, and now Sue Dunworthy was wielding it like a machine gun.

"I suppose you want to keep this just between us?"

I didn't want to agree, but this was a secret I wanted kept. I'd done nothing wrong. There were no rules against keeping letters from before the war, but I also knew it might cast suspicion on me. I was stationed in a combat theater. There were spies everywhere.

"I'm good with that," Sue said, not waiting for a reply. "And maybe you'll do me a favor sometime? In return?"

Before I could answer, Sue winked, then strolled through the arched doorway and into the recesses of the convent walls. A shadow flitting through the night, my most prized possession in her greedy hands.

I listened to the sound of Sue's shoes on the stairs, then a door closing. I was alone again. More alone than I'd been since arriving in Algiers.

I remembered Ruth's face that last time I'd seen her. She'd looked worried. She'd asked to meet me after curfew. Was that meeting about Sue Dunworthy? Did Sue have some kind of dirt on Ruth as well?

Had Sue threatened Ruth the way she'd threatened me? Could they have fought on the balcony and Ruth went over the edge?

It sounded fantastical, but I couldn't rule it out. I also couldn't share that suspicion with Captain Devlin without exposing my past.

I'd known it was a bad idea to keep the letter. Even back home, Americans were suspicious of anyone with strong ties to Germany. There were plenty of German American soldiers in the Army, but I suspected I might be the only one carrying around a letter mailed from Nazi Germany and written in the enemy's language. The letter was perfectly innocent, but Sue didn't understand the German language, and I understood why she'd jumped to the conclusion that I might be up to something. Unfortunately, she might not be the only one who'd jump to that conclusion.

However, any Army translator would quickly dismiss the allegation. *Unless.* Unless the Army decided the letter was some coded message from the enemy. Somehow, carrying the letter with me all this time, I had never imagined that possible complication. Until now.

I was still married to Konrad. After he'd left me for dead, there'd been no avenue to divorce. The law required I wait three years before I could file for abandonment and get a divorce.

I had to get that letter back. What's more, I had to destroy it. As painful as it would be to lose the last piece I had of Sadie, I couldn't risk it being discovered again. Ever since Konrad's violent exit, I'd been frightened. The Army had offered me some sanctuary. Before Ruth's death, I'd felt safe with the Double Deuces. But now, who could I trust? And how long did I have before Sue told Captain Devlin about her suspicions? My sanctuary was shattered. I sank into the nearest chair and sobbed silently into my olive drab coat.

# Chapter 21

When Captain Devlin pulled up outside the convent wall the next morning, I fumbled my way into the jeep. My eyes were gritted with fatigue that not even two cups of Lindley's instant coffee could fix. It was going to be a long day.

I'd had a restless night after Sue's accusation. And I felt the loss of my letter like a physical pain.

Captain Devlin headed straight to the 805th Signal Company office. Private Shottler was at his desk, a telephone to his ear with one hand and a single finger pecking at a typewriter with the other.

"Did Private Rivera get back from his top secret mission yet?"

Private Shottler set the handset back into its cradle, ending his call. "No, sir. I'm not sure when he'll be back."

"You're not sure when he'll be back?" Captain Devlin looked to the ceiling. "Listen, Shottler, I know you're not supposed to talk, but would I be right in assuming that Private Rivera has been sent east?"

Private Shottler's eyes shifted to me. I kept my face stony. "You might be, sir. I couldn't say."

"Mm-hmm." Captain Devlin cocked his head. "Tebessa?"

Shottler shook his head.

"Constantine?"

Private Shottler licked his lips. His knee bounced up and down like beans in a hot skillet. "I can't tell you that, sir."

Captain Devlin quirked a smile. "Keep up the good work, Private. You're doing a fine job here. I won't forget it."

Shottler shifted his position and set the other knee to bouncing. "Yes, sir. Thank you, sir."

Devlin headed out the door and I followed. Only when we were back outside did I ask the question. "What was that all about, sir?"

"Rivera's in Constantine."

"Do you think he's running away?"

Captain Devlin chuckled. "No, Lincoln. He hasn't gone AWOL. My guess is he's been reassigned. He's been ordered to Constantine, and judging by what I'm hearing about this new German assault, that's not surprising. Communications are vital during an offensive."

"Right. Of course." I reddened. I should have known that. "So he gets away with it," I said, feeling defeated.

"We don't even know if he did it, Lincoln."

"But he's our most likely suspect."

"He is," Devlin agreed, tapping the side of the jeep. "But the war comes first. We'll have to wait it out. I'll inform Colonel Cantry that our investigation has to be suspended until Private Rivera returns to Allied Force Headquarters."

Captain Devlin pulled out his sunglasses and climbed into the jeep. I remained motionless, standing on the busy sidewalk, my mind racing.

"Get in, Lincoln. I'll take you back to the Adjutant General's office."

I rubbed at my scar, closing my eyes briefly, shielding myself from his gaze for just a moment while I gathered the courage to say what I had to say. Finally I shook my head and said the word running through my mind. "No."

Devlin pulled his sunglasses down. His blue eyes blinked in surprise.

"Sir," I added, a bit late. I pulled at my collar, straightened my uniform jacket. "I'm not going back. We have to find out who killed Ruth. We have two more days."

Captain Devlin flung his arm across the back of the seat, as if bracing for a sharp turn. "Lincoln, the investigation is at a standstill. Our prime suspect is at the front, fighting for his country. We have no idea how long his mission will last. He could be out there for weeks. If or when he returns to Algiers, then we'll question him."

I pressed my lips together. I had an idea. A crazy idea, but it was the only option. I leaned over the jeep's door frame. "We can't wait, sir. This is our chance to catch Ruth's killer. Maybe our only chance. If Private Rivera didn't kill her, maybe he knows who did. We need to go to him."

"To Constantine? That's crazy!"

"No," I said, drawing out the word, my mind racing. "It's thorough. We go out to the command post and find Rivera. We interview him. We find out if he had anything to do with Ruth's murder. If he did, we arrest him and bring him back. Case closed."

Captain Devlin dropped his arm from the back of the seat, shaking his head. He scrubbed at his face. I waited. I'd go out there by myself if I had to. Maybe Kirksey would drive.

"This is crazy," Devlin finally said. "You know that, right?"

"Yes," I admitted. "But it's also our only option. We can't stop the investigation. If we stop now, it'll never be reopened. Colonel Cantry didn't want you to spend these three days. If we stop now, the case will be forgotten, and Ruth's killer gets away with it."

Captain Devlin twisted his lips. "That's probably true. I can't see the colonel reopening the investigation." He tapped his fingers on the steering wheel. "All right, fine. We'll go. But I don't think you know what you're asking. The trip will be hell, for one thing. It's four hours to Constantine, maybe more if the roads are clogged up, which they probably are, with the Army on the move. But let's say we make good time and don't encounter too many roadblocks. That's eight hours, give or take. If we're lucky, we find him right away. Talk to him. If we don't, we might have to spend the night."

"I can do that."

Devlin rolled his eyes, but his mouth quirked up in a smile. "Okay, but that's just the first problem. Constantine is General Eisenhower's forward command post. I have no idea how far the Germans are from Ike's front line at this point. It might be dangerous."

I gave a curt nod. "Right. Do I need to pack a bag?"

"No time for that. Besides, you won't need it. We'll scrap for supplies on the road and I've got a couple C-rations in the jeep." Captain Devlin looked at his watch. "It's eight o'clock now. If all goes well, we could be back in Algiers by midnight."

"And if we don't find Private Rivera right away? What if he's not there?"

"We'll jump off that bridge when we get there. With any luck, we'll make an arrest and the case will be over. You hungry?"

"Always, sir."

"Me too." He slipped his sunglasses down, his mouth twisted into a frown. "We're going to need fuel to make it all the way to Constantine. Let's pop over to the club and see what's being served up at the snack bar."

Captain Devlin drove to the American Red Cross Club. The large, six-story building had once been home to the student's association of the University of Algiers. I knew the Americans had requisitioned the club just hours before the British had prepared to take it over. Despite being allies, the British and American brass argued over everything from supply issues to administrative decisions in the running of Allied Force Headquarters. I had seen more than one letter between the two countries debating territorial rights in Algiers, like two hyenas fighting over a fresh kill.

The vaulted foyer was tiled in colorful Moorish designs. Cane chairs and accent tables were spaced around the lobby, offering a place for soldiers to sit and read or write letters. A young brunette in a Red Cross Uniform and two pretty French girls, dressed in civvies, ran a busy information desk. The snack bar was at the far end of the lobby just beside a set of French doors leading to an outdoor seating area.

Captain Devlin walked to the back of the foyer. "Right. Stay here. I'll grab us a couple burgers."

"Yes, sir." I had been to the snack bar once before, but by the time I'd made it to the front of the line, the food was gone. I suspected Captain Devlin wouldn't have to wait, being an officer and an MP. Plus it was early in the day. Supplies wouldn't have run out just yet. I waited, my mouth already watering. I was tired, and the thought of a burger had my stomach growling. Powdered eggs just didn't offer much in the way of energy, but red meat would clear my head. If only the Army were able to ship Coca-Cola to Algiers.

The thought of a fizzy drink made my mouth more than water: it made me ache with homesickness. When Sadie was old enough, we would meet Konrad at the soda shop across from his office. We'd share a sandwich and a Coke. Money had been tight, but I had always been grateful Konrad was employed. I'd thought myself lucky. Until the day he'd left me with a scar on my forehead and a hole in my heart.

I glanced around the lobby, looking for an open seat, and saw Private Wainwright standing at the information desk located just inside the front doors. I smiled and gave a little wave. Wainwright blushed red, waved back and headed over.

"Hello again, Miss Lincoln."

"Private Wainwright, what a pleasant surprise."

He grinned, his eyes raking over me. "Isn't it? I got an assignment right here at AFHQ. How about that?"

"That is a surprise. Where did you get assigned?"

"Signal. It's an important job, Miss Lincoln."

"It is," I agreed. He must feel bad about not being sent to the front, and I didn't want to make him feel worse. "An Army runs on information."

He nodded vigorously. "Exactly. It's not like I'm shirking, you know. I want to win this war as much as anybody."

"I'm sure you do." I saw Corporal Pinski out of the corner of my eye. "Good luck to you, Private."

"Abyssinia, Miss Lincoln. Promise me a dance at the next do?"

"Of course," I said, hoping we wouldn't cross paths again. I didn't want to encourage any kind of romance. "Abyssinia."

Corporal Pinski stood in line at the Postal Section clerk's office. I walked over and waved a hand to get his attention. He looked up from the papers in his hand.

"Hey, Corporal. Getting yourself a burger?"

Corporal Pinski grinned and held up a hamburger wrapped in wax paper. "You know it. Thought I'd send some money back home, then head to the office."

The Army paid better than most jobs back home, and there wasn't much to buy in Algiers. Most families back home were still suffering the effects of the Depression, and Army pay helped. "How are things going at the office? I hope the workload isn't too heavy."

"We're doing okay. We'll be glad to have you back, though. Are you still due back Thursday?"

"I am."

"I guess they have to investigate these things. But it must be hard for you, Ruth being a friend and all."

"Yes, it is. But I feel a responsibility too."

"Of course you do. We all miss her." The line moved and we moved with it.

"How is everyone at the office holding up?"

Corporal Pinski shrugged. "Okay, I guess. Mary still doesn't feel well. I don't think the climate agrees with her. And Sue complains nonstop about the extra work."

That wasn't exactly what I meant, but I guessed Corporal Pinski was trying to spare me from feeling bad about leaving the squad at such a difficult time. "I'm sorry, Corporal. I know you're already short-staffed because of Ruth."

"No, it's okay. You'll be back in a couple of days. And anyway, Sue's problem isn't the work. She's just lazy."

I laughed. I couldn't contradict that statement. Sue was lazy. She liked the dances and exploring the city, but at work Sue was always lethargic and watching the clock for quitting time.

"Maybe it's more noticeable without you and Ruth to pick up the slack."

I felt another twinge of guilt for abandoning my post at the Adjutant General's office. "Maybe she's upset about Ruth."

"Maybe." Corporal Pinski quirked his lip in a half smile. "I can't really see her being upset, though, can you? I mean, the rest of us are upset, of course. But Sue? Nothing ever really seems to bother her."

"That's true." I saw Captain Devlin returning, a paper sack in his grip. "Listen, Corporal, I've got to go."

Corporal Pinski saw Captain Devlin and raised a quick salute. "All right, Dottie. See you in a couple of days. Good luck. And hurry back, if you can. We need all hands on deck."

# Chapter 22

Captain Devlin donned his sunglasses and took the coastal highway. The road was plagued by potholes, and I held on to the side of the jeep for dear life, bouncing around like a tail gunner. "They should name this road Popcorn Highway."

Devlin brayed with laughter. "We should make a sign."

I cracked a smile.

The road was busy with jeeps and deuce-and-a-half trucks. Beyond the highway stretched nothing but sand and stone as far as the eye could see. The dust was unbearable. My eyes burned with it. Without slowing, Captain Devlin leaned over, snapped open the glove compartment, and handed me a pair of sunglasses. I put them on. "Thanks."

The roar of trucks became like a rainstorm, white noise that lulled me into a daze. More than once, Captain Devlin had to steer the jeep off the road and onto the shoulder to pass slower traffic. Columns of marching men. Tanks. Heavy artillery. The offensive in the east was definitely picking up steam.

We turned west at a town called Thema. The countryside reminded me of a postcard I'd once seen of Arizona, minus the saguaro cactus. We passed a large open-air market sprawling along the side of the road. Carpet vendors had spread their wares on the dusty ground. Carts filled with everything from fruit to copper pots were parked around the perimeter. Camels sat beside the carts or stood among throngs of men wearing vibrant indigo robes with turbans wound around the lower half of their face, shielding their mouths and nostrils from the blowing sand and desert wind.

My thoughts turned back to Sue and the letter. Sue wanted a favor. What kind of favor? At least I was safe for the time being. Sue wanted something, so it wouldn't be in her interest to turn the letter over to Officer Fitzgerald. Not yet, anyway. My initial panic over Sue's accusation had subsided. The letter dated from before the war. I could translate its innocuous contents if anyone asked. What worried me more than anything was the look in Sue's eye when she challenged me about the letter. The probing into my personal life, looking for cracks and vulnerabilities. There was no question Sue was a woman on the hunt. I couldn't help but wonder if Sue had found something incriminating to threaten Ruth with. And if so, had it led to Ruth's death?

Soon we were gaining elevation, climbing the foothills of the Atlas Mountains. Traffic cleared and I was lulled to sleep in a sitting position. Army life meant finding sleep where you could, so I dozed, occasionally jerking awake when the jeep bounced too hard or swayed into the ditch to pass slower vehicles.

After a couple of hours, I gave up on the effort and sat up straight. The sun beat down. I'd probably end up with a sunburn. I readjusted my sunglasses. The winding road had cleared somewhat. Ambulances and medical trucks trundled past from the opposite direction, but the number of trucks and military vehicles had dwindled. Green fields stretched across the landscape, overtaking the dry, rocky ground. Saharan and Mediterranean cypress trees huddled around sand-colored villas. Feral dogs roamed tiny neighborhoods along the road. Large white birds with black wings flew overhead, diving, then gaining altitude, like reconnaissance planes on patrol.

"We're almost there," Captain Devlin shouted above the roar of the engine and the desert wind.

"You've been here before?"

"Once. Deserter."

I was too exhausted to shout out a conversation. I assumed he meant he'd had to pick up a deserter.

Finally, I spotted signs of civilization. A few roadside stands gave way to larger blocks of housing and businesses. Suddenly, a city much like Algiers appeared in the near distance. Whitewashed buildings, blinding in the sun. French colonial structures packed together with much older, boxy designs. The road widened, but it was only when we crossed the large iron-railed bridge that I caught the true splendor of Constantine.

A large canyon cleaved the city of Constantine in two, as if a giant had come through with an immense saber and slashed the land. I marveled that long ago, long-dead tribespeople decided to build a city balanced precariously on rock outcroppings that had to be crossed by multiple bridges.

Traffic slowed to a crawl on the bridge, then stopped. I licked my dry lips. My skin felt sucked of all moisture. Captain Devlin handed over his canteen, and I took it gratefully. I swirled the water in the canteen, judging it to be half full. This time my taste buds sang the moment the chlorine water touched my tongue. I took three long swallows, then handed it back to Captain Devlin. He put the jeep in park and took a long draft. "We'll get more at the command post."

I rummaged in my bag for my Army-issue anti-chap lip balm. I ran it over my lips three times for good measure, then handed it to the captain.

He took it and swiped it across his lips, pressing them together, then handed it back to me. It was an oddly personal moment, sharing a ChapStick. When the lip balm was tucked into the side pocket of my utility bag, Captain Devlin shut down the engine. "I think we have a few minutes. Wanna stretch your legs?"

"Sure."

I got out of the jeep and brushed off the sand that had accumulated in the folds of my uniform. I lifted my knees a few times. The guys in the truck behind us did the same. I staggered to the iron railing bordering the sidewalk and looked over the side. The gorge was a beautiful butter-colored stone that plunged at least five hundred feet down. At the bottom, a green trickle of a river crawled through the gorge.

"It sure is something, isn't it?"

"It's beautiful." We both stood looking down the gorge, each lost in our own thoughts.

Captain Devlin shook his head. "I can't wrap my head around this one, if I'm honest, Lincoln. From all accounts, your friend was a level-headed sort of gal. Private Rivera is a known flirt. But it's inexplicable to me that a randy private was so enraged by one rejection that he threw her off a building. It just doesn't make sense."

I gazed out one last time at the gorge below. "Maybe there's more we don't know," I said, remembering Sue's accusation. "Maybe Ruth was wrapped up in something."

"Maybe. But if she was, nobody seems to know about it. And I doubt Rivera will shed much light on it, assuming he didn't go into a rage and kill her."

"How will you get it out of him if he did?"

"Carefully, Lincoln. Very carefully."

After a few minutes, the truck ahead of us rumbled into action.

"Looks like it's time to gear up." The captain's shoulders sagged, and I suspected fatigue was hitting him hard.

"You okay, Captain? Want me to drive?"

"You know how to drive a jeep?"

"No," I admitted. "Doesn't look too hard, though. I can learn."

Captain Devlin threw back his head and laughed heartily. "Spoken like a true soldier."

* * *

The Advanced Command Post for Allied Force Headquarters operated out of an orphanage at the top of one of Constantine's many hills. Next door was a bustling villa, with jeeps and staff cars coming and going.

Surprisingly, once we arrived at the command post, finding Private Rivera was relatively quick and easy. As always, Captain Devlin shouted at the nearest GI, a British Tommy. "I'm looking for a Private Rivera with the 805th Signal Company."

"American, sir?"

"Of course, American."

"Check one of those lorries there," he said, pointing to a line of mobile communication units. Whip antennas on top of the trucks swayed with the wind. Each truck had an open cab; the mobile generator chugged just a few feet behind the cab. Radiomen sat on cushions inside, surrounded by their equipment.

Captain Devlin nodded his thanks and pulled up next to the last SCR 299 in the line. The SCR 299 was a mobile communications unit used by the Signal Corps to provide long-range communication across the thousands of miles of the North African front.

We found Private Rivera in the third panel van with the back doors wide open. He sat on the cushioned seat in the middle of the cab, speaking into a handset. Another man sat behind him. Rivera glanced up, and his eyes went wide when he saw me. He finished his transmission and nudged his buddy. "Hey, Rocky, can you take over for a minute?"

Rivera jumped down from the van, reaching up to button his collar. He smoothed his hair back and snapped a quick salute to

Devlin, then returned to his buttons. "Captain," he said, giving me a concerned glance.

"At ease, soldier. I don't care about your slovenly appearance. I'm here about Auxiliary Wentz. Is there someplace we can talk? In private?"

Private Rivera looked away, a muscle in his jaw twitching like a live wire. "Sure thing, Captain. This way." He led us to a line of olive trees shading several empty ammo crates serving as makeshift chairs. Nobody sat down.

"You look familiar," Rivera said, squinting my way. The last time we'd met had been in a darkened auditorium. I pulled off my sunglasses, and recognition flared in his eyes.

"She should," Captain Devlin snapped. "You pushed her down at the dance a couple nights ago."

Private Rivera's scrubbed a hand over his handsome face. "I'm so sorry. I don't know what happened. I never meant to send you sprawling like that. I'm really sorry, miss."

He sounded sincere enough. "It's okay. No harm done."

Captain Devlin got right to the point. "We understand you had an altercation with Auxiliary Wentz just minutes before she was killed."

Rivera's head snapped back to Devlin. "Killed? Who said anything about killed? I heard she committed suicide."

"You heard wrong."

Private Rivera didn't speak for a few moments. His hand rubbed his chest as if he had sudden heartburn. Captain Devlin watched him closely.

Private Rivera closed his eyes, looking as if he were struggling to breathe.

"Word is, you were pushing her around, just like you pushed Auxiliary Lincoln here."

Rivera's nostrils flared. "Hey," he said, his voice cracking, "I didn't do anything to that sweet girl."

"That's not what I've been told. I've got a dozen witnesses that say you were forcing your attentions on Auxiliary Wentz shortly before she died."

Rivera shook his head. "It wasn't like that. I just wanted a dance."

"Maybe you didn't want to take no for an answer," Captain Devlin said. His demeanor was calm, but I saw the hard granite in his eyes.

"C'mon, sir. Even if that were true, I don't need to force anyone. The Army provides condoms, and Algiers has plenty of nice-looking broads willing to give a guy a little something in exchange for cigarettes or a few francs. Only good thing about Algiers, sir—anyone can get laid anytime." Private Rivera tried for a light, joking tone. But I could see his heart wasn't in it and the words fell flat.

"Careful, Private," Devlin warned, a muscle twitching in his jaw. I didn't know if he was trying to protect my sensitivities or if he was warning Private Rivera against lying to the police.

Private Rivera's shoulders sagged. "Look, after Ruth turned me down, I went to Madame Carree's. But just because it was easy, that's all." He looked at me. "No offense, ma'am."

"Who were you with? Do you have a name?"

"Yvette. She was sweet. Talked a lot about her family." He rummaged in his pockets and pulled out a cigarette. "Think she was gunning for more money."

"Did you give it to her?"

Rivera took his time lighting a cigarette. He blew out a smoke ring, squinting up at Devlin. "Of course. What am I gonna do with it? Especially now that I'm out here."

"And you resent that?"

"No. Being out here is a damn sight better than being stuck in Algiers. Thought I was gonna be stuck behind the lines the whole war, you know? I'm glad to see some action."

"So maybe you wanted to get it on with a girl in uniform. A nice girl from home, right? Maybe things got out of hand and you pushed her."

Rivera dropped his gaze to his combat boots. Licked his lips. Heaved a sigh. When he looked up and met my gaze, his face was etched with pain. He rubbed at his forehead as if he had a sudden itch.

"It would be better for all of us if you just told us the truth, Private," Captain Devlin said, not unkindly. "What was the situation between you and Auxiliary Wentz?"

"I love her, okay? I didn't hurt her."

"Loved her?" Devlin sounded skeptical.

Private Rivera's shoulders sagged. "Yeah. I wanted her to marry me, okay? But she wouldn't do it. Said her job came first. She said we both had a job to do, and she wasn't going back to the States. So I asked her to wait for me. She said she didn't know where the war would take us. She thought it was a mistake to make promises we might not be able to keep."

"So you were angry?"

"Hell, yes, it made me angry. She got me, ya know? She saw through my bullshit. And . . ." He swallowed hard. "And she loved me too. I know she did."

"So you proposed at this dance?"

"No, before. I'd written to her, but she never responded. So I got leave to go to the dance. I thought maybe my letter got lost or she wanted to hear it in person. Instead, she turned me down."

"Do you have any proof of this marriage proposal?"

"Are you serious?"

Captain Devlin inclined his head.

Rivera threw up his hands. "I don't have the letter, obviously. It's probably with her things." He said this last quietly.

My heart went out to him. He hadn't killed Ruth. He'd loved her. It was written all over his face.

"What happened then?" Captain Devlin asked, more gently this time.

"I'm ashamed to say I left. I was mad. I told her if she didn't want to be with me, there were plenty of other girls who did. Which is crap because there's nobody else in the world like Ruth. She's tough, ya know? But soft and sweet inside. She got my jokes. We just fit, ya know? Like the guide channels in a tuning unit." Rivera sniffed and sucked a drag off his cigarette.

"So you went to the brothel."

Rivera winced. "Yeah, but not like that. I went there, but I just went to have a drink. I didn't know what to do with myself. There's not a lot of places a man can be alone in Algiers, ya know?"

Devlin nodded as if he understood. "Privacy does seem to be a casualty of the war. Did anybody see you there?"

"Saw lots of guys. And I paid for that girl Yvette. Just to sit in her room, though. She'll remember me. I'll bet dollars to daisies I'm the only customer she had who didn't want the usual services."

He looked up, first at Captain Devlin, then at me. "Look, I know what you're thinking, but that's not where my head was that night. I didn't want to be with anyone else. I wanted to be with Ruth. Madame Carree's was the only place I could go and just . . ." His voice trailed off.

"Cry?" I asked, softly.

"Hell, no. I didn't cry," Rivera snapped. "I just went there to have a few drinks. Get some quiet so I could think. Christ. I'm not a weepy dame, okay?"

"Okay," I said.

He was silent for a moment. "I can't believe she's really gone. She was so alive. Another reason I fell for her. Everything was so intense with her. I never met a woman like that before." Then Rivera did get tears in his eyes. "I know you're just doing your job. Maybe you came out here to arrest me. But I did not kill Ruth. I loved her. I wanted her to marry me."

Captain Devlin cleared his throat and looked away, clearly uncomfortable with Private Rivera's show of emotion. "Did you see anything suspicious that night?"

Rivera tilted his head back and chewed his bottom lip. "She was worried about that girl Mary. Said the girl didn't have the sense God gave a goat. I know she went up after the girl. I saw her go up those stairs. I guess she thought Mary was having a meetup with her fella. That Brit. She talked to the vixen at the bottom of the stairs on her way up."

"Wait a minute," Captain Devlin interrupted. "What vixen? Mary?"

Private Rivera laughed. "Mary's a great-looking broad, but she's no vixen. That dark-haired girl with the Southern accent. Wears too much makeup."

"Sue Dunworthy," I said, thinking that Private Rivera was a good judge of character if he knew to steer clear of Sue.

"Yeah, that one. She was at the bottom of the stairs there, in the little alcove, and she called me over. Her and that MP."

"Why'd she call you over?"

Rivera shifted his eyes away, tilted his head, and pressed his lips together. He bounced on his heels. I had the distinct impression he was deciding just how much to tell us. "She always had something to sell, that girl. She had some stuff to show me."

"You're talking about the black market," Devlin said, raising an eyebrow.

Private Rivera gave Devlin a sardonic look. "I think you know what goes on, Captain."

Captain Devlin shifted his feet.

"Anyway, Ruth said something to that girl Sue and then went upstairs. She didn't have any time for me, that's for sure. So I took off for Madame Carree's. When I left, I guess I thought I'd rent a girl for the night. But when I got there, I just couldn't do it. I love her." He took a drag off his cigarette and stared out into the desert. Then he turned to Devlin. "You're sure she was murdered?"

"We're sure," I said.

"And you're gonna find out who did this? Make 'em pay?"

"We're going to try to find out what—

"Yes, Private," I said. "We'll find out what happened to Ruth. We'll see that justice is done."

Rivera held my gaze for a long beat, then let out a shaky breath and nodded. "Good. She didn't deserve this. She was a good woman."

"Yes, she was."

Rivera sniffed, ran a hand across his forehead, and tossed his cigarette aside. "You know, when I signed up, I'd come to terms with maybe not getting back, ya know? Never thought one of you girls would . . ." he stopped, blinking rapidly. "I gotta get back to work. Germans are on the move. I don't know why I got moved out two weeks before my CO told me I'd be staying in Algiers for the duration. Not that I'm complaining. I wanted to get into the fight anyway. But Ruth? It's just not right."

"Stay safe, Private," I said.

"You too."

I turned to head back toward the jeep.

"Hey, wait up," Rivera said. "The Army doesn't issue weapons to WAACs. Do you have anything for protection?"

I glanced at Captain Devlin. Despite the sunglasses, I had the distinct impression he was rolling his eyes. "No, not really. I mean, no."

"Here." He reached into his pocket and pulled out a small, curved dagger with a brass cover. "I got this off an A-rab. He didn't speak English, so he didn't say much, but he showed me how to use it."

I took the knife. I ran my fingers over three empty holes where I suspected jewels had once been embedded. Small brass rings on either side of the sheath would have been used to tie the knife to a man's body. "Thank you, Private Rivera. I don't know that I'll ever have cause to use it, but thank you."

Rivera gave her a grim smile. "Let's hope you don't, but after what happened to Ruth, I'd feel better knowing you have it. Find out who did it, miss. Make 'em pay."

Private Rivera climbed back into the van, indicating that the interview was over.

Captain Devlin tucked a cigarette into his mouth and spoke around it. "Congratulations, Lincoln. You're the first WAAC in this man's Army to carry a weapon. A-rab issued."

"They were here before we were, sir. And long before the French."

"Well, that doesn't amount to a hill of beans right now, does it?"

Captain Devlin reached into the back of the jeep and pulled out a canvas bag. Inside were C-rations. My grumbling stomach told me to skip the history lesson. Captain Devlin didn't care about the French occupation, and I supposed with my empty stomach and exhaustion sitting on my shoulders like an anvil, I didn't either at the moment.

We ate quickly. I scarfed down cold pork and beans, then dug into the vanilla caramels.

"We'll have to grab some water on the way out." He glanced at his watch. "We'd better get a move on. Don't want to be sleeping on a road in the middle of the desert."

"You'll be okay to drive?"

Captain Devlin chuckled. "First thing you learn in basic training. Keep marching, stay alert. Besides, I've got a little help if I need it."

"You're ready to teach me to drive?"

He grinned and patted his breast pocket. "Not that kind of help. Got a few bennies from one of the Brits."

"Oh," I said, trying to keep the disapproval out of my voice. Benzedrine was an amphetamine the British Army supplied to its troops. Word was, General Eisenhower was trying to get the War Department to distribute the drug to American troops in the field, but so far it hadn't happened. The British seemed all too happy to share their supply, for a price.

"Don't worry, Lincoln. Haven't had to take one yet. I'll be fine to get us back in one piece."

Somehow that wasn't very reassuring. I decided I'd better stay wide awake for the trip back. No more dozing upright. I needed to help Devlin keep his eyes open and on the road. I had no intention of dying in a jeep accident in the middle of the Algerian desert.

Captain Devlin steered the jeep out of the courtyard and down the steep winding road.

A staff car approached from the opposite direction. Despite the glaring sun, I could make out the four stars on the license plate. As we passed, I stared right into the face of General Dwight D. Eisenhower. Suddenly I was wide awake. I'd never seen the general in the field before. It was thrilling. The general's head turned as we drove past, and then we were going around the rock outcropping and down the hill toward the desert plain below.

"He didn't do it," I said after we'd cleared the city.

"No, I guess he didn't," Devlin agreed.

"We need to talk to Sue."

"She never mentioned seeing Ruth that night."

"Why would Sue kill Ruth?"

"Jealousy?"

"What would she have to be jealous of? Ruth didn't have anything Sue wanted." Even as I said the words, I wasn't so sure. Sue was trying to blackmail me for the letter. Maybe Ruth had something Sue thought could make money for her? I remembered the silk hankie in Ruth's utility bag. Had Sue discovered Ruth dealing in the black market? I doubted it. Ruth didn't break regulations.

"Did Sue ever have a thing for Private Rivera?" Captain Devlin asked.

"Not that I ever noticed," I said, squinting against the wind and the sand kicking up from the desert floor. "She was always talking to Gar Mitchell."

"Huh. Well, guess we'll just have to ask her."

"Stop the car!"

"What is it?" Devlin slammed down the brake, pitching us both forward.

"Look!" I pointed at a line of soldiers wearing desert tan, marching along the roadside, hands on their heads. The sun had settled just behind the craggy rockfaces, hiding the men's faces. I had a burning desire to jump out of the jeep and check every single one. To look for a tall man with piercing blue eyes and a cruel chin.

"Germans," Captain Devlin spat like a curse. "Guess it wasn't a total loss then."

"What wasn't a total loss?"

"The fight to the east."

I tried to scan each face, looking for Konrad. I knew the chances of him being here were a million to one, but still, I scanned. The clouds and the setting sun worked against me. "How many of them do you think there are?"

"Two hundred? Who knows? Believe me, they have way more prisoners than we do." Devlin pulled out his pack of Luckys. I folded my shaking hands against my stomach, grateful for the increasing darkness. He wouldn't be able to see the emotion coursing through me. Fear. Longing. An urgent desire to check each man, to interrogate each one. Did they know Konrad von Raven? Was he alive? Where had he left Sadie?

"They're grinding us into the ground out there, Lincoln. We're not winning this particular battle. Word has it, we're taking a beating."

"Will there be more, do you think?" I dared a look at the captain. "German prisoners?"

"I damn well hope so. We're in this to win, right?"

I let out a shrill laugh. "That we are, Captain. That we are."

"You okay, Lincoln?"

I dragged my eyes away from the soldiers. There was no way for me to check each face. There were too many of them, and Captain Devlin would think me insane if I got out to confront the enemy. Besides, I had no idea where Konrad had ended up. Now that the initial shock of seeing German soldiers marching down the road had settled, I realized the chance of Konrad being here, in North Africa, was so unlikely as to be impossible. He could be anywhere. He could be in Germany. Or fighting in Russia. Or bombing the United Kingdom. Or he could be in Paris, as part of the occupying forces. I gave Devlin a watery smile. "It's been a long day."

Devlin lifted his chin in agreement. "That it has. Let's get back. We need to check Rivera's alibi, just to be sure he's telling the truth. And then we'll find your Auxiliary Dunworthy."

I tucked my hands under my armpits. The temperature had dropped with the setting sun, but I knew my sudden shaking had more to do with Sue. When confronted with Captain Devlin's questions, would Sue pull out my letter? She might think it would save her from a murder inquiry. Pulling my uniform jacket tight around my shivering body, I wondered if Sue would brandish the letter to Captain Devlin or threaten me later. We didn't have time to get off track now, and I suspected my letter might cause a bit of an uproar. I had no doubt that Private Rivera's alibi would check out. That left us with Sue Dunworthy as our most likely suspect. A member of my company, my own squad, a part of the family I was trying to build in the Army, held my darkest secret. And she was now our prime suspect in a murder investigation.

# Chapter 23

The 577th MP Company headquarters was quiet when we pulled up outside the office building. Devlin killed the engine. The engine ticked, cooling down from its long workout.

I climbed out of the jeep, every muscle screaming in protest. All I wanted to do was get back to barracks, wash up, and go to bed. My body felt like a deflated life vest. For a fleeting moment, I wished for a hot bath in a large tub. I pushed the image away. A hot bath was a distant dream. Maybe if I had a Coke, I'd wake up and be ready to interrogate Sue Dunworthy. Instead, I'd have to find some coffee.

I followed Captain Devlin into MP headquarters with thoughts of hot coffee dancing in my head. Private Venturi manned the front desk. When he saw us, he leaped to his feet. "There you are, Captain. The colonel wants to see you ASAP!"

"Hey, Venturi. Any news on the panty bandit case?"

"He said you need to come in now, sir." Private Venturi stepped closer and lowered his voice ominously. "He's been waiting for you all evening."

"Goddammit. All right."

"Her too," Venturi said. Something in Venturi's face made me think Colonel Cantry including me in this meeting was not good news.

I followed Devlin down the hall to Colonel Cantry's office. Private Venturi stayed at his desk.

The colonel's door was open. Cantry stood at his office window, smoking his pipe. When he turned to face us, I flinched. He glared at me and then turned his furious gaze to Captain Devlin.

"What the hell do you think you're doing taking a WAAC to Constantine?" the colonel shouted, thrusting his pipe in our direction.

"Sir." Captain Devlin saluted. I followed suit. "We had a suspect to interview."

"This girl died here in Algiers. What the hell reason would you have to go out there?"

Captain Devlin pulled out the cigarette tucked behind his ear and held it in two hands, rolling it between his fingers.

"Sir," I said, hoping to stave off Colonel Cantry's anger, "our prime suspect was just transferred to Constantine."

The colonel's eyes bulged at this pronouncement. "Our suspect? *Our?* You are not an MP, little lady."

Captain Devlin cleared his throat. "Sir, Private Rivera was our prime suspect. We had no choice but to interview him. Unfortunately, he was transferred to Constantine late last night."

"There's a goddamn war on, captain. Of course we're transferring every man we can spare to the front."

"Of course, sir. And we have eliminated him from our suspect list. He didn't do it."

Colonel Cantry's cheeks bellowed. "You had no authorization to take a WAAC to a forwarding operating command post."

"Colonel, with all due respect, WAACs drive to Constantine all the time. One of Auxiliary Lincoln's colleagues is a driver for the general. I'm sure she's made a few trips to the CP."

I didn't know if Kirksey had driven the general to Constantine, but it was entirely probable that she had. The colonel, however, was not impressed.

"I don't give a god damn what her *colleague* is doing. When I get a call from the general himself, asking me what a military police vehicle is doing at his CP with a WAAC in the jump seat, I goddamn better know what the answer is!" Colonel Cantry shouted.

"I'm sorry, Colonel. I didn't think it would be a problem."

I remembered the staff car we'd passed on our way out of the command post and General Eisenhower turning his head. It was my fault the colonel was so upset. If I hadn't been in the jeep, the general wouldn't have thought anything of the MP jeep at his CP.

"Devlin, this investigation is over."

My heart sank. "But, sir—"

Colonel Cantry held out a wavering index finger. "Not another word, young lady." He was shaking with fury. He lowered his arm and turned to Captain Devlin. "And you, Captain—you had no business taking a WAAC to a forward operating base. She does not have clearance."

"She's GI."

"Like hell she is," the colonel roared back. "She's a secretary. You don't take a secretary into the field."

I swallowed back my fear. "I am a soldier, sir."

"Soldier?" Spittle flew from his lips. His face was an alarming tomato color. "A soldier of what? The typing pool? You know what happens to me if you get killed out there? Did you ever think about that, Devlin? What happens when the Germans kill a WAAC? It would be a PR nightmare."

"Sir, I'm sorry you got reamed by the general, but I assure you, the WAACs here in North Africa have the necessary clearance to be on post. The drivers—"

"The drivers are with high-ranking officers who are protected, Devlin. Use your head!"

I cleared my throat, summoning the last of my courage. "Sir, we came here with the understanding that we are risking our lives."

"Is that so?" Colonel Cantry breathed in through his nose like a dragon ready to fire. "Are you ladies ready to be sent home? Because I guaran-god-damn-tee that if you were killed out there, General Eisenhower would cancel this ridiculous experiment and send you all packing. Which wouldn't be the worst thing in the world, if you ask me. You don't belong here anyway. But it's not gonna happen on my watch, I tell you that. I will not be responsible for Ike's precious war brides getting killed. This investigation is over. Young lady, you will return to your regular duties. Your temporary duty is over forthwith. You are excused. Devlin, a word."

I opened my mouth to respond, my eyes burning with unshed tears, but Devlin put a hand on my arm and shook his head.

I snapped a quick salute and did an about-face, biting down hard on the inside of my cheek, fighting the urge to lash out at Colonel Cantry. I didn't know what I might say, but if I started speaking, I wasn't sure I'd be able to stop. I had to get out of there double time, before I got myself booted out of the Army for insubordination.

* * *

I was too agitated to sit down. I paced beside the jeep. When Captain Devlin finally emerged from the building, he jumped gracefully into the jeep. "Get in, Lincoln."

Disappointment flooded through me when he turned toward the convent. The street was empty. Darkness closed in on all sides. I tried to gather my thoughts while Captain Devlin drove the short distance back to my barracks. I needed to muster my arguments against abandoning the investigation.

I couldn't argue with a colonel. I was a lowly auxiliary with no standing to challenge him or his orders. I knew Captain Devlin was eager to get back to his panty bandit case. But we couldn't just abandon the investigation. Ruth's killer had to be brought to justice.

Devlin parked the jeep a few feet away from the entrance gate and turned off the engine. "I know how you feel."

"No, you don't. Sir."

Captain Devlin chuckled softly. "Okay, maybe I don't know exactly how you feel, but I'm frustrated too."

"What did the colonel say?"

"About what you'd expect. The investigation is over. Wentz's death will be ruled accidental."

"I guess that's better than suicide," I said bitterly.

"It is. I had to fight for that, if you wanna know."

"Oh. Thank you." I turned to face him. "There's no way we can stop investigating."

"There's no way we can *keep* investigating. Right or wrong, Cantry is furious. The last thing a man in his position wants is to get a reprimand from the supreme commander."

"I understand that, but I can't let this go, Captain Devlin."

"You have to. You don't have a choice."

"We didn't even talk to Sue. She lied to us. She said the last time she talked to Ruth was on the dance floor. Private Rivera says otherwise. She was at the bottom of those stairs. She talked to Ruth right before she died."

"We have no reason to suspect Sue Dunworthy. So what if she lied? Maybe she forgot. It was a busy night, what with the bombardment and all."

"But she lied about it."

"Do you have any evidence that Dunworthy had a reason to kill?"

I bit my bottom lip. I didn't know the answer to that question. And what I couldn't tell Captain Devlin was that Sue was dangerous. She was trying to blackmail me. It was entirely possible she had been blackmailing Ruth for some reason. But I couldn't say any of that without revealing my own secrets. There was one thing I could say, though. "I think Ruth was on to Sue."

"What do you mean?"

"Sue's up to no good. She always has things she shouldn't. Silk handkerchiefs and perfume."

"What do silk handkerchiefs and perfume have to do with anything?"

"Think about it. Ruth had a silk handkerchief in her utility bag. I think she confiscated it from Sue. Maybe the night of the dance. Maybe that's what she wanted to talk to me about after curfew. You're having a problem with panties being stolen off ships, and Sue has been selling silk handkerchiefs to the girls. She says she gets them from the Casbah. Or rather, she says her boyfriend gets them."

"Her boyfriend being Private Mitchell?"

"Yes," I said. Here was a way to keep the investigation going. Captain Devlin wanted to catch the panty bandits. Maybe Private Mitchell had something to do with trading American goods on the black market. It was possible.

"There's no way Private Mitchell is involved with the black market. He's an MP, for Christ's sake. And you never told me the victim was selling on the black market."

"I don't think she was selling anything. I think maybe she confiscated the silk hankie. Probably from Sue Dunworthy."

"You have no evidence of that, I presume."

"No, but it's possible, isn't it? Maybe Sue is dealing with someone besides Private Mitchell. Someone dangerous. Ruth had the silk handkerchief in her utility bag. If Ruth confiscated it, maybe Sue was angry. If Ruth was about to turn her in, she might have had a reason to silence her."

"That's a lot of *ifs*, Lincoln."

"I know, but they're things we should explore, right?"

"Maybe. If there was still an investigation, which there isn't. I'm sorry, but my hands are tied. The colonel's orders are to close the lid on this thing. There's nothing I can do."

"Maybe there's something *I* can do," I muttered.

"You better get that out of your head, and pronto. If you care about your job here and you want to stay. You seem like a dedicated"—he hesitated—"auxiliary. You need to move on."

"She was in my squad, Captain. It was my job to protect her."

"And you did the best you could. As an officer, I'll tell you this: you'll find out, like everywhere else in life, you can't account for the unexpected. You can't foresee every possible eventuality. There was no way for you know Wentz was in danger. And you can't discount the probability that she was depressed or upset that night. Maybe she did jump. Maybe in a moment of despair after turning down her boyfriend, she climbed out on that ledge and thought about jumping. Maybe she changed her mind at the last minute, but it was too late."

"That's a lot of *maybes*."

"There's no way for us to know what happened, Lincoln. You have to move on. We still have a war to win. That's what we're here for, right?"

I pulled myself out of the jeep. There was no point continuing the conversation. He wasn't listening. He'd made his decision. Even if I told him about Sue's blackmail, it wouldn't change his mind. Not with Colonel Cantry calling the shots. I was on my own now.

"Hey, Lincoln."

I turned around and waited.

"It was interesting working with you, Lincoln."

"Interesting?"

"Yeah. You were my first female"—he paused, searching for the correct term—"assistant. You did good. Except for one thing."

"Oh yeah? What's that?"

"You really need to learn to salute."

I gave a quick salute. "Thanks, Captain. Abyssinia."

"I doubt it," he called, driving away, leaving me alone and in the dark.

# CHAPTER 24

I woke up the next morning determined to find out what Ruth discussed with Sue at the bottom of the stairs on the night of her death. I shortened my physical training, but when I was done, Sue was already gone.

Mary was in the squad room, getting ready for work.

"How are you feeling, Mary?" Even though I wasn't squad leader anymore, I still felt protective of the girls. I wanted to make sure Mary was okay and had recovered from her illness.

"I'm fine."

"Are you sure? You look a little pale."

"I said I'm fine. You don't have any right to question me anymore. You're not squad leader."

"I'm just concerned about you."

"Well, don't be."

I decided to change the subject. "So, who took my place?"

"Cornfeld, if you can believe it."

"Mabel? Really?" I was surprised. Mabel Cornfeld was a sweet girl. Obedient. A little jumpy. She had a nervous disposition. But Fitzgerald had avoided Sue Dunworthy, which I had to give her credit for. Sue would have been a terrible choice, even without my suspicions that she might have killed Ruth. Kirksey was unreliable.

Mary was too young. I was out, and Ruth was dead. Mabel was the best choice. "She'll do a good job."

Mary rolled her eyes. "I guess. If she doesn't drive us all to distraction with her constant worrying."

"She can be a little anxious, but she cares about the squad."

"I guess. Anyway, I'm off. I'll see you at the office. Pesky will be glad to see you."

"If you wait a minute, we can walk together."

Mary frowned. "I don't think you realize how much paperwork has piled up since you left. Pesky won't like it if I'm late."

I didn't think Mary would be late. It was only seven thirty. But I didn't argue. I'd left the office in the lurch. I didn't have a right to keep Mary waiting. "Of course, you're right. I'll see you there."

Mary gave a tight smile and left. I hurried to change and fix my hair. I didn't know yet what I was going to do about Ruth. I needed a plan. I could try to have lunch with Sue and ask some questions. But until then, I needed to help Corporal Pinski with the paperwork piling up at the Adjutant General's office. I'd seen the congestion on the road to Constantine firsthand. For every vehicle and every man moving between Allied Force Headquarters and the various battle stations in the east, there was a pile of paperwork back at the office.

I grabbed my utility bag and headed out the door. Walking down Rue Florian, I saw Mary several hundred yards ahead. I hustled, hoping to catch up. I could ask Mary about her interactions with Sue that night. I hadn't asked Mary if she'd noticed any tension between Ruth and Sue. Maybe there was something more I could learn about Ruth's movements that night.

But instead of turning right onto Boulevard Gallieni, toward the Hotel Alexandra, Mary turned left toward Avenue Georges Clemenceau. I followed, wondering where in the world Mary Jordan was headed.

My feet ached. The temperature was still cool, but I was sweating under my wool olive drab. I ducked behind cars and buildings more than once as Mary made her way through the streets of Algiers. For reasons I couldn't explain, I felt certain Mary did not wish to be seen. Where was she going? Maybe she was skipping work to meet Captain Haywynn.

Almost an hour later, I watched with wonder and deep concern as Mary walked into the Casbah. She walked right past the sign painted in big black letters, "CASBAH OUT OF BOUNDS. OFF LIMITS."

Whatever Mary was doing, I very much doubted that Captain Haywynn waited at the end of this journey. I couldn't imagine any scenario where the overprotective, overprivileged earl would send his girlfriend into the most dangerous place in Algiers for Allied soldiers.

Rumors around Allied Force Headquarters painted a picture of spies and saboteurs hiding within its labyrinth of narrow streets and dead-end alleyways. Thieves and pickpockets were said to be waiting to strip American service personnel clean, like vultures on a fresh kill. Signs were posted on every street and alley that led into the Casbah saying "Off Limits" and "Casbah Out of Bounds." Why in the world would young Mary Jordan venture into the forbidden zone?

Mary stopped suddenly, taking stock of her surroundings. I darted behind the nearest wall, riddled with bullet holes, heart pounding. After I'd caught my breath, I peered around and saw Mary pull a piece of paper from her utility bag. She looked up at the blue street signs attached to the tall buildings. From where I stood, I couldn't see the paper in Mary's hands, but when Mary turned decidedly to the left, I assumed she was following directions written on the piece of paper. Or a map. Who had drawn Mary a map of the Casbah? And for what reason?

Two women dressed in the traditional white haik passed by. Their dark eyes roamed over me, but their steps did not falter.

I hurried on after Mary as she worked her way deeper and deeper into the old city. A rancid smell filled the air. I entered a small open area where goats wandered aimlessly and a butcher shop displayed fresh meat. I reached into my bag for Ruth's silk handkerchief and covered my nose and mouth. Mary hurried past the butcher's shop and made another turn. I followed.

When I peeked around the corner this time, I saw Mary bent over, retching into the gutter. I didn't blame her. I put a hand on my stomach, breathing shallowly, fighting my own urge to vomit. When it finally passed and I looked up, Mary was gone.

"Damn." I went down the little street. Laundry hung between the buildings, a gentle breeze setting them to fanning passersby below.

A young boy came careening around the corner, colliding with me. His eyes went wide, and he scampered off. Two Algerian policemen soon followed. I pressed myself against the wall, my mind racing with excuses about why I was walking through the forbidden Casbah. But the two policemen ran right past me, apparently chasing the boy. Their red fezzes bounced through the narrow, crooked street like a patrol car's flashing lights. Their heavy black boots pounded the pavement, echoing through the alleyways.

I waited until my racing heartbeat righted itself and continued on. I came to a fork in the walkway. On the left side, a set of small steps led to crooked house. Beyond that the sundrenched cobblestone walkway continued. To my right, a narrow alley disappeared into darkness. Mary was nowhere to be seen. *Damn.* I had lost her. The hairs on the back of my neck prickled. I wasn't safe here. What's more, Mary wasn't safe here. What the hell was she doing, wandering around in the Casbah alone? And where had she gone? I should have called out to her instead of sneaking around like a schoolgirl.

As I contemplated my next move, I heard a popping sound. The mud bricks beside me exploded in a spray of masonry. I ducked as another shot rang out. I spun around and flattened myself against the wall next to the residence.

Was someone shooting at me? It was entirely possible. The Casbah was off-limits to American personnel for a reason. There were still German operatives in Algiers and Frenchmen still loyal to Vichy. I wondered if those two women had reported seeing American women in their territory. Or had the young boy told a father or brother who was a member of the Algerian People's Party?

I had no idea where Mary had gone, but I couldn't stay where I was without risking my own safety. With one last look back down the darkened alleyway, I turned and ran for the sunlight.

★ ★ ★

I arrived at the Hotel Alexandra almost two hours late for work, sweaty, disheveled, and exhausted. I was also mortified. I'd run away like a frightened rabbit and left Mary alone in the Casbah.

I entered the building, knowing I had to tell Corporal Pinski to send out a search party to find Mary. I couldn't leave her there alone with someone taking potshots at Americans. But when I walked into the office, Mary sat at her desk, typing as if she'd been there all morning.

"Hey, Corporal, I should get a raise. Seems I'm the only one who can get to work on time," Sue said, tapping her red nails on her chin.

"It's not my fault Fitzy sent me to order the flowers for the funeral," Mary said, giving Sue the stink-eye.

"The funeral?" I asked. "Do you mean Ruth's funeral?"

"Of course Ruth's funeral," Mary said, never taking her eyes off her typewriter. "Who else would I mean?"

My head swam and I felt faint. How had I not known Ruth's funeral was already scheduled? Someone must have made the arrangements and let the company know while I was in Constantine. I hadn't seen First Officer Fitzgerald since I'd received my temporary duty orders.

Corporal Pinski gave me the once-over and frowned. "Are you okay, Dottie? Looks like you had a rough morning."

I smiled weakly at the sergeant. "I'm fine, Corporal. Sorry I'm late. Won't happen again."

"No problem. Glad to have you back."

I went to my desk. There were piles of files stacked beside my typewriter. With shaking hands, I rolled a stencil into my machine and opened the first file. There was no way on earth First Officer Fitzgerald had sent Mary Jordan to the Casbah alone. Not for flowers or anything else. She was lying. But why? I didn't dare ask Mary what she'd been doing in the Casbah or how she'd gotten back to the office so quickly, with everyone listening. But I was damn sure going to find out.

# CHAPTER 25

That afternoon, I stood with my fellow soldiers at Ruth's gravesite. There was a storm rolling in from the west, bringing with it a strong, cold breeze.

El Alia Cemetery was located south of Algiers, on the road to El Harrach, thirteen kilometers from the city's center. A single American flag snapped in the wind above the little plot of graves south of the main road. Saplings strapped to stabilizing posts had been planted along a pathway of crushed quartz. Someday those saplings would grow, and the graveyard would be shaded by trees, but today I felt like we might as well be on the face of the moon. The ground was dry and rocky; dust blew against my shins.

Each plot was marked out with white stones and filled with mounded gravel, a white cross at the head. I glanced at the names. Each man's name, company, and date of death was burned into the white cross. Most of them had died during the invasion of North Africa in early November. Casualties of our successful takeover. Almost five hundred Allied soldiers had been killed by the French during the invasion. Most Americans didn't trust the French after their meager resistance, even though the French military now fought with the Allies.

The women of the 22$^{nd}$ Post Headquarters Company gathered in small groups, talking and smoking. The girls wore olive drab, and the cold wind pulled at the pins holding our caps. I found myself standing alone next to the trucks parked on the verge beside a row of palm trees. A rifle company and a bugler stood on the verge with me but didn't try to make conversation, for which I was grateful. Soldiers spoke in soft tones, the wind whipping around them like mist.

At precisely fifteen hundred hours, two men climbed out of the first truck, walked around to the back of their vehicle, and dropped the leaf. When they pulled out a pine box, the Double Deuces stubbed out their cigarettes, pulled their uniforms straight, and walked solemnly toward the coffin.

Two soldiers jumped down from the second truck, all business, until they caught sight, one after the other, of the women walking toward them. They froze, shovels in hand. Meeting each other's eyes, they tossed the shovels back into the truck and folded their arms.

Wanda Wooten had tears streaming down her face, but she didn't make a sound. Mabel Cornfeld's fists were clenched, and her lips pursed, as if she were physically battling a breakdown. Kirksey's eyes were wet. The rest of the female soldiers were stoic.

The two men holding Ruth's coffin lowered it to the ground in the face of the procession.

"We'll take it from here," Kirksey said.

Ruth's honor guard included me, Auxiliary Kirksey, Auxiliary Jordan, Auxiliary Dunworthy, Auxiliary Wooten, Auxiliary Cornfeld, and two other women from Communications who had bunked with Ruth back in Daytona Beach.

The rest of the mourners—about thirty WAACs—stood lined up along the pathway, facing Ruth's open grave. Corporal Pinski was there, standing beside First Officer Fitzgerald.

Across from the line of WAACs stood a bugle man and an honor guard of eight men assigned to fire the three-volley salute.

Auxiliary Wooten signaled the WAAC honor guard to take their places. Together we lifted Ruth's coffin and made our way to the open grave. The pine box was surprisingly heavy. The weight tore at my heart.

Chaplain Lieutenant Winslow led the service. The wind whipped through the tiny graveyard. The sun picked out diamonds in the quartz below our feet, but the wind drove through my olive drab jacket. My teeth chattered and I resisted the urge to hug some warmth into my arms. Overhead the palm trees rustled like hushed voices.

I studied the faces of the women shivering stoically in the cold. My gaze settled on each face. Mary's chin was lifted, as if in defiance, but I saw her bottom lip wobbled. Wanda's brown eyes filled with tears. Kirksey's brows were drawn, but she stood at attention, no other emotion in her face.

I watched Dunworthy. Sue looked bored. She caught the weight of my gaze and winked. My cheeks burst with fresh heat. My stomach twisted. How dare she? Was Sue openly taunting me? Threatening me? Was she crowing over her spoils, claiming victory as Ruth's killer?

We carried Ruth toward the open grave. Anger coursed through me. Everything about this was wrong. Ruth didn't deserve to spend eternity in this desolate, dry, dusty place.

When this was over, I would find a way to make Sue pay for what she'd done. For there could be no question that Sue Dunworthy had killed Ruth. Private Rivera had seen Sue at the bottom of the stairs, talking with Ruth, and Sue had lied about it. She had to be responsible for Ruth's death. What's more, instead of showing remorse, she appeared proud of her crime. I had always known Sue was trouble, but I'd never imagined the girl was a monster.

I heard a clatter of metal on metal and realized the men from the second truck were pulling out shovels.

Swallowing back a lump in my throat, I hoisted the coffin more securely onto my left shoulder. I needed to be strong for Ruth.

After the funeral, I'd find a way to get to the truth. If my suspicious were right, I'd make sure Sue paid for what she'd done. But now was not the time. Ruth deserved to be honored here.

We set the coffin down next to the open grave. First Officer Fitzgerald stepped forward, and it was only then that I noticed the American flag tucked under her arm. She withdrew it, and we helped her unfold it and lay it over the pine box.

Lieutenant Winslow stepped forward with an open Bible. He began the service. I kept my eyes on my shoes, thinking about Ruth. I missed her dependability and enthusiasm. In my rush to find Ruth's killer, I'd barely had time to contemplate the very real hole left by Ruth's passing. The 22nd would miss her. Yes, she'd been annoying in her constant reprimands about regulations. But she'd been kindhearted and an enthusiastic soldier. She had always been ready to buoy a WAACs flagging energy with her own. Ruth's absence was a great loss to the company.

When the service was over, the firing squad gave a three-volley gun salute. Cracking the still air, the shots jolted my bones. The wind had died down, and the sound echoed across the desert. A silence fell then, but I could still hear the echo of the last shot. And I felt as if something had ended here. Something more than Ruth's life. We were soldiers in a war zone, and we had lost one of our own. The women of the 22nd Post worked hard and played hard, but somehow, with Ruth's death, we were in the war now. In the war, and at risk, like any other soldier in this man's Army.

Wanda stepped forward and began to play "Taps." The male bugler echoed for her. The mournful sound on this bright sunny day made the reason for our gathering all the more grievous.

The song ended. Mary stepped forward with a basket full of flowers. The women lined up to take a flower or two. First Officer Fitzgerald went first. She reverently laid a bunch of freesias on top of the American flag. Corporal Pinski laid down a single daisy.

One WAAC after another followed suit. I wondered if anyone had told Private Rivera the date for the funeral. Somehow I doubted it and wished I'd known to tell him. Soon a respectably sized bouquet of English daisies, gladioli, and chrysanthemums heaped on top of the coffin. Ruth would have loved the flowers. For all her strictly GI philosophy and no-nonsense work ethic, Ruth had been a kind woman. I wondered if it was that kindness that had somehow gotten her killed.

It wasn't until the grieving party dispersed that I saw Captain Devlin standing underneath the palm trees. I walked over to greet him.

"Thank you for coming."

"I had some time," he said around the unlit Lucky Strike in his mouth.

"I guess you're hot on the trail of your panty bandits." I didn't mean for the words to sound so harsh, as if I were mocking him.

"We're working on it. I wanted to tell you. I did check out Private Rivera's alibi. He was telling the truth."

I nodded. I'd expected as much.

"I am really sorry about Ruth." He squinted into the sun. I smiled as he pulled out his sunglasses. I surmised he'd taken them off out of respect. "From what I hear, your office is going to be jumping this week."

"Yes, I'm sure we'll be busy."

There was so much I wanted to say. I wanted to tell him that Sue had winked at me during the funeral. I wanted to tell him about my adventure in the Casbah and the shots exploding beside my head. I even wanted to tell him about Sadie, and Sue trying to blackmail me for a perfectly innocent letter. I wanted to beg him to continue the investigation. But I knew it was pointless, and so I kept my mouth shut. Captain Devin would not defy Colonel Cantry's direct order that he wrap up the investigation. There wasn't anything left to say.

He adjusted his hat and gave me a defeated smile. "Well, I would say I hope I'll be seeing you, but really I hope you won't need me again."

I shook my head, never thinking I'd needed him at all. But he was right, of course. The moment Ruth's body hit the ground, I'd needed him. I'd huddled close to him during the bombardment. I'd cajoled him into an investigation. I'd tracked him down at the Church Villa. "I hope so too, Captain Devlin. Thank you for trying."

He rubbed a hand across his face in a gesture I now knew meant he was uncomfortable. "Goodbye, Auxiliary Lincoln. Have a good war."

I watched him stride to his jeep and hop in. He gave a final wave and then he was gone, the jeep kicking up a cloud of dust behind him.

That was that, then. My work as assistant to the military police was officially at an end.

I joined the girls on a truck ride back to barracks. It was like old times, in a way. All of us on a truck to the barracks. From there, we'd all head to our respective offices. It was time to get back to work.

It was time for me to corner Sue Dunworthy and find out why she'd killed one of our own.

# CHAPTER 26

I was the last to arrive back at the Adjutant General's office after the funeral. We still had five hours left before our shift ended. We'd all agreed to work late to make up for the time we'd missed during the funeral. I'd have to wait and talk to Sue after work. I had no doubt I could get Sue to agree to a meeting on the back patio. She would probably assume I wanted to talk about the letter. I still wanted it back, but first I wanted to know why she'd lied about talking to Ruth the night she was killed.

I suspected Sue had followed Ruth up the stairs that night. Mary and the earl made no mention of seeing Sue upstairs, so she must have gone up after they left. I had seen Gar Mitchell on the steps of the opera house, smoking with Captain Haywynn, just minutes before Ruth fell to the pavement. That eliminated them as suspects. But Sue had not been there. The only thing I didn't know is *why* Sue went up there. She may have gone up to blackmail Ruth, but try as I might, I couldn't think what Sue would blackmail Ruth *for.* Of course, it was possible Ruth had a secret. But if she did, I had no idea what it might be. The more likely scenario was that Ruth had threatened to expose Sue's dealing in the black market. I felt fairly certain that Sue would do anything for money and much more to keep the money flowing. Maybe that's how Ruth had acquired the silk handkerchief. Had she confiscated it that night, shortly before her death?

I walked into the office, the weight of the day heavy on my shoulders. Kirksey, Mary, Sue, and Corporal Pinski were all there, along with Wanda Wooten, who had been assigned to take Ruth's place for the time being. I went to my own desk. The place was eerily quiet. Nobody was in the mood to work, but there was a war raging in the east.

Sergeant Gilmore leaned against the doorjamb to his office with his hand on his hip, eyes narrowed. After I'd settled at my typewriter, the sergeant cleared his throat and walked to the front of the room, next to Corporal Pinski's desk. "Ladies, I'm sorry for your loss. I've been informed that the investigation into Auxiliary Wentz's death has been concluded. Her death was a terrible tragedy. It's a sad thing, but unfortunately, not everyone is equipped to deal with the hardships of war. Now let's get back to work."

Nobody knew quite how to take this little speech. Sergeant Gilmore's calm demeanor was so outside the norm of what we were used to.

"It wasn't suicide, Sergeant," I pointed out. "Her death was ruled accidental."

Sergeant Gilmore clasped his hands behind his back. I had the distinct feeling he wanted to hit something, but his tone stayed steady and even. "Yes, well. It's very sad, but as you all know, the Krauts are pushing west as we speak. Word is the Desert Fox has had some success near the Faid Pass. We have a lot of work to do, and I need all hands on deck."

"I have to get back to the motor pool, but I thought we could have a toast first." Kirksey held up a bottle of wine. "To Ruth?"

"We don't have time for a damn cocktail," Sergeant Gilmore growled, his usual demeanor returning.

"Sergeant," I said, unable to disguise my frustration, "Ruth was a soldier who lost her life serving her country. Surely we can make time for a simple toast?"

"It's just one toast, sir," Corporal Pinski said.

Gilmore frowned but gave Pinski a nod.

"We'll get back to work right after, Sarge," said Kirksey, uncorking the bottle. "We know how important this push is. We want to do our part."

"All right, but make it quick."

"Thank you, Sergeant Gilmore."

Sergeant Gilmore returned to his office, muttering under his breath.

Corporal Pinski lined up our coffee cups on the side table. Kirksey poured a small amount into each cup and passed them down the line. We all stood up from our desks. Mary sniffed at her cup. Sue reached for the cup with both hands, her eyes darting around the room like a soldier trapped behind enemy lines. Had the brutality of Ruth's death finally hit her?

I leaned closer. "Are you all right, Sue?"

"Of course I'm all right. Mind your business, Lincoln."

Kirksey cleared her throat and raised her tin cup. "I just want to say that Ruth was a really good soldier. She was also a good friend. It's hard to accept that she's gone, and we're all going to miss her. She was a stickler for the rules, and sometimes she could be a bit bossy, but she was a one of us, one of the Double D's. And I think that's all she really wanted to be."

"Here, here," I said, smiling at Kirksey.

Corporal Pinski raised his cup. "She was a valuable member of our team."

"That's a laugh," Sue sneered.

Everyone froze.

"Nobody liked her," Sue said, sloshing wine from her coffee cup. "We're all sitting here pretending we miss her and we're sad she's dead? Did anybody really like the woman?"

Corporal Pinski frowned. "Sue, that's enough."

Sue laughed, a harsh, grating sound, like truck tires on gravel. "What a funny expression. It's never enough."

"That's not true," Kirksey said. "I liked Ruth."

Sue walked up to Kirksey, standing almost toe to toe. "Did you really, Kirksey? Did you just love the way she was always bossing you around? The way she poked her nose into everybody's business. Did you like the fact she threatened to report you for loose lips?"

"Sue, stop this," I said, stepping between Sue and Kirksey. "Ruth was only trying to be a good soldier. We're here to honor her memory, not drag her name through the mud."

"We're not soldiers. We're secretaries." Sue enunciated the word *secretaries* as if we were all hard of hearing. "In really bad clothing, I might add. Nobody really wants to be here. I don't want to be here. Do you want to be here?" Sue's eyes were wild. Her words ran together like an onrushing train.

"Sue, calm down." Something was wrong. Sue was always defiant, but in a controlled, sultry way. This out-of-control ranting was alarming. I'd never seen her this way.

"Don't tell me to calm down. What are we even doing here, in this filthy, Arab-infested place? It's a joke. We don't want to be here. Dottie, you don't want to be here. Mary wants to get married and go back to merry old England, right? Run away with your earl? Pinski wants to go home to his mama." She cackled like a witch over a cauldron, her eyes wide and somewhat mad. "Kirksey wants to get away from her Podunk town in Mississippi. I get that. Girl just wants to live the high life in this fake French Riviera, right, Kirks?"

"I do not," Kirksey said, outraged.

"What about you, Dottie?" Sue went on. "What do you want? Hmm? Who are you fighting for?"

I grabbed her by the elbow and steered the hysterical girl back to her chair. She was trembling, the way Kirksey did after a bombardment. "Sit down, Sue. Get control of yourself."

Sue slumped into her chair, suddenly deflated. She took a sip of her wine and closed her eyes, her head moving from side to side to an invisible song.

"Sue, what's wrong? Are you sick?"

Behind me, Mary let out a stifled moan, then leaned over and was sick all over the floor at her feet.

"Ugh, gross!" Kirksey exclaimed, stepping away from the pool of vomit on the floor.

Mary put a hand over her mouth. "I'm so sorry. I just feel so dizzy."

The smell of vomit clouded the air. I stepped around the puddle on the floor and put a hand to Mary's forehead. "You're clammy."

Sue bent over, dropping her hands to her desk. Saliva dripped from Sue's open mouth.

"Oh my god, Sue!" What was happening? I steered Mary to the nearest chair. Wanda Wooten stood with her coffee cup between two fists, blinking rapidly, as if her brain couldn't catch up with the locomotive speed of events happening all around her.

I knelt beside Sue and took her hand. She was shaking like a planted flag. She slumped back in the chair, her head lolled back, and I watched in horror as her eyes rolled back in her head. If I hadn't been holding on to her, she would have fallen backward onto the floor.

"Dottie," Kirksey gasped, "what's wrong with them?"

"Someone should get a doctor," Corporal Pinski said. He still stood with his coffee cup raised, his eyes shifting between Sue and Mary, confusion clouding his face. "Maybe they got the dysentery."

"Sue! Oh god, what's wrong with her? Is it the wine?" Wanda threw her cup, the contents splashing onto the tiled floor like a wash of blood.

"What the devil is going on out here?" Sergeant Gilmore growled from his office, then stopped short, eyes widened at the tableau.

Sue jerked back and tried to stand. She collapsed. I tried to cushion the fall, but Sue was dead weight in my arms. Her body jerked. She opened and closed her mouth like a beached fish gasping for breath. Spittle flew from her mouth.

"We need to get her to the hospital," I said with a calm I did not feel. "Corporal Pinski, can you carry her?"

Corporal Pinski blinked, then put down his coffee cup and moved into action. "Yes. Yes, of course."

He reached down and scooped Sue into his arms. Sue's head lolled away from Pinski's body, and I smoothed a hand over her brow, laying her head gently against Pinski's chest.

Corporal Pinski headed for the door.

"You too, Mary. Let's go." Mary stood and allowed me to steer her toward the office door.

Corporal Pinski walked in quick, steady strides to the Church Villa hospital across the street and up the hill from the St. George Hotel. I straggled behind with Mary leaning against me. Gratitude flooded through me, watching Corporal Pinski move quickly. Nobody else could have carried Sue, and there was no telling how long it might have taken for Medical to come with a stretcher. The nurse manning the front desk at the Church Villa jumped up when she saw Corporal Pinski carrying Sue in his arms, and beckoned him to follow her down the hall into an exam room.

A second nurse coming down the hall helped Mary to a nearby chair. Mary pushed at the woman and insisted she was just fine, thank you very much. "It's just a stomach bug. I'm fine," Mary cried. "Leave me alone."

"Does she need to see the doctor?" the nurse asked. I shook my head. The nurse gave Mary one last look and nodded before heading back toward the examination rooms. The sound of murmured voices drifted from the interior of the hospital, but the lobby was strangely quiet. The chaos of the past few minutes died down like a bombardment ending abruptly.

"What the hell just happened?"

I jumped at Kirksey's question. I hadn't realized Kirksey had followed us from the office. "I don't know. Malaria maybe?"

"It didn't look like malaria."

"No, it didn't. Maybe Corporal Pinski is right. Maybe it's dysentery. Did they eat in town today?"

"Not that I know of. Dottie, Sue . . . I've never seen her like that before."

"Neither have I," I admitted. Even before she'd collapsed, she'd been shaking. Shaking implied malaria. "Maybe she has a fever."

Kirksey nodded. "Fevers can make you lose your mind."

"She hasn't lost her mind, Kirksey."

Jeannie met my gaze, her eyes solemn. "You heard all those mean things she said. It wasn't normal for her. You can lose your mind and still keep it, Dottie."

"What do you mean?"

"You can lose your mind for a little while and find it again when things calm down. Something set her off, Dottie. Something made her lose her mind. What if it wasn't a sickness?"

"What else could it be?"

"I don't know, but I have a bad feeling."

I put my arm around her shoulders, hoping to comfort her. But she was right. Something was off with Sue. She was calculating and mischievous. She was straightforward and opinionated, but I'd never heard her lash out in that panicked way. Was it guilt? Had the reality of her actions hit her at Ruth's funeral? "Illness can make you act strangely. I'm sure that's all it was."

"First Ruth, and now Sue." Kirksey leaned against me and sighed heavily. "Dottie, are we in danger here?"

# CHAPTER 27

Kirksey went back to work at the St. George. I kept Mary in the waiting room until her color returned. I wanted a few minutes alone with the girl. I wasn't squad leader anymore, but Mabel wasn't equipped to deal with the conversation that needed to happen.

I sank into the cane chair next to Mary, pushing aside the exhaustion pulsing behind my eyes. I was too tired to beat around the bush. "Mary, I think I know the answer to this question, but I have to ask: Are you in trouble?"

Mary's heart-shaped face crumpled, and tears swelled and dropped down her pale cheeks. She didn't deny it. "How did you know?"

"Just a guess. Is that why you were in the Casbah?"

Mary's head snapped up. "How did you know about that? Were you following me?"

I brushed the accusation aside. "I saw you on the way to work. I was going to catch up so we could walk together. When I saw you go into the Casbah, I was worried, so I followed you. Just to make sure you were safe."

Mary looked away. She bit her lip and a tear coursed down her cheek. I resisted the urge to hug the girl close. Mary was touchy and vulnerable. I understood the feeling and knew from experience that close contact wasn't always wanted in times like this.

Mary sniffed and swallowed hard. "I'm not a hundred percent sure, but . . . maybe. I didn't know what to do. Sue told me there was a woman there who might—"

I didn't need Mary to finish the sentence to know what Sue had suggested. It made me sick to my stomach, thinking of Mary seeking the services of a back-alley doctor in the Casbah. She might have died. Thankfully, it seemed Mary had been unsuccessful in her attempts.

"Is it Captain Haywynn's?"

"Of course it is! Who else would it be?"

"I thought you liked him."

"I love him." Mary began to cry harder. "But I don't want him to think I'm trying to trap him. If I am . . . in trouble, I didn't do it on purpose, Dottie."

"Of course you didn't. I think he'll know that, Mary."

"But he won't," she wailed. "He's told me. So many girls try to trap an earl. I don't even understand what an earl is—do you?" She blinked her wide blue eyes in genuine confusion.

I stifled a laugh. "It's not important. Do you truly love him?"

"I do. He's sweet to me, you know? He's not like the other boys."

I resisted the urge to roll my eyes. Captain Haywynn was hardly a boy.

Mary sniffed and swiped her arm across her wet face. "He treats me like I'm special. Like I matter. He says he thinks I'm smart."

It would have been sad if it wasn't so sweet. "Mary, did you drink any of the wine today?"

"No. Did you?"

"No."

"I pretended to drink it. You know, for Ruth. But it was so cold at the funeral. Too cold to drink wine. It would have been nice to have a Coke. Or hot chocolate. Real hot chocolate, right? Not that powdered stuff the Army gives us. Sometimes I think I'd give anything for a real cup of hot chocolate."

I nodded, feeling a wave of sympathy for Mary. She was a small-town girl who'd run away from home to join the Army. And now she was miserable. She didn't belong in North Africa. Captain Haywynn had been right about that. I would never admit it to Captain Devlin, but Mary wasn't suited to Army life.

I thought about my next question carefully. "Mary, do you know if Ruth and Sue had any kind of trouble between them?"

Mary turned her head, sadness turning to suspicion. "Why do you ask that?"

I smiled, hoping I looked self-deprecating. "I don't know. What Sue said about nobody liking Ruth."

Mary's lip wobbled again, the suspicion vanishing like flare smoke. "She accused me of killing her, when it first happened. She said I must have pushed her, but I didn't! I'd never do that! I didn't like Ruth much, but I wouldn't *kill* anybody. I don't even like to squish bugs."

"Do you have an idea of who would?"

Mary shook her head and wiped her nose with the back of her hand. I thought about giving her a hankie, but I only had the silk one from Ruth's bag, and that was evidence. Mary's next words were unexpected and strangely insightful. "Honestly, I think it might have been Sue herself."

"Why?"

"Because." Mary shrugged, her delicate shoulders holding their position while she thought things over. "I don't know. Ruth had this way of getting into everybody's business. Sue was right about that. And Sue . . ." Mary's shoulders drooped.

"Yes?"

"Sue wasn't the kind of person to like that. I think she has secrets."

A cold alarm spread up my spine. "Mary, if you know something, you need to tell me."

"I don't *know* anything."

"But you suspect something?"

"I don't know. Sue always had stuff, you know? The handkerchiefs. Stockings. Real silk stockings too. Not these thick nylons." She plucked at her stockinged leg. "Things she wasn't supposed to have. I think she was maybe making a little money on the side? Ruth wouldn't have liked that."

"No, she wouldn't."

"I know technically we're not supposed to buy anything off the black market, and Sue always said the stuff came from the Casbah. But who really knows? She made it sound like it was okay, but I always wondered."

"So you think Sue was getting these things illegally, and Ruth found out?" Mary was detailing my own theory of the crime. I should have felt elated. Vindicated. But I didn't. Instead, doubts knocked around in my head. It was too simple. If Sue didn't like Ruth poking her nose in her black-market dealings, wouldn't she have told her to mind her own business? Even if Ruth threatened to turn her in, wouldn't Sue have some kind of backup plan for that scenario? I couldn't put my finger on it exactly, but Sue was a street-smart girl. Would she be so naive as to share her activities with the company and not have a plan to escape Army punishment? Was murder really the only way out?

"She *always* had stuff she wasn't supposed to, Dottie. Maybe Gar gave it to her. He acts like her boyfriend, but I don't really think he is. Not in Sue's mind, anyway."

"Why do you say that?"

Mary shrugged and sniffed. "They're always together, and they talk and stuff. But I never saw them kiss, or even hold hands."

Mary was right. Sue and Gar were always together at every dance, but I'd never seen them be intimate. Were they very private? I had a hard time imagining Sue guarding her privacy in that arena. She was flirtatious and sexual like no other WAAC in the 22$^{nd}$.

"They're going to send me away, aren't they?"

"You can't stay here in your condition, Mary. If you are pregnant, that is. You might not be." I tried to do some math in my head. We'd been in Algiers for just a few weeks. How fast had Mary jumped into Captain Haywynn's bed? "In any case, you need to tell Captain Haywynn what's going on. That's the first thing."

"Are you going to tell Fitzgerald?"

"No. I'm going to leave that for you to do. But I suggest you tell Captain Haywynn first. And soon."

Mary drew in a heavy sigh and released it slowly. "I guess I don't have a choice. Do you think he'll be angry with me?"

"I don't know, but I don't think so. I think he loves you. But there's only one way to find out."

"Right. The hard way. I guess nothing is easy in war."

I smiled. "I think the earl is right. You are a smart girl. And a soldier in the United States Army. You're going to be okay, Mary."

Mary gave a wan smile, and a burst of color hit her cheeks. I put an arm around her shoulders and gave her a tight squeeze. I wasn't lying. Mary was going to be all right. She had Captain Haywynn to look after her, and I hoped she'd find happiness in Warwickshire. I felt more like myself in that moment, hugging Mary, silently saying goodbye to the youngest member of my squad. The moment was interrupted by Corporal Pinski. He walked through the double doors and into the lobby.

I released Mary and got to my feet. "How is she? How's Sue?"

Corporal Pinski shook his head. "She didn't look too good, but she's with the doctor now. Mary, are you feeling any better?"

Mary gave a weak smile. "I'm fine, Corporal, thank you."

"Corporal Pinski, can you take Mary back to barracks? I think she's all done in for the day, and I don't want to send her alone, in case she gets sick again."

"Of course. You'll be okay here?"

"I just want to talk to the doctor."

Corporal Pinski frowned. "Are you sure you're okay to be alone?"

"I'll be fine, thanks, Corporal."

He looked unsure about leaving, but he did as I asked. Mary let herself be led away. She gave me a little wave as she left, and I smiled encouragingly. "Chin up, Mary. Everything's going to work out."

Mary smiled and walked out the door, leaning on Corporal Pinski's arm.

The roar of an engine sounded outside. Captain Devlin hopped out of his jeep and strode into the building, sunglasses shielding his eyes. "Lincoln! What the hell happened?"

# Chapter 28

"How did you know I was here?"

"Your Sergeant Gilmore called the 577th."

"He reported a crime?"

Captain Devlin shook his head. "He reported you all AWOL. Said his WAACs had abandoned post."

"Bastard," I muttered.

I told Captain Devlin everything I could remember about the events in the Adjutant General's office after the funeral. I also shared Mary's theory of the crime. With a pang of regret, I left out the detail about my letter and Sue's request for a favor. It had nothing to do with Sue's illness or Ruth's murder.

"Cheese and crackers," Devlin exclaimed, when I was finished.

I suppressed a smile, but he noticed.

"I know," he said, rolling his eyes. "I'm a good Catholic boy, Lincoln, if you can believe it. It's been drilled into my head since the cradle not to take the Lord's name in vain. The guys give me hell about it, but sometimes it just slips out."

"There are worse things." My heart warmed at his confession. He was a good man, and those were few and far between in my experience.

"Is it possible Dunworthy collapsed from exhaustion?" he asked, rubbing his chin. "Or stress?"

"I don't think so. She wasn't acting exhausted. She was acting manic. She looked scared, Captain."

"It doesn't sound like she was close to our victim."

I was glad to hear Captain Devlin referring to Ruth as a victim. Even though her death had been ruled an accident, he at least still believed Ruth had been murdered. "Not at all. She wasn't upset. Mary Jordan thinks Sue may have killed Ruth."

Captain Devlin's brows rose. "That's quite an accusation."

"She thinks Ruth was interfering with Sue's sales."

"Did you know Dunworthy was dealing on the black market?" Captain Devlin asked.

"I suspected."

"That is a detail you should've shared with me."

"I know. I'm sorry. But I did tell you about the silk handkerchiefs."

"So, Sue was dealing in the black market?"

"Yes, I think that's fair to assume at this point."

Dr. Edwards came through the double doors, looking exhausted, running a hand through his dark hair. "She's stable."

"That's good news," I said.

The doctor pressed his lips together. "Maybe. I thought I should tell you, when the nurse brought Auxiliary Dunworthy in, she had this on her." Dr. Edwards held out a jewel-encrusted pill case. "Did you know she was taking Benzedrine?"

"I had no idea."

"I've seen enough of this to know the signs. It's definitely an amphetamine overdose."

I knew some of the girls had been given Benzos by the British servicemen. They used them to stay awake during their long working hours. Captain Devlin himself had his emergency dose. But I'd never seen any sign that Sue was taking it, or any of the girls in the Adjutant General's office.

"I've given her a sedative. Sometimes that brings them down. But she took a sizable dose, I'm afraid."

"Will she be okay?"

Dr. Edwards shook his head. "It depends on a lot of factors: how much she took, how much damage it caused to her nervous system. We'll keep her here and treat her as best we can, but I wouldn't get your hopes up."

"Did she tell you where she got it?"

"I don't think you understand, miss. She's not conscious. To be honest, I'll be surprised if she makes it through the night, which is what I told the corporal who brought her in."

"Oh my god." Something like panic pounded in my chest. *Not another one.*

"Do you know of any other WAACs taking these?" Dr. Edwards asked. "I mean, they're pretty widely available to the men. I'm guessing it's the same for the girls."

I shook my head. "I've never seen anyone taking drugs. Except for aspirin."

"Might not be aspirin," Captain Devlin said. "The stuff is everywhere."

"Doctor Edwards, can we see her?"

"I don't think that's wise. Like I said, she's unconscious. Best to let her rest. But I thought I should tell you, when I asked her how much Benzedrine she's taken, the girl insisted she was poisoned."

"Did she say how?" Captain Devlin asked with a measured calm that didn't fool either me or the doctor. "Or who might have poisoned her?"

"No. I asked her how much she took, and she said the word *poisoned*."

"Oh my God," I said, replaying the events of the day. "It must have been the wine."

"What wine?" Devlin demanded.

"We had a toast for Ruth."

"Who suggested the toast?"

"Kirksey did, but she would never hurt anyone."

"Where did she get the wine?"

"I don't know."

"We'll have to ask her."

"Captain, I'll leave this in your capable hands." Dr. Edwards deposited the pill case into Captain Devlin's outstretched hand. "I need to get back to my patients."

"Doctor!" I resisted the urge to pull on his arm and make him face me. "Can we please see her? Just for a minute. I want her to know she's not alone."

Dr. Edwards frowned. "I suppose it wouldn't do any harm. But keep it short. The girl needs rest if she's to pull through this."

"Thank you, Doctor."

"Yes, yes." Dr. Edwards was already walking away. "I'll send a nurse to come and fetch you when she's ready," he said over his shoulder, then disappeared behind the double doors and into the ward.

"Well done, Lincoln. You got us an interview." Devlin stuffed his hands in his pockets and leaned back on his heels. He pulled a cigarette from his front pocket and rolled it between his fingers.

"Have you made any progress on your panty bandit case?" I asked, to distract him and help pass the time.

"From what we've gleaned so far, the panty bandits are Americans, and they're selling American goods from ships docked in the harbor. I'm guessing American sailors are the culprits, stealing cargo and smuggling it out of the ships to sell to civilians."

"And you think Sue might be wrapped up in that somehow?"

"I don't know. It's a possibility. She's got to be getting the silk from somewhere. She never said anything about dating any sailors?"

"No." I shook my head. "I'm sure she's danced with a few sailors over the past couple of weeks, but nobody sticks out in my mind. The only soldier she seemed to spend time with was Private Mitchell."

"Well, I think it's time we talk to Private Mitchell."

An Army nurse entered the foyer, carrying a clipboard. "You can come back and see her now."

Captain Devlin tucked his unlit cigarette back into his pocket. But when we moved to follow her, the nurse stopped and held up her clipboard. "Only one visitor is allowed. Doctor's orders."

"You go ahead, Lincoln. I'll be waiting outside for you to report back."

"Thank you, sir."

Sue's room was the first one on the left. I didn't know what I'd expected, but the sight of Sue lying prone under a single sheet, her skin filmed in sweat, was a shock. She was worse than before. No wonder the doctor didn't want visitors.

The nurse made a notation on her clipboard and said, "You have five minutes."

I sat down on the edge of the bed. I could feel the heat coming off Sue's overworked body. Underneath her eyelids, her eyeballs danced like water in oil. I laid a hand across Sue's sweaty forehead. "Sue, it's Dottie. I'm here. You're going to be okay, Sue."

Sue swung her head from side to side, as if struggling with some invisible monster. When she opened her eyes, they were wild, the pupils dilated. "Ruth," she said. "Ruth ordered me to."

"Shh." I rubbed a hand across Sue's arm, trying to calm her. "It's okay, Sue. Don't worry about Ruth right now."

"My orders, Ruth. My orders were—were—" Sue let out a long breath, then went limp.

I kept rubbing Sue's arm, hoping it was calming her down, my mind racing. What were Sue's orders? Orders from whom? All this time I'd thought Sue had hurt Ruth. But now I wondered. Had Ruth ordered Sue to do something she didn't want to do? I couldn't imagine that Ruth would violate regulations, so it would have to be something personal. Ruth had been a stickler for the rules, but there was no mistaking the fear in Sue's voice.

I was deep in thought when I met Captain Devlin outside the Church Villa. He was fiddling with his cigarette again, leaning against a tree planted in the sidewalk. "How'd it go?"

I relayed Sue's words. "She sounded scared, Captain."

"Maybe she's scared of getting caught? Do you think Dunworthy did it? That she threw a fellow WAAC off the roof? Is she even capable of such a thing?"

I chewed my bottom lip. "If she got Ruth up against the balustrade and took her off guard? Yes, I think it's possible. But why would she do it?"

"Because Ruth was going to turn her in for dealing in the black market?"

That was the theory I'd formed in my mind, but now doubts niggled. "Sue was constantly telling us about things we could buy. She wasn't quiet about her activities. She even confronted me once, telling me there was nothing the Army could do if she was selling black market items, because auxiliaries aren't real Army. We can't be court-martialed."

"Jealousy? Something about a boyfriend maybe? Private Rivera says he was going to marry Ruth. Did Sue want him for herself?"

"No," I said, shaking my head, "definitely not. Whatever happened between them, it wasn't about a man."

"Well," Captain Devlin said, clapping his hands together and shifting his feet, "if Sue was hopped up on Bennies, she'd definitely be capable of picking Ruth up and throwing her over. It's a powerful drug. It gives you energy and strength."

"You know a lot about this."

Devlin laughed. "I've arrested a few men on Bennies. They're surprisingly strong. Some say that's why the Krauts are such good combat soldiers. The drug gives them the energy to blitz."

"That's just a wild rumor."

"Don't be so sure. The Brits are supplying it to their men and there's a big push to get the War Department to distribute it to our boys in the field."

"Does this mean the investigation is back on?"

"Definitely not, Lincoln. Colonel Cantry closed that case. But according to Doc Edwards, someone might have poisoned Auxiliary Dunworthy. That's a separate case. We need to talk to Auxiliary Kirksey and find out where she got that wine. But first I want to talk to Gar Mitchell. He's one of my men, and if he saw any indication that Dunworthy was dealing on the black market, I want to know about it. I'll need a notetaker. You game?"

# CHAPTER 29

Captain Devlin radioed Private Venturi and found out that Private Mitchell was patrolling the docks. "Well, that's interesting," he said, tossing the handset in the back seat.

"How so?"

"Private Mitchell's girlfriend is possibly dealing in the black market, and he's patrolling the docks."

"You think he's involved."

"Seems a likely scenario."

"Mary says he's not her boyfriend, but they're always together at social events."

"What makes her think he's not the boyfriend?" Captain Devlin asked.

"Mary has a very juvenile idea of love. She said they never hold hands."

Devlin barked a laugh.

"I know," I said, "but it does make me wonder. I never have seen Sue show any affection for Mitchell. In fact, now that Mary mentioned it, I can't stop thinking about how bizarre that is."

"So they weren't sweethearts. They were in business together."

"Maybe. But even if Sue was dealing in the black market, why would she kill Ruth? And what did Ruth order her to do?" I massaged my temples. My brain hurt. There were too many unknowns to get a solid footing on exactly what had transpired between Ruth and Sue Dunworthy. "If Ruth threatened to expose Sue, what would it mean? What would the Army do?"

"Honestly? Not much," Devlin admitted. "I'd want to interview her about any contacts she might have, but I don't have jurisdiction over the WAACs. Like you said, you girls are an auxiliary force. I suspect the most the Army would be able to do is issue an immediate discharge and send her home. Assuming your commander, Fitzgerald, decided the action was warranted. Would Dunworthy kill to stay in Algiers?"

"She might. I guess it depends on how much money she was making."

"If she's doing what we think she's doing, I'd guess she's making a tidy bundle."

I sighed. "From what I've seen, money is the most important thing to Sue Dunworthy."

"So she might kill for it."

"She might." Disappointment and a feeling of despair hit me in the stomach. Is that what had happened? Had Ruth been killed for money? There were no good reasons for murder, but somehow money seemed like the most trivial reason of all. I tried to picture Sue lifting Ruth up and over the balustrade. I didn't think she'd be able to do it unless she was on those Benzedrine tablets. And after Ruth's death? Sue had been so flippant about the whole thing. Sue was greedy, but it would take a special kind of monster to be that coldhearted.

Captain Devlin drove down to the docks and parked outside the Gare Alger, the main train station in Algiers. Seagulls swooped across the blue sky, calling to one another against the backdrop of the white city.

The port of Algiers had a northern and a southern pier, two dry docks, and the train station. The docks were bustling with activity. British destroyers sat alongside American battleships. French naval vessels looked small and derelict next to the more robust Allied ships. Behind the train station was the train yard, with three running rail lines.

American military police guarded the train station, along with the French police force. Half a dozen Arab men worked nearby, loading five-hundred-pound bombs onto trucks that would undoubtedly be moved to the front.

Captain Devlin parked in the street between a black Bentley coupe and a British staff car. We climbed out of the jeep. "We'll check the train station first."

"Captain, look!" I saw an MP standing with Captain Haywynn on the sidewalk at the other end of the station building. "There he is."

Captain Haywynn, Private Mitchell, and a French civilian stood huddled together. The civilian wore a dark suit and a wide-brimmed felt hat. He carried a battered briefcase, which he waved in the air as they spoke. Private Mitchell pointed an angry finger in the civilian's face.

"Hey!" Captain Devlin shouted. "Mitchell!"

Private Mitchell's head jerked up at the sound of Captain Devlin's voice. To my complete surprise, he turned and ran. The Frenchman looked from Mitchell to Devlin. He pulled the brim of his hat down low and clutched his briefcase to his chest.

Captain Devlin ran after Mitchell, shouting at two other MPs to guard the front door of the station house. He pulled his whistle from his shirt pocket and sounded the alarm.

Captain Haywynn stuffed something into his uniform pocket and sauntered toward his staff car, parked just behind Devlin's jeep, one hand up in greeting. I couldn't see his face. Captain Devlin could have easily intercepted him, but instead he made a run at Private Mitchell.

The Frenchman headed my way, then made a hard right, onto the street. I sprinted toward him, blocking his way before he skirted a parked car. If the man had lifted his head, he might have seen me, but he was looking at his feet.

I'd never tackled a man before. I had always cowered. But the last few days had changed everything. If this man was somehow involved in Ruth's death, I had to stop him. I had no clear plan. There wasn't time. I simply lunged at him, crashing into him with all the force I could muster. He tried to throw me off, losing his grip on his briefcase. The case hit the asphalt and cracked open. White handkerchiefs billowed out and scattered, along with dozens of glass pill bottles. A couple bottles broke open, spilling little white pills onto the pavement. Amber shards of glass glinted in the sun.

I scrambled to my feet. I placed the heel of my Oxford onto the man's neck but underestimated his strength. He twisted, grabbed my foot, and threw me to the ground. My teeth gnashed painfully against one another. My elbow burned. The man turned away, but I'd glimpsed his face. The shock of it stunned me still for a moment.

The group of Arab men loading the bombs broke off and grabbed the Frenchman, hooking his arms behind his back. In the short scuffle, the man's hat was knocked off, and I stared at the man I'd been fighting.

"Henri?" The proprietor of Chez Pilar. Held firmly in place by the arms of two dock workers, Henri's face was sheened in sweat.

"I hope you are not injured, mademoiselle," he gasped, breathing heavily. "I did not intend to damage you."

I straightened my skirt and smoothed my hair. I'd lost my cap in the scuffle. "I'm fine."

Henri refused to meet my gaze. Instead, he spoke to the asphalt beneath his feet. "I am deeply sorry to involve you in this sordid business. My shame is immense, madame."

I looked down at the silk handkerchiefs fluttering down the sidewalk. A couple of the Arab dock workers followed my gaze, and two of them scrambled forward to gather the items. I knelt down and picked out the white pills, avoiding the glass shards. I let the men take the handkerchiefs. Casting furtive glances down the sidewalk, they stuffed them into their pockets lightning fast. I glanced at Captain Devlin. He had Private Mitchell by the arm, his back turned. We had moments at best.

I rubbed at my hip and studied Henri's flushed face. "You're trading on the black market."

Henri lifted his chin, defiant. "My family has been in this country for almost one hundred years. It's a beautiful, complicated country. There is much wealth in the land. Or there was. Then the Germans came and stripped it bare, leaving my country like a carcass in the sun."

"But the Germans are gone now."

"Yes, and what have the Allies done for us? I have a family to feed, and the Americans give us scraps while they do the same as the Germans. Taking what they need from our country, with no thought to the people who live here."

"But surely you can get some assistance. The North African Trade Board helps civilians."

Henri shook his head, a sad smile curling his lip. "Ah, mademoiselle, you think that Robert Murphy is here to help us? No, he is here to help Vichy. To keep order while you Americans fight the war."

"You're mistaken, Henri. And even if that's true, dealing on the black market is wrong."

"What else can I do? I must feed my family."

Two French policemen ambled out of the train station lobby and stopped when they saw Captain Devlin arguing with Private Mitchell. They spoke to Captain Devlin, undoubtedly to find out what was going on and how it might affect them. I had only moments to make a decision. I didn't want Henri to go to jail for dealing in the black market. I believed Captain Devlin when he said that Henri was one of the good guys. He was just trying to feed his family.

"Let him go," I said in French to the two Arabs holding Henri. "Thank you for your assistance. You can get back to work now." The two men exchanged a look, then released Henri. The boys who'd scooped up the handkerchiefs gave me a wary look. I nodded toward the trucks they'd been loading. "You can go too."

They retreated a few steps, then turned and jogged back to their worksite.

Henri retrieved his hat and studied my face.

"Listen up, Henri. You heard someone was dealing drugs to civilians. You came here to find out who," I said in French. "Do you understand? You came here to put a stop to it."

Henri blinked rapidly. He glanced behind me. I turned and saw Captain Devlin striding toward us. The two French officers stood with Private Mitchell. Though no guns had been drawn and no cuffs were in sight, I had no doubt that Captain Devlin had enlisted the French soldiers to guard Private Mitchell.

I turned back to Henri. "Let's store the evidence."

Henri looked down at the remaining handkerchiefs fluttering in the breeze and the pill bottles and broken shards. He dropped to his knees and began to gather the silk. "Mademoiselle, you have my eternal gratitude," he said quietly. Tears shone in his eyes. "Merci mille fois."

"Find another way, monsieur. If the French authorities find out what you're doing, you'll be arrested."

Henri blinked rapidly and nodded his head vigorously.

"Courage, monsieur," I said, not looking up from my task of dropping the pill bottles into the briefcase. "You must show courage."

# CHAPTER 30

"So you took it upon yourself to investigate this illegal activity between allied forces and planned to get the goods and bring them to me? That's your story?"

Henri darted a glance my way. I did everything in my power to keep my expression neutral. "Yes, Captain." Henri nodded vigorously. "You yourself said I should tell you if I see anything. I did not want to bring you bad information, so when I heard of this arrangement, I had to see for myself."

Captain Devlin leaned back in his chair, steepling his fingers together under his chin, and contemplated Henri.

We sat in a small office adjacent to the main ticket booth. Two members of the French police guarded Private Mitchell outside in the lobby. Devlin had more faith in the French police than I did. But I supposed if Private Mitchell were to run, Captain Devlin knew where to find him.

"And you purchased these items"—Devlin waved a hand at the open briefcase on the desk, the handkerchiefs and pill bottles jumbled together—"in order to prove this illegal activity was happening."

Henri bobbed his head up and down. "Yes, yes, that is it exactly."

Captain Devlin didn't say anything. I crossed my fingers in my lap, willing Henri not to look in my direction. Thankfully, this time Henri stared placidly back at the captain.

Devlin took in a deep breath and let it out slowly, his eyes narrowed. Coming to a conclusion, he slapped his hands on the desk. "All right, Henri. Thanks for the goods. You've done a great service for the war effort."

Henri's mouth fell open at this pronouncement, but he quickly recovered. "I am happy to hear it, Captain. I hope I can be of use to you again."

Captain Devlin frowned and rubbed at his chin. "Yes, well, thanks again, old pal." The note of sarcasm was inescapable, but Henri smiled widely, as if he hadn't heard. I was sure that he had, and I wondered if Captain Devlin would ever pay Henri for information again.

Captain Devlin slapped Henri on the back, ushering him out the door. "Be good, Henri."

Henri ducked his head and hurried across the station lobby.

"That was quick work," Devlin said, still staring out the open door.

"Yes, sir." I didn't dare say anything else. My legs shook, and I resisted the urge to fall into the chair Henri had just vacated.

"Mitchell!" Devlin barked. "Get in here."

I bowed my head, hiding a smile. It was clear that Captain Devlin knew what I'd done, but he was going to overlook it. I didn't know why I'd felt the need to spare Henri. I supposed I believed Captain Devlin's insistence that Henri was one of the good guys.

Private Mitchell strode into the tiny office, his fists clenched, and snapped a salute to Captain Devlin.

Private Mitchell scowled at me. "What's she doing here?"

Captain Devlin got straight to the point. "Mitchell, are you the panty bandit we've been looking for all this time?"

Mitchell dragged his gaze away from me. He swallowed hard. "You got bigger problems than me."

Captain Devlin gave a wry smile. "Haywynn isn't in our jurisdiction, and you know it." He softened his voice. "You're in a world of hurt right now, Private. Giving me guff isn't going to help you."

Private Mitchell swallowed hard. "Hey, you need to know—"

"What I need to know," Devlin said, his words falling like shrapnel, "the *only* thing I need to know is this: Are you the panty bandit, wise guy?"

Mitchell dropped his head. He rubbed his hands on his trousers and blew out his cheeks. "Okay, yeah. But it wasn't just me, Captain. You gotta know that."

Captain Devlin switched gears. "We can get to your accomplices at a later date. We have more important things to discuss. You're acquainted with Auxiliary Dunworthy. Is that correct?"

"Sue?" Gar snapped his gaze to Devlin. "She didn't have nothing to do with this."

"You wouldn't be using her to deal Benzos, now, would you, Mitchell?"

"Benzos? No way, Captain. Wait a minute," he said, glancing at me. "What happened? Is she okay?"

Devlin held up a hand, "Calm down, there, bucko."

"Did something happen to Sue?"

"She's in the hospital," I said.

Private Mitchell clasped his hands above his head, eyes darting between me and Captain Devlin. "No, no, no, no."

He was shocked. And upset. There could be no mistaking his obvious distress. Mary must be wrong. He must care for Sue, after all.

"What the hell happened? What did you do?" he yelled, jabbing his finger at me with each word, fury coming off him in waves.

"Did you give Auxiliary Dunworthy the Benzedrine?" Captain Devlin said, stepping between us.

Private Mitchell shook his head as if to clear it. "No."

"You're not a very good liar."

Private Mitchell stepped back, arms flailing. His large frame seemed to grow with his anger. "Okay, okay. She needs them for work. So what?"

"I'm afraid Sue took too many," I said.

The fury went out of Private Mitchell like air from a bursting barrage balloon. "Oh God. Is she okay?"

Captain Devlin put a hand on his chest and pushed him back. "Sit down, Mitchell." Captain Devlin sat on the desk. He placed a firm hand on Mitchell's shoulder. "This is important. How many bennies did you give her?"

Mitchell shook his head as if to clear it. "She doesn't really care about me, but I like her. She's fun, ya know? She doesn't take this war shit too seriously, for one thing."

"How many pills, Mitchell?"

Mitchell put his head in his hands. "Oh man, I'm done for. You're gonna send me to the pig pen."

The "pig pen" was the stockade, and I suspected Mitchell was right. Devlin didn't confirm or deny it.

Mitchell's head popped up. His eyes were wet. "I didn't give her too many. Just a couple pills every now and then."

"Could she have been getting them from someone else?"

"I don't think so, but maybe. You don't think she tried to off herself, do you? Because she would never do that."

A chill ran through me. Everyone had assumed Ruth committed suicide. Now Private Mitchell was worried the same would be said of Sue Dunworthy. Someone was staging these attacks to look like suicide. But who?

"Was she upset about anything? Did you ever have a reason to think she might need a lot of those pills?"

"No. She was happy. Excited, if you want the truth." Private Mitchell hesitated. "Look, she told me she was about to come into a lot of money. Said she saw something and that someone was going to pay."

Captain Devlin stood up off the desk. "What did she see?"

"I don't know. She never would tell me. Said it was safer that way. She kept things close to the vest. That was just her way."

"Think hard, Mitchell. Do you have any suspicions about who it might have been?"

"That girl Mary? I don't know. She's a piece of work. Acts all innocent, but I don't think I've ever met anyone less innocent. She's a game player, that girl."

"Do you know if Sue was seeing anyone else?"

"She likes me," Mitchell said, not sounding entirely convinced. "For now, anyway. She didn't want to get serious with anyone, though. She was clear about that from the get-go."

"Do you know of anyone who might have wanted to hurt her?"

Mitchell laughed. "This one right here, sir." He pointed at me. "This is the one you're looking for. So help me God, if you hurt Sue, I'll fucking kill you."

"Stand down, Mitchell."

"She's the one you need to be asking questions. Look at her face! Sue was right. She's a German spy."

"Don't be ridiculous," Devlin said. "Making wild accusations isn't going to get you out of this, Mitchell."

"It's the truth. Just ask her."

Devlin rolled his eyes my way. But something must have shown on my face, because he paused.

"Sue told me. She has a letter from the Krauts. With a swastika on it!" Gar lunged toward me. "What did you do, you Nazi bitch?"

"No!" I stumbled back. Captain Devlin grabbed the back of Private Mitchell's shirt and yanked him backward. I fell against the radiator running behind me.

"She's a security threat," Mitchell huffed. "She's a goddamned spy!"

"No!"

Captain Devlin, brows furrowed, cocked his head and studied my face. Private Mitchell glared at me, hate coming off him like rays from a hot sun.

I was back in my bungalow in Houston, Konrad standing over me, his fists clenched and bloody.

I couldn't move.

I couldn't speak.

Like an animal caught in a trap, I stood frozen, my fate in the hands of the men standing over me.

# Chapter 31

Leaving Private Mitchell in the temporary custody of the French police, Devlin grabbed my arm, his face stony, and steered me out of the train station. "Let's go, Lincoln."

I followed, knowing I had a problem.

I felt like a prisoner.

I tried to still the fluttering panic blooming in my chest as memories of Konrad gripping my arm so hard it left bruises reared up like a loaded howitzer.

"You're hurting me, Captain."

Devlin ignored my words but released me once we were standing beside the jeep. "Is it true?"

The fear had dissipated like so much smoke, and I was in control of myself again. I forced myself to remain calm. I would clear this up. I'd find the letter in Sue's footlocker and hand it over. Captain Devlin was a reasonable man. He would understand. I cleared my throat before speaking. "Private Mitchell doesn't have all the facts."

"Don't give me that bullshit, Lincoln. Is it true? Are you working for the Krauts?"

"Of course not."

Captain Devlin paced the sidewalk, then came to a standstill, hands on his hips. "Then what's all this about a letter?"

I swallowed the lump in my throat, threatening to choke off my words. Sue had told Private Mitchell. Had she told anyone else? I realized it didn't matter. Captain Devlin knew, and as my current superior officer, his opinion mattered more than anyone else's. And judging by Devlin's face, I was going to have a hard time convincing him of my innocence.

I had to tell him everything about the letter, but my mouth felt like a dry canteen, a metallic taste coating my tongue. Taking a deep breath, I met his gaze head on. I had nothing to hide here. I'd done nothing wrong.

I told him about my disastrous marriage, leaving out the most lurid details, and explained about the letter. How it was the only link I had to Sadie. I detailed everything that happened after I found out Konrad had left and taken Sadie to Germany. I didn't tell him about the days before, when I woke up in the hospital. There was no reason to share that particular shame, and those events played no role in my actions after Sadie was taken.

Captain Devlin didn't speak for some time, rolling a cigarette between his fingers. I stood awkwardly beside the jeep, shifting my feet, clasping my hands behind my back. Finally, he spoke. "Did you know he was a Nazi when you married him?"

"Of course not. I'm not sure he is a Nazi. Not really. I think he felt duty bound to return home and help the war effort. I'm not saying he's a good man. He's not. He's . . ." I paused, searching for the right words. "He was not kind to me."

Captain Devlin met my gaze and held it. I saw the questions there but said nothing more. Finally, he cleared his throat and rubbed at his chin.

"I cannot ignore Private Mitchell's allegation, Lincoln, whatever I might think. There will have to be an investigation."

My heart sank to my toes. What did that mean? I wanted to ask, but the words wouldn't come.

"So, Auxiliary Lincoln," he said, tucking the cigarette behind his ear, "are you a spy for the German government?"

I wasn't sure what I'd expected, but it wasn't such a forthright question. "No, of course not."

"And if I were able to question Dunworthy further, what reason would she give for making such an accusation? An accusation, I might add, that could lead you to a firing squad."

Cold sweat pooled around my waist. "She went through my things and found the letter. She saw the postage stamp of Hitler and the postmark with a swastika on it, and assumed I was communicating with the enemy."

"That's a fair assumption, given the facts. The Army doesn't deliver letters from Germany or any other enemy territory."

"No, sir. It was sent before the war. That is, it was sent before the United States entered the war."

"Where is this letter?"

"I don't know. Sue wouldn't give it back to me. I expect she has it in her footlocker, but I haven't checked."

"And now Sue Dunworthy is incapacitated and unable to answer questions. Did you have something to do with that development?"

"Of course not," I said, flinching at his icy demeanor. "I'm not a spy, and I would never hurt anyone in my company, sir."

"Did Ruth know about this letter?"

"Ruth? No, nobody knew."

"Well, that's not true. Mitchell and Dunworthy knew. How had they gotten their hands on the letter?"

"Sue must have gone through my footlocker. Or I might have dropped it," I admitted, embarrassed that I'd been so careless.

"And you have no idea where it is now." It wasn't a question.

I clenched my fists but kept my voice calm. "I assume it's migrated to Sue's footlocker. We can go back to barracks and I'll show it to you."

"I don't read Kraut," Captain Devlin snapped.

I stepped back, feeling as if he'd slapped me. The truth was, I'd concealed my past from the Army. I hadn't done it for any nefarious reasons. After Konrad left, I'd felt divorced, even if technically it was impossible for me to file any legal paperwork. I'd joined the Army to start a new life, and I didn't want to bring Konrad's name with me. But to my fellow soldiers, the letter was proof of ties to the enemy.

"You can give it to a translator. You'll see—it has nothing to do with the war."

Captain Devlin walked around the front of the jeep and climbed into the driver's seat. "Get in."

I did as he asked, my stomach spinning.

He started the jeep and threw it into drive. He didn't say another word as he wound his way back up the windy roads of El Biar.

I didn't know what to say. Did he believe me?

Devlin drove like a demon. It didn't take long to pull up to the convent walls. He slammed on the brakes, and I held on tight to the side of the vehicle, planting my feet against the floorboards, to keep from flying through the windshield.

Captain Devlin killed the ignition and jumped out of the jeep.

"What are you doing?" I scrambled after him.

But Captain Devlin didn't answer. He marched into the main courtyard and on into Officer Fitzgerald's office. Fitzy was at her desk. When she saw the captain, she got to her feet, her gaze flicking between us.

"Captain Devlin," Fitzgerald said, giving Devlin a half-hearted salute, "is everything okay? I heard about Auxiliary Dunworthy."

Captain Devlin gave a curt salute in return. "Yes, ma'am. Auxiliary Dunworthy is under the doctor's care. Hopefully we'll see some improvement in the morning. I didn't come to talk about Dunworthy, though. I've come to inform you that Auxiliary

Lincoln has been accused of spying for the enemy." Captain Devlin's tone was matter-of-fact. "I'm requesting that you confine her to barracks while I investigate the allegation."

"Captain!" I cried, trying to meet his gaze. "I told you, I'm not a spy."

"That may be, but an accusation has been made. You yourself admit—"

"I admitted that I have a letter from Germany. That is not a crime. The postmark is from 1941. Before we even entered the war!"

"The truth is, you could have been working for the enemy before we even got into this war. Until I can see the letter and have it translated, I have to take this accusation seriously, Lincoln. We're in a war here. Credible accusations of espionage must be investigated. I joke about this being the silly side of the war, but this is serious. I have to look into this and confirm you're telling me the truth. It's my *job*."

"It's not a crime to keep family mementoes," I said, eyes blazing, "even if they were mailed from enemy territory."

"Did you disclose your ties to Germany to your superior officer?"

"She most definitely did not," Fitzgerald said.

"Then I have no choice."

"Where is this letter?" Fitzgerald asked.

"It was last known to be in Sue Dunworthy's possession."

"Oh." Fitzgerald's eyes went wide.

Suddenly I realized the gravity of my situation. Sue had possibly been poisoned. Ruth had been killed. Private Mitchell had accused me of being a spy based on information provided by Sue, who was now unconscious in the hospital. "I couldn't have killed Ruth. I was outside with you and Kirksey."

"I'm not accusing you of killing Auxiliary Wentz. The Army has determined that her death was accidental. You're the one who started talking about murder. Maybe you were trying to cover up your own crimes."

"What crimes? Please, Captain Devlin"—I put a hand out to him, but the captain moved away—"just go through Sue's things and find the letter. I didn't do anything wrong."

"That, Auxiliary Lincoln, remains to be seen."

"You're wasting valuable time, sir. Someone killed Ruth, and now Sue has been poisoned. The WAACs are in danger. There's someone out there trying to kill us."

"I don't think you understand, Lincoln," Captain Devlin said, his eyes frosty. "*You* are now my prime suspect."

# Chapter 32

Wanda Wooten stood guard over me while First Officer Fitzgerald and Captain Devlin searched the squad room for the letter. I waited in the darkening courtyard, blinking back tears, wishing I could sink into the concrete beneath my feet.

I was certain that Devlin would return with the letter and take it to a translator. He would see I had no affiliation with any German spies or government agents, and we could get back to solving Ruth's murder. If Sue had indeed been poisoned, the only possible suspect had to be the person who pushed Ruth Wentz off the third floor of the opera house.

But the shame of being made a fool in front of the captain would never go away. Bringing a letter bearing the enemy's markings into Allied Force Headquarters was the most boneheaded thing I could have done. Only a foolish, weak-willed woman would do such a thing, and all the old feelings came rushing back to me. Feelings of inadequacy. Feelings of shame. Feelings I thought I'd left behind when I joined the Army. I could only hope Captain Devlin would understand and forgive me for my lack of judgment. I should have left the envelope behind. I should have kept better care of Sadie's letter. Pushing aside what could not be changed, I shifted my thoughts to the crime.

I ran the details of Private Mitchell's interview over in my mind. He'd admitted to giving Sue the Benzedrine, and I believed him. He obviously thought of Sue as his girl, even if Sue didn't reciprocate the feeling. Mitchell insisted he'd given Sue only a couple of pills now and then, and I was inclined to believe that as well. He'd been caught red-handed, running the panty bandit thefts. If he'd sold the pills to Sue, why not admit it? No, he'd given them to his girl. And if that were true, then it was doubtful Sue had enough pills to overdose herself. I couldn't think of a single time Sue had seemed intoxicated. In fact, the only time I'd seen Sue impaired was after Ruth's funeral. Someone else must have given Sue the Bennies. But who? And how was the drug added to the wine? If Kirksey had something to do with it, how had she managed to target Sue and nobody else? And why in the world would Kirksey kill?

Private Mitchell had accused Mary Jordan of being a game player, but I couldn't agree with him there. Mary was manipulative, especially where men were concerned, but she didn't seem intelligent enough to play games with Sue Dunworthy. But Sue had seen something. Something that she expected would pay off. What had she seen?

Sue had told Dr. Edwards she was poisoned. She'd also said that Ruth ordered her to do something. But do what? Had Ruth ordered Sue to stop selling black-market items to the women in the 22nd? Had she ordered her to stop taking Benzedrine? If Ruth knew about either of those things, I had no trouble imagining Ruth taking charge and ordering Sue to follow Army regulations.

I was missing something. I didn't think Sue—sick and possibly dying of an overdose—would waste precious words telling me about a fight with Ruth because she'd failed to follow regulations. There had to be something more, but I could not come up with a suspect who would poison Sue Dunworthy. It didn't make sense.

Nothing made sense anymore.

It had been a long day. My hip ached. Mess Leader Lindley and her crew began setting up for dinner. My mouth watered, and I hoped Devlin and Fitzgerald would be back down and have this whole mess cleared up in time for chow. I hadn't eaten since before the funeral. All I wanted to do was grab some grub and go for a run. Exercise always cleared my mind.

But when Captain Devlin and First Officer Fitzgerald came back down the stairs and into the courtyard, they returned empty-handed.

"Where is it, Lincoln?" Captain Devlin asked, his mouth grim.

"I told you: Sue took it. Did you look in her footlocker?"

"We did." Captain Devlin's usual good humor was gone, his eyes distant and cold.

I shook my head, confused and exhausted. Where would Sue hide it? "Did you check under her mattress?" The WAACs lingering in the courtyard stopped and watched the scene unfolding before them. "Did you check under *my* mattress?"

Devlin and Fitzgerald exchanged a look.

Fitzgerald lifted her chin and said, "Auxiliary Wooten, take"—she paused to clear her throat—"*Auxiliary* Lincoln to her squad room. I'm ordering you to stay with her and stand guard."

"But—" I didn't know what to say. "This is a mistake. Captain Devlin. I promise, there's a simple explanation for this."

But Captain Devlin had turned away. It was First Officer Fitzgerald who now took control, although she didn't look happy about it.

A wide-eyed Wanda Wooten shot a nervous glance my way, then snapped a salute and shouted, "Yes, ma'am, First Officer."

It was the snappiest salute I had ever seen Wooten, or any other WAAC, make.

Wooten reached out to grasp my arm. I pulled away. "I can walk by myself, Wooten. I'm not going to disobey a direct order."

Wooten looked to Fitzgerald, who dipped her chin toward the staircase. With as much courage as I could muster, and a last glance at Captain Devlin, I walked across the lobby, head held high.

All the WAACs watched me pass. The mess crew stopped clanging their pots to watch. Some girls came out from the day room, possibly drawn by the sudden stillness in the courtyard.

I smiled at Mabel Cornfeld, but the girl looked away. Word must have gotten around already. Somehow they all knew. I saw it in the eyes of the women I passed. They knew what Captain Devlin and First Officer Fitzgerald had been looking for, and they despised me for it. Without knowing anything about the contents of the letter, they'd already branded me a traitor. They'd decided my guilt. I swallowed hard. I'd never realized before how an accusation wounds as much as a condemnation and conviction. Even after I proved the allegations were false, how many of my friends would still suspect me?

I'd never felt more alone. I'd been beaten and abandoned by my husband, but this was worse. The 22nd had become my family these past few weeks. I'd relied on them for support and companionship. And now, with one unfounded accusation, I stood alone outside their warm circle.

I walked up the stairs, blinking back tears, feeling as if the world crumbled at my feet with each step. The tiny place I'd made for myself in the Army was now nothing but an empty crater. After Konrad left, I'd thought I'd lost everything. I'd lost Sadie, the most important person in my world. I'd joined the Army to keep my darkest thoughts at bay. Joining the Army had given me a purpose, a reason to wake up in the morning. And it was all being ripped away.

I was innocent. But without the letter, I had no way to prove it.

Walking down the hall to the squad room, the crushing weight of failure pressed down on me. I'd failed to protect my squad. I'd failed to find Ruth's killer. I'd failed to protect Sue. I never should have accepted being squad leader. I couldn't protect my own daughter. How could I protect an entire squad of soldiers?

# Chapter 33

Cold night air crept into the barracks room, dropping the temperature, setting my jaw clacking. I sat on the edge of my bed, a blanket draped across my shoulders. I looked at my watch. It was just past twenty hundred hours. I had been sitting alone in the squad room for almost two hours. I'd expected Mary and Kirksey to return, but so far neither had shown her face. Were they avoiding me? Squad Leader Mabel Cornfeld was also AWOL. Maybe First Officer Fitzgerald had assigned the girls to another room, effectively turning Squad Room B into a temporary prison.

Footsteps sounded in the corridor. Kirksey walked in, and I felt a flood of relief. I got to my feet, letting the blanket slip off my shoulders.

"Kirksey, thank god you're here." I hated the eager desperation in my voice, but I needed a friend. Kirksey gave me a grim smile. I swallowed back an uneasiness brewing in the pit of my stomach. "I guess you heard."

"Everyone's talking about it downstairs. It's a good thing you have a guard. I think they're ready to break out the pitchforks." The joke fell flat. Kirksey's eyes were wary and she remained standing just inside the doorway.

"Where's Mabel? Is Mary okay?"

Kirksey dropped her eyes. "They asked to bunk with Squad F."

I rubbed at my forehead as if I could rub away the hurt. I had been branded a traitor. That hurt more than being branded a fool by Konrad. How could my fellow soldiers believe I would betray my country? How could they believe I'd betray the WAAC or the 22nd Post after everything we'd been through together?

"I'm not a German spy, Kirksey. I thought you, of all people, would trust me. You know me."

"Do I?"

"Jeannie, please." My eyes stung but I blinked back the tears.

Kirksey folded her hands, as if in prayer, and rested her chin on them. "Oh, Dottie, what did you do?"

I paced the room, wishing we could go outside. I'd be able to think better outside. I rubbed at the scar on my forehead. So many decisions had led to this moment. Some of them good, some foolish. I turned back to Kirksey. "Sit down. Let me explain."

Kirksey hesitated, but when she sat on my bed, relief washed over me, a relief so big it almost overwhelmed me. I swallowed back the lump forming in my throat and willed myself not to cry. Good soldiers don't cry.

I joined Kirksey on the bed. I heaved out a sigh, searching my mind for where to begin. "You've heard about the letter?"

"Yes."

"I received that letter before the war. I've had no contact with any German since '41, since before Pearl Harbor."

Kirksey nodded, staring at her lap. I waited, hoping my friend would believe me, trust me. I resisted the urge to tell Kirksey I was innocent. I needed to give Kirksey time to think over what I was saying, to ask questions.

"Who's it from?"

This was the hard part. I hadn't told anyone about my marriage. "It's from a family member. Remember I said I have family from Alsace Lorraine?"

Kirksey nodded.

"Well, that wasn't the whole truth." I heaved a sign and plunged ahead. "I also have family from Germany."

"Oh," she exclaimed, brown eyes widening. "And you're still in touch with them?"

"No, not now. But before the war started, I received a letter."

Kirksey lowered her head and laced her fingers together. She cracked her knuckles absentmindedly. Then she reached into her utility bag.

She unzipped the inside pocket and pulled out the letter. I gasped, my hands flying to my mouth. Kirksey gave me an apologetic smile. "I don't know what I was thinking, taking it. I guess I wanted to ask you first. If this letter proved you were a traitor, I wasn't ready to let them have it. I couldn't bear to see you being put in front of a firing squad." Kirksey's lips trembled at this last statement.

"Oh, Jeannie." I wrapped an arm across her shoulders. "Even if I were a traitor, I don't think they'd shoot a woman."

"Don't you?"

I hugged her close, and Jeannie fell into me. "I'm sorry, Dottie. That night you went running, I went out to join you. Even though I think you're a little nuts to do so much PT, I couldn't sleep, and I thought we could talk. But as I was coming down the stairs, I saw Sue walk out to the patio. I heard what she said."

"So you took the letter?"

"No. I didn't know what to think. I didn't find the letter until after Sue got sick."

"You were worried I had something to do with Sue being poisoned?"

Kirksey threw up her hands. "I don't know. I don't know what I was thinking. It seemed outrageous to believe you, of all people, would be spying for the Germans. You're not, though, right? You can't be a spy."

"No," I said, "I'm not a spy. You have my word, Jeannie." Kirksey was such a trusting, sweet soul. If I got out of this mess unscathed, I would have to look out for Kirksey, even if I wasn't her squad leader anymore. That trusting sweetness could so easily be trampled on and taken advantage of.

"Are you Jewish?"

"No."

"After Sue was poisoned, I went through her things. To get the Bennies so that nobody would know."

"Are you the one who sold Sue the Benzedrine?"

"No. She sold a couple of pills to me. And a few others."

"*Sue* was selling them?"

"Yes."

"Are you sure? How do you know?"

"I saw her making a deal with Captain Haywynn at the dance. He gets it from the British dispensary and sells it to Americans."

I remembered Captain Haywynn asking me if I needed a little extra help when he'd given me a ride the morning after Ruth's murder. Is that what he'd meant?

"So, you're taking them?"

"I can't sleep. You know that, Dottie. The wine doesn't help at all anymore. I have to be able to stay awake during the day, to do my job."

"Oh, Jeannie."

"I'm afraid if I shut my eyes I'll never open them again. That bomb was meant for me. What if it still has my name on it? What if I was meant to die here?"

"You're not meant to die. It was a fluke."

"But maybe I was," Kirksey insisted. "I was supposed to be in bed that night. Instead, I was with Sue, doing things I shouldn't be doing."

"The Bennies."

"No, we snuck out that night to meet some boys," Kirksey said, giving me a rueful smile. "I keep thinking about it. If I had been a good girl, I'd be dead."

"Jeannie, if there's one thing I've learned, there's no rhyme or reason to misfortune. Bad things sometimes happen. Not because you deserved it or you were meant to be there."

"You don't think so? I have to disagree with you there, Dottie. I think God does watch out for us and puts us where he wants us to be. And I think I was supposed to be in my bed that night."

I thought about Kirksey's words. "Maybe God wanted you out of that bed. Maybe he sent Sue to get you out of harm's way. Did you ever think of that?"

Kirksey's lips parted. "Do you think so?"

"I do," I said, giving her arm a squeeze. "Anyway, I'm glad you weren't in that bed. What would I do without you?"

"So, what is it? What is your tie to Nazis? Why do you have this letter with a swastika on it?"

I looked longingly at the letter.

"You still want it?" Kirksey's brow creased.

"It's the last communication I had from my daughter."

"Daughter?"

"I was married. This was before the war. His name was Konrad von Raven. He's German. I met him in Houston when I worked for Baker Hughes."

"You're married to a German?"

"Back then we weren't enemies. Yet. But when Hitler took power, Konrad kept talking about wanting to go back to the Fatherland. I thought he was joking at first. We had a life in Houston, with our daughter. I didn't realize how serious he was about it until it was too late. One day I came home from work, and he was gone." That wasn't the whole truth, but it was close enough. "I'd left Sadie—that's my daughter—with a neighbor. When I came home, they were gone. *She* was gone. They just vanished. I was frantic. I called the police, but they didn't care. Then about a month later, I received this letter. He told me that he had taken Sadie back where she belonged."

"To the Fatherland?"

I nodded. "She belonged with me. She belonged at home, where she was born. I wanted to get to Germany, to get her back, but I didn't have any money. I couldn't afford the ticket. Then war broke out, and there was no way for me to get there. She was lost to me."

"Is that why you joined the WAACs?"

"No. I wasn't foolish enough to think I could get to Germany by fighting the whole war myself. I was just feeling really lost. I did think if I joined the Army, I could make a difference. I could help defeat Germany faster, and that was better than sitting at home waiting for it to be over. When it's over, when we've won, I'll find her."

"Good God, Dottie."

"Believe me, Kirksey, I have no loyalty to the Third Reich. I've never even been there. When I met Konrad, I was young. He was dashing. He convinced me we were meant for each other." I released a bitter laugh. "I married him against my father's wishes. Dad thought I was too young, and he was right. But I was determined, and before I knew it, I was pregnant. I didn't find out until later what a cruel man Konrad really was."

"Oh, Dottie, I'm so sorry. A daughter. You must miss her terribly."

"I do. Sadie was my gift. She was the only joy in my life, and he took her away from me. So no, I am not spying for the Germans. I have more reasons than most to want to see them defeated. If they're not, I'll probably never see Sadie again." My voice broke, and I sniffed back the tears trying to form. I shook my head to clear away the memories and stood. "Kirksey, I need you to do something for me. I need you to take this letter and give it to Captain Devlin. Only Captain Devlin."

"Why? It's evidence against you!"

"Because he'll get a translator. He'll read it and see that I'm not the enemy. Somebody's poisoned Sue. I think it's the same person who killed Ruth. I have to find out who's doing these horrible things before they hurt another girl."

"You trust him? This captain?"

"I do."

"Okay." Kirksey said, getting to her feet. "Of course I'll do it."

"Be careful. Don't talk to anyone else. We don't know who's hurt Sue."

"So it's not an overdose? You think someone did this to her on purpose?"

"Unfortunately, yes, that's exactly what I think. Wouldn't she know not to take too much?"

"That's true. I think she would. And she wouldn't be distraught over Ruth's death. I don't think she cares about anybody but herself," Kirksey said.

"Exactly. So I can't see her taking too much out of grief. I think somebody gave it to her. Where did you get the wine anyway?"

"I bought if from a street vendor."

"When?"

"On the way back from the funeral."

"Was it in your possession the whole time?"

"Yes."

"So it couldn't have been spiked. Sue was poisoned some other way."

"But Mary was sick too."

I shook my head. "She's been ill. Her sickness had nothing to do with Benzos."

"That's a relief, I guess."

I walked Kirksey to the door. "Why don't you take Mabel with you? She's strong. I don't think it's safe to walk through the streets alone. Go straight to the MP's office. It's not far. Give Devlin the letter, and tell him I need to talk to him."

Kirksey chewed her bottom lip but nodded and carefully tucked the letter back into her utility bag. "Okay, I'll be careful."

She reached out and gave me a quick hug. “I’m glad you’re not a spy. I would have been really disappointed.”

I laughed. “Thanks. And Kirksey, you need to get off these Bennies. They’re dangerous.”

She gave me a rueful smile. “I know. Guess I’ll have to find a way to sleep.”

“We’ll think of something.”

“Sure we will, Dottie.” But Kirksey didn’t look convinced.

“Okay, hurry. And don’t stop to talk to anyone. Remember, straight to the MP’s office.”

“Got it. Don’t worry, Dottie. I grew up on the dark streets of Jackson, Mississippi. I know how to handle myself.”

“Hurry, Kirksey. I’m counting on you!”

# Chapter 34

After Kirksey left, I sank back down onto my bed. I was grateful that Kirksey believed me. I had at least one friend left in the WAAC. I only hoped Captain Devlin was at 577th MP Company headquarters. If Kirksey couldn't find Devlin, I would have to wait even longer. The longer it took to prove my innocence, the harder it would be for the other girls to accept that the accusation was unfounded. Doubts and suspicions would act as a festering wound. I wanted it cleaned out before the rot infected my company. I'd have a lot of explaining to do once it became public knowledge that I'd married a German before the war. I knew it would be a hard pill for most of the girls to swallow. But if Kirksey could find Captain Devlin quickly and clear up the mess I'd made, hopefully the girls would forgive me and understand.

I glanced at my watch. I hated to admit it, but the chances of Devlin finding a translator and getting to the convent before lights out weren't good. Though I knew the captain didn't let the clock dictate an investigation, I wondered how eager he would be to prove my innocence. The panty bandit case was solved, but I suspected the captain had a lot of paperwork in his immediate future. I also realized he might need to track down other American and British servicemen who sold goods illegally. There were the sailors on the ships, making goods available. And that didn't even begin to cover the French civilian population. Of course, Henri and others like him weren't under US Army jurisdiction, but it seemed to me it would be in the Army's best interest to know who was working the black market and where those goods were being sold.

And then there were the Bennies. How many other WAACs were taking the drug to stay awake during their increasingly long hours at work? Dr. Edwards had recognized the signs of Benzedrine overdose in Sue because he'd seen it before. Plenty of it. I wondered if General Eisenhower was aware of the drug problem plaguing Allied Force Headquarters.

Was Captain Devlin opening an investigation into the drug trade in Algiers? If so, why should he care about a fifth-column GI Jane confined to barracks? I realized I was most likely a back-burner item right now.

But what else could I do? I had to wait for Kirksey to find Devlin, then wait for Devlin to find an interpreter. Once that was done, would he make his way to the convent immediately? Or wait until morning? I had no idea.

Sue was in the hospital. Mary and Mabel had requested another squad room. Wanda Wooten guarded the door, and Ruth was dead. I had utterly failed as a squad leader. I never should have accepted the position. But of course, Leader Fitzgerald had not asked. I'd been assigned. Still, I should have told Fitzgerald I was a bad choice. I should have told the truth about my past. I should have insisted Ruth be assigned as squad leader. I'd almost said as much when Fitzgerald told me about the assignment, but some part of me had wanted the position. I'd wanted to take care of these girls, to prove to myself that I was capable of doing so. But I'd been as successful at leading a squad as I'd been as a mother.

The sound of footsteps pounded up the stairs. A group of women were making their way back to their squad rooms after smoking on the patio or washing their hair beside the well in the courtyard. Usually the WAACs were loud, laughing, shouting at one another, blowing off steam after long days at their desks or driving trucks or working in the kitchens. Today they were subdued. I didn't have to guess why. A few peeked their heads into the door to my squad room, then quickly withdrew. Not one of them spoke to me or met my eye.

Sue's footlocker was open. Her extra skirt and stockings were strewn across the bed. We'd all been in a hurry to get ready for the funeral. Still, Sue would have gotten a dressing down for leaving her bed in such a state if any of the officers had seen it. I was always threatening Sue with KP duty for not making her bed or being in proper uniform, but I'd rarely followed through on the threats. Would things be different if I'd been a stronger leader? Would Ruth still be alive?

Ruth. I missed her. And I still didn't know what had happened up on that balcony. I was certain Ruth would never be involved with the black market, and the thought of Ruth Wentz using drugs was laughable. But if Ruth discovered that Sue was dealing in the black market, she would have done everything in her power to put a stop to it. Sue Dunworthy was cunning, but was she a murderer? Despite her laziness and unmistakable greed, I had a hard time picturing Sue physically throwing Ruth off that balcony. It was possible but unlikely. The more I thought about it, the more far-fetched it seemed. That left me without a real suspect.

I paced the floor, my Oxford browns clicking against the concrete. My mind felt like a ball of tangled twine. If only I pulled the right thread, maybe I could solve this crime. But no single thread presented itself.

Pushing aside my jumbled thoughts, I knelt down in front of Sue's locker and began organizing its contents. I had nothing else to do. Physical activity always calmed my body and stilled my mind. I pulled out the wadded-up shirts and stockings and laid them on the floor beside me. Next, I took out a stack of letters. I didn't want to pry, but couldn't help but notice they were from GIs. A lot of GIs. I stacked them into a neat pile.

Underneath the clothing and stockings, I found a woven bag. It looked like the messenger bags carried by local news boys. I pulled it out. Inside I found two boxes of Kotex. Two heavy boxes. Much too heavy to hold sanitary napkins. I opened a box. It was stuffed with money. Rolls and rolls of money. French francs and American dollars. Resting at the bottom of the flimsy cardboard box were three gold coins engraved with Arabic writing. Underneath the bag, folded neatly, were a stack of women's panties.

I blinked. We knew that Private Mitchell was part of the panty bandits. Now I knew Sue was most definitely a distributor. The girls in the 22nd Post wore GI panties—cheap, uncomfortable things that we all complained about. I knew many of my fellow WAACs would pay handsomely for a pair of the silky-smooth rayon panties sitting at the bottom of Sue Dunworthy's footlocker.

Again I wondered if Sue would really kill Ruth to keep her illegal activities a secret. I still didn't have an answer.

I had no doubt if Ruth found out about Sue's illegal activities, she would have notified the Army. But if that were the case, Sue would have been arrested or charged. Instead, Ruth wound up dead. I couldn't imagine Sue killing Ruth over a stack of panties, no matter how valuable they were in a combat theater.

Sue had been standing at the bottom of the stairs at the opera house that night, but there was no evidence she'd ever gone up to the roof.

I fingered the woven bag, my mind racing. There was something Kirksey had said about bags. About Sue's utility bag.

I moved over to Ruth's footlocker. Lifting the latch, I saw that Ruth's locker was immaculate. No surprise there. Her extra clothing was folded neatly with crisp corners. I'd seen Ruth ironing her uniform every night, and the girls had teased Ruth for ironing her GI-issued panties as well.

I felt a pang of regret as I lifted the items and placed them on the bed as carefully as I could. Ruth's locker contained a packet of letters from her family. I knew how much Ruth valued the few letters she'd received from her brothers. Her mother had sent her a knitted blanket and socks. She also had a small blue-and-white tin with a Zouave on horseback painted on the lid. I held it in my hands, puzzled. When I opened it, a smile pulled at the corners of my mouth. Inside were hard candies. She'd probably purchased the tin from the sous market in Algiers, but the candies were all American. Somehow I'd forgotten Ruth had a sweet tooth.

At the bottom of the footlocker was a packet of letters tied with an indigo ribbon woven with a jacquard design. With shaking hands, I retrieved the letters and untied the ribbon. The first letter was just a folded piece of paper. *Sweet Girl, Please, please reconsider. I love you more than these words here can say . . .*

I did not need to read on. These were the letters from Private Rivera. Ashamed to trespass upon Ruth's personal life, I returned the love letters to their resting place at the bottom of the locker.

There was nothing else in the footlocker of note. No money, no secret letters, nothing that could explain why someone wanted her dead. I wondered if she'd bought the candy tin in the market when she was with Rivera. Did it have any sentimental value to her? Had it been a romantic day in Algiers with her fella? For despite Ruth's insistence that they keep the relationship a secret, and her refusal to marry him in Algiers, I had no doubt that Ruth had loved Private Rivera. She'd just loved the Army—and the opportunities the Army gave her—more.

That night, when she'd argued with Rivera, she must have been heartbroken. Was that what she'd wanted to talk about in the courtyard after hours? I doubted it. Ruth hadn't shared the relationship with anybody. Why would she spill everything after it was over?

I slumped back onto my bed and threw an arm across my eyes, blocking out the lamplight. I looked at my watch. Kirksey had been gone almost an hour.

Kirksey, who blurted out confidential information about General Eisenhower. Kirksey, my only real friend in the Army. Kirksey, who took the letter and Sue's utility bag in an effort to protect me. And yet, Kirksey's actions had done nothing but cast suspicion on me and possibly ended my career in the Army. I hoped Kirksey was working fast. I needed to get out of here. There were still so many questions to be answered.

What would I do if they kicked me out of the Women's Army Auxiliary Corps?

There would be jobs aplenty back in the States. I'd just have to start over. But if I was charged or if anyone found out I'd been accused of espionage? Who would hire me then? Nobody, that's who. Thank God Kirksey had retrieved the letter and kept it safe.

My mind wandered. I thought of Sadie and her drawing. What would Captain Devlin think when he saw it?

Ruth's family would be notified of her death. They might have already had word from the War Department. I had Ruth's letter in my footlocker.

I swung my feet to the floor and sat bolt upright. The letter. There was something different about Ruth's letter. It had nagged at my mind for days and suddenly I saw it clearly.

*To be opened in the event of my death.*

No name. No address. On the ship, sailing to North Africa, Officer Fitzgerald told us to write a letter to our loved ones in case we got sick, went missing or were killed in action. Some of the girls laughed. Others worked silently and soberly on their letter. But we'd all believed it was only a precaution, a silly Army rule we had to follow. Algiers was a thousand miles from the front. We were safe. Or so we'd thought. Then we'd experienced our first aerial bombardment our second night in Algiers, and the letters made perfect sense.

But Ruth's letter didn't have a name or address.

*Ruth's letter did not follow regulations.*

The night of her murder, Ruth had made a point of handing over her utility bag. She'd been firm, pressing the bag into my hands. Was there a reason she'd handed it over? At the time, I'd thought she didn't want to wear it while dancing. But looking back, I wondered if Ruth had been trying to tell me something.

I went to my own footlocker and fished out Ruth's belongings. That night, after the murder, after Sue's accusation, I'd thrown everything into my locker and fallen asleep fully dressed. I hadn't thought about Ruth's utility bag since.

Sitting on my bed, I glanced at the doorway, to make sure nobody was watching, then spread the contents of Ruth's bag on my bed.

The tube of ChapStick. Dentyne. Ruth's passbook. Sunglasses. And two envelopes.

Ruth had *two* letters.

*Mrs. Hannah Wentz* was written across the top of one, per regulations.

The second letter read, *To be opened in the event of my death.* No address. No names.

I had some scruples about opening it. The letter did not have my name on it. But Ruth had given me the bag. Ruth had trusted me with it moments before her death. I'd been investigating Ruth's murder for days. If anyone was concerned, it was me. I decided Ruth wouldn't mind if I opened the letter. If I was wrong, I'd seal it back up and hand it over to First Officer Fitzgerald to forward to Ruth's family.

It wasn't sealed.

I lifted the flap.

Inside, I found two sheets of carbon paper. *Used* carbon paper. I frowned. There was no letter.

I spread the carbons out on my bed. Then I held one up to the light. One sheet was well used with typed letters and numbers embossed so heavily, the piece of paper was almost transparent. Corporal Pinski and Sergeant Gilmore would be proud: they were constantly admonishing us to conserve precious resources. I could make out the usual list of names and assignments. Orders directing men to units in the field, to forward operations in Constantine, to assignments in Signal and Medical at Allied Force Headquarters. It was impossible to read because of the multiple orders, each one typed over the last.

The other carbon sheet had a single order typed on it.

Special Order Number Forty-Nine. A pristine carbon that should have been reused. Why would Ruth have kept the carbons from these two order sheets?

I held the carbon up to the light.

*SPECIAL ORDER)*

*NUMBER 49)*

1. *Pvt THOMAS A. WAINWRIGHT, 361723564, Hq Co AF, is transferred in grade to 63rd Signal Bn, and will report to the Commanding Officer thereof for duty.*

Private Tommy Wainwright, the handsy young man I'd danced with the night Ruth died, had been ordered to report to the 63rd Signal Battalion. When we'd met up at the Red Cross Club, he'd told me as much. Why would Ruth keep a copy of the carbon? It didn't make sense.

I slumped back against the wooden bed frame. We typed up dozens of orders every day. Ruth had kept the carbon for Private

Wainwright's order. Was there some kind of discrepancy between the carbons and the original?

I looked over the carbons again. Two sheets. The sheet with a single order typed on it was highly unusual. The WAACs used the carbons until they were practically falling apart. Supplies were short, and orders were to get as much use out of them as possible. I tried to read the orders on the worn, much-used sheet, but didn't see Private Wainwright's name.

Why had Ruth taken these out of the office?

There was only one answer I could think of. There was something significant about this particular order. But what?

And how could I find out?

Footsteps approached outside the squad room. I pulled my blanket over to cover the carbons. I looked back to the door. Nobody entered.

Quickly, I returned the carbons to their envelope and placed it in my own utility bag, enclosing it in the zippered pocket. Then I laid Ruth's letter to her mother in my footlocker. Whatever happened, I would make sure it was sent, along with my own letter, telling Ruth's family what a wonderful soldier and friend she'd been to the women in the 22nd Post Headquarters Company.

But right now I had a tough call to make. I'd been confined to barracks. To leave would be to disobey a direct order. I would be going absent without leave—AWOL. Leaving might also confirm to my fellow WAACs that I was guilty of spying for the enemy. Officer Fitzgerald might think I'd gone off to join fifth-column Germans in Algiers. But I had to go. I had to go to the office and find the original Special Order Number Forty-Nine. I had to find out why Auxiliary Ruth Wentz had disregarded Army regulations on two fronts.

# Chapter 35

I had to act fast.

Sue might have recovered and could return from the hospital at any time. Butch could decide she needed something from her footlocker before bedding down for the evening. Mary as well. I wrote a quick note to Kirksey explaining that I had a lead and I'd gone to the office. I quickly made my bed and left the note in the middle, clear for anyone to see.

Next, I dug into my footlocker and found the knife Private Rivera had given me in Constantine. I felt a little foolish tucking it into my stocking, securing it with my garter. The knife was small enough not to show through my khaki skirt. But the streets of Algiers could be dangerous at night, and a whisper of fear worked its way inside my head. If what I suspected was true, going to the office might be a dangerous proposition. I doubted the knife would be necessary. There were plenty of personnel working all hours at the Hotel Alexandra. But it was better to be safe than dead.

I went to the single window in our squad room and looked outside. The antiaircraft gun was silent. A puff of smoke drifted from the other side of the gun. The men manning the gun were smoking. I didn't think they could see me. Their eyes would be trained to the skies, not to the WAAC barracks windows.

I estimated the drop to the ground below was about six feet. During basic training, we had practiced dropping from a five-foot-high wall. Down and to the right was an awning over the entrance door. If I could swing my body to the awning, I could use that to dangle myself down safely. Of course, it was also possible the distance to the awning was longer than it looked. I could slip, fall, and break an ankle. Or my leg.

It was a risk I had to take. There was no other way out of the convent.

I was ready. Closing my eyes for a moment, I took a steadying breath and walked to the doorway where Wanda Wooten stood guard just outside the squad room door. Wooten tensed when I approached but did not turn around.

"Wanda, I'm exhausted. I think I'll get some shut-eye. Can I close the door while I change?"

Wooten frowned. "Make it quick."

Wooten was getting better at being a jailer. There was no eye contact and no hesitation.

"Will do." I closed the door and grabbed my utility bag. I slung it over my shoulder, wearing it cross-body, and quickly made my way to the window. I had to move fast.

Once Wooten opened the door and saw my absence, she'd raise the alarm. I had minutes to get the hell out of here and hurry to the Hotel Alexandra as fast as my legs would carry me.

Heaving a bracing breath, I sat on the windowsill and spun my legs around to dangle over the side of the wall. I glanced once more at the antiaircraft gun. No movement. No shouts. That was a good sign.

Heart thudding in my chest like a cannon, I gripped the windowsill and eased myself off the edge. The joints in my hands pulsed with pain.

Best-laid plans.

I miscalculated the jarring weight of my body and the weathered wood of the sill cut into my hands. I gripped tighter, teeth clenched against the sharp pain. My knuckles screamed. My palms dug into the wood.

I kicked against the wall, sending a sharp pain through my bruised knees. Still, I kicked wildly, trying to find purchase. Trying to anchor myself somehow.

I paused and forced myself to stay still. It was excruciating. I fought against the urge to kick, to climb back inside. I dangled there, trying to relax my body while holding tight to the windowsill.

Taking a shallow, shaking breath, I did what the Army taught me.

I dropped and rolled.

Instead of landing gracefully in a tight ball, I again miscalculated. I hit the awning, bounced off immediately, and did a belly flop onto the packed earth. Hard.

The fall knocked the wind out of me. I gasped like a beached fish, willing air into my lungs. An eternity passed before my stunned body was able to draw in a breath.

I lay in the dark, trying to catch my breath. I knew the GIs at the gun couldn't see me now. But Wooten could open that door at any minute.

I had to get moving.

Struggling to regulate my breathing, I got to my feet. I leaned against the wall for a minute more. With shaking hands, I put on my overseas cap and brushed the dirt from my uniform. I needed to appear calm. I was just a WAAC on my way to work. The front was afire in Tunisia, and I was doing my job, working a late shift to help the war effort. That was my story if anyone asked.

I took a few staggered steps, then hurried along the wall, heading toward the tree-lined drive that emptied onto Rue Florian. I slipped through the iron gate, grateful that Mabel Cornfeld had oiled it just last week. No screeching metal broadcast my departure.

Outside the convent's wall, the dark pressed in. Walking alone down the deserted streets of El Biar, I made my way toward the office. The streetcars were hulking shadows on the tracks, their service shut down at eighteen hundred hours. A pair of drunk French sailors stumbled up the hill. They asked me for a date. I told them in icy tones that I was on my way to work. I was glad to have the knife tucked reassuringly into my stocking. Thankfully, the sailors moved on, cracking jokes about manly American women. I didn't mind the teasing—I preferred that to their continued attentions.

The Hotel Alexandra was three kilometers away. It would take about half an hour to get there. My knees ached. The closer I got to the hotel, the busier the streets became. I wasn't worried about being recognized. The blackout was in full effect, and there were too many soldiers and civilians milling about to pick me out.

When I reached Boulevard Gallieni, a donkey cart pulled up beside me. The driver, an Arab man wearing a striped jillaba robe, asked me in French if I needed a ride.

"Merci." I started for the back of the wagon, but the man stopped me.

"Sit with me, miss," he said in perfectly accented French. "No need to endure a bumpy ride with the tins."

"You are very kind." I bowed my thanks and climbed into the driver's seat. I smoothed my skirt over my aching knees and gripped the bench.

The cart moved at a surprisingly rapid clip, and less than ten minutes later, the man reigned his donkey to a halt at the St. George Hotel. The traffic cop watched me descend from the cart but didn't stop me when I thanked the driver and hurried across the street to the Hotel Alexandra.

I strode past the MP manning the front gate and ducked my head down as I made for the stairs.

As expected, the building was busy. Phones rang. Teletype machines hummed and clacked. Voices murmured. More than one department was running a full shift tonight. But when I got to our office, the door was closed. I rapped on the wood softly and leaned an ear against the door. I heard nothing, and no voice called out.

I turned the knob, creaked open the door, and slipped inside, closing the door behind me. The place was dark and empty, thank God.

I went straight for Ruth's desk and sat. I clicked on the desk lamp and surveyed the items laid out on the desktop.

But there were no orders on Ruth's desk. Corporal Pinski said that Sue was complaining about her workload, so she must have been shouldering the bulk of Ruth's work after I was transferred to temporary duty with Captain Devlin.

I went to Sue's desk, sifting through the paperwork carefully, looking for Special Order Forty-Nine.

Nothing.

Glancing at the office door, my heart firing away, I went to the last place I might find the order. The file cabinets along the back wall contained the enlisted 201 files, which contained communications and reports pertaining to each individual soldier, including orders, transfers, travel orders, and any disciplinary actions. Another file cabinet contained copies of all General Orders and Special Orders that were routinely batched and forwarded to the War Department for their records.

I pulled open the cabinet marked "201 Files" and found Private Wainwright's personnel file. I flipped open the folder and scanned through the documents within. Payroll, travel orders, his Soldier Qualification card, furlough requests.

The last sheet in the file was a copy of the Special Order Forty-Nine assigning him to the 63rd Signal Battalion in Algiers. This order matched the pristine carbon copy in Ruth's possession.

The Adjutant General fielded orders from the War Department and from the various commands in North Africa. Each day, his office sent over a master list of orders that we then typed up and distributed. I needed to see the master list. I had a sneaking suspicion, and I needed to confirm it or put it to rest.

I opened the file cabinet marked "Special Orders and Files." Rifling through the sheets of paper, I finally found what I was looking for: the Assignments List for the past week, when Private Wainwright was assigned to Algiers. It was several pages long, but I found his name on the second page.

Special Order Forty-Eight. The order stated that Private Thomas Wainwright was assigned to the 133rd Infantry, 2nd Battalion.

*The front.*

Private Wainwright's original order was to report to an infantry division.

I looked back at Special Order Forty-Nine. This was the same order reflected in the pristine carbon copy. *Private Thomas A. Wainwright, assigned to the 63rd Signal Bn, AFHQ.*

*Two orders.*

Two separate and quite different orders had been typed up for Private Thomas Wainwright.

It wasn't unusual for men to be moved from one company to another at the front, but I had never seen a soldier moved *from* an infantry division to the rear. Usually, the orders moved men from rear-echelon assignments to frontline companies, not the other way around.

I laid the carbon order beside the original. Both were dated February 12, 1943. They'd both been typed on the same day. The day of the dance. The day Ruth Wentz lost her life.

I remembered Tommy's joke about getting me to assign him to headquarters. Had he already asked someone else in the Adjutant General's office to get him reassigned? It appeared so. And someone must have taken him up on it. The order filed assigned him to Allied Force Headquarters. The Assignments List was the only proof he'd ever been assigned to a combat unit.

But who would ever think to look?

*Ruth.*

Auxiliary Ruth Wentz, the company's most dedicated soldier. The woman who followed regulations to a tee. She must have discovered the discrepancy. Did she go to Sergeant Gilmore to clarify the order?

No.

Going to Sergeant Gilmore would break chain of command.

Nobody else in the office cared about such things, but Ruth cared. She would have gone to her superior. She would have gone to—

"Hello, Dottie."

# Chapter 36

"I don't suppose I can persuade you to be reasonable?"

I stood up, my chair scraping against the floor, breaking the silence. I glanced at the closed office door. For the first time, I wished Sergeant Gilmore would burst out of his office in his usual rage.

But I was alone.

Corporal Pinski chuckled. "I didn't think so. All you WAACs are so goddamned patriotic. Some of us don't have that luxury. Some of us are going to get sent to the front because of you."

Corporal Pinski and Tommy Wainwright. Why would Pinski reassign Tommy? I hadn't seen any indication they'd known each other before the war. I remembered Pinski sending money to his mother at the Red Cross Club. And Tommy, flushed with triumph at being assigned to AFHQ.

An icy cold sweat broke out across my back. My heart pounded so hard that his words sounded distant.

*Cornered.*

My mind raced. I struggled to slow my breathing and sought out his face in the dark. He was all shadow. "You reassigned Tommy Wainwright to HQ."

"Tommy was reassigned, yes."

"You transferred Private Wainwright from a combat unit to Allied Force Headquarters. But why? Did you pull strings for him?"

Corporal Pinski threw back his head and laughed. "Oh, Dottie. That's just sad. I thought you might be different, but you really are just another gullible female. I didn't have to pull strings, as you put it. I just had to dangle the option and put a price tag on it."

"To save him?" Had Pinski transferred Private Wainwright because he was young? Were they friends?

"I don't give a shit where Tommy waits out the war. Do you have any idea what it's like to have your life ripped out from under your feet? To have your life torn apart by the government?"

I knew all too well what it was like to have my life torn apart, but I wasn't going to share that with Corporal Pinski.

"You don't get it, do you? Of course you don't. You were stupid enough to volunteer for this sideshow. They draft me into the Army, pay me half of my salary, and don't give a damn about the consequences."

That drew me up short. "You killed Ruth for money?"

"No." Corporal Pinski came into the weak light cast by Ruth's desk lamp. His eyes gleamed with a cold certainty I had never seen before. "No, I reassigned Tommy Wainwright for money."

I blinked. Suddenly it all made sense. Private Wainwright asking for a transfer, afraid to fight. Special Order Forty-Eight and Forty-Nine. The carbons in Ruth's utility bag. Corporal Pinski was selling orders. Offering cushy jobs at Allied Force Headquarters, far away from the fighting, to anyone who would pay. And Ruth had found him out.

"Plenty of guys will pay just about everything they have to stay away from the front. You girls are so eager to serve. To prove yourselves. I get it, I guess. But you don't actually have to risk anything, do you?"

"Ruth risked everything. You killed her because she found out you were selling orders."

"She was going to tell the brass." He sounded like a petulant child. "I knew you'd figure it out. You girls are too smart by half."

"How could you do it? You were always so good to us."

"What else was I supposed to do? It's not like I had a choice about it. The Army foisted you girls into our office, putting my job in jeopardy. Do you know how many meetings I had to have to prove to Sergeant Gilmore that he still needed me? He wanted to ship me off to the front the week you girls arrived. So I played nice. Seemed the best way to stay put and avoid transfer to a combat unit. I let Gilmore know I'd deal with the WAACs, and he was only too happy to agree. It let him off the hook."

"But you underestimated Ruth," I said, feeling some satisfaction that Ruth had seen through Pinski's veneer.

"I underestimated her curiosity. I saw her put those carbons aside. I had to do something. I did try to make her see sense. There are plenty of other men who can serve at the front. Why should she care?"

"But she did care. She knew General Eisenhower requested us because he's short on men, Corporal Pinski. Surely you know that." Ruth would never have ignored such a flagrant violation of Army regulations and articles of war. What Corporal Pinski had done was criminal. Selling orders, transferring men from the front to desk jobs behind the lines, risked the war effort.

"She made the same ridiculous argument. You girls really are full of self-importance. The Army wants you here to boost morale, nothing more. I told her she might as well make some cash before the Army sends you home. But she wouldn't listen. I just wanted her to listen. I don't like killing. I'm a pacifist, really. And I'm trying to save lives, Dottie. Not all men are cut out for combat."

"But, Corporal," I said, my mind racing. I had to find a way out of this office. Corporal Pinski was not of sound mind. "By reassigning these men, you're putting other men's lives at risk."

"No, I'm not. That doesn't track. The Army needs thousands of men. It's not going to affect the war effort if a couple get reassigned to HQ. They need them here anyway, to run this whole operation."

"That's not your decision to make. General Eisenhower—"

"General Eisenhower," Pinski snapped. "General Eisenhower sits comfortably in his villa or his plush apartment at the George, sending thousands of men to fight and face death."

"He's trying to win a war."

"Maybe if we were fighting the Japs, it would be different. The Japs actually did something to us. But the Germans? Why are we fighting Germans? I mean, you're working for the enemy, for Christ sakes! I'd think you of all people would understand."

I ignored the jab about my past. "I thought you wanted to serve at the front."

"Where did you get that idea? Do you really think anybody wants to fight and die, get slaughtered on the battlefield? For what?"

Red-hot anger coursed through me. "It's a sacrifice, yes. But it's the only way to defeat the Nazis."

"Do *you* want to fight? If they gave you a gun today, would you really use it? Why should we care about the damn Germans anyway? What difference does it make to me—to you even—if they occupy all of Europe? We shouldn't even be here in the first place."

"How can you say that? Germans are killing our soldiers faster than we can replace them."

"Let me ask you this, Dottie. What difference is one soldier going to make? Or five soldiers? You've seen the scale of this thing. Thousands of boys are going to the front. Thousands will die. It's not going to change anything to keep a few of the boys safe behind the lines. You're a smart girl. Do the math."

Corporal Pinski had moved closer. My heart hammered rabbit fast.

I needed to calm down.

I needed to make a plan.

I needed to get out of this room.

"How are you any different, Dottie?"

I jerked my gaze to his. "I'm not a killer, for starters."

Corporal Pinski smiled and for a moment he looked like the old Pinski, like the man I thought I'd known. For the second time in my life, I felt tricked by a man. I'd trusted Pinski. He'd used the same kind of charm my husband had used to woo me all those years ago. Corporal Pinski wasn't handsome, and he didn't have a movie-star smile like Konrad, but he had projected a gentle smile and a steady courtesy to the WAACs. We'd all thought he was on our side. But it had all been a lie. Corporal Pinski wasn't a good man looking out for the WAACs. He was a selfish killer looking out for himself.

"What do you know? You're just a girl looking for adventure. A bored, lonely woman with nothing better to do."

"No. I'm a woman serving my country, because I believe in it."

"Well, you're a fool." Corporal Pinski walked toward the outer door. "I'm sorry, Dottie. I don't want to have to do this. I've always liked you. It would've been easier if I'd been able to shoot you."

"The Casbah? That was you?"

Corporal Pinski shrugged. "It was a worth a try. I was outside for a smoke and saw the two of you. I'm not very skilled with guns. I wish I'd brought it here tonight, but I didn't expect to see you. I figured that MP would have you locked up for espionage."

"So you weren't after Mary?"

"Of course not. She's just a child. She doesn't really belong here. I'm sure you'd agree. They'll probably send the WAACs home after this. You gals are dropping like flies." He chuckled to himself.

My stomach roiled with those flippant words.

Pinski leaned over, yanked at the thick black telephone wire and pulled it free from the wall. When he straightened, I watched him pull the phone cord tight between his fists. "I think I'm going to have to make this one look like a rape. I'm sorry about that too."

# Chapter 37

"I don't think anyone will care too much. You're a suspected German spy. The Army will probably be glad to be rid of you, if you want to know the truth."

My legs felt like powdered eggs. The filing cabinet handles dug into my back. I'd retreated as far as I could without melting into the wall. I held the carbon in my hands. I couldn't let it go. It was the only evidence I had that proved Corporal Pinski's crimes.

The knife in my stocking burned against my skin. Could I pull the knife fast enough? Corporal Pinski was a big man, but I didn't believe he'd just stand there and watch me draw a weapon. I needed to think. I needed a plan, and fast.

Corporal Pinski stood before me, gripping the telephone cord, studying me as if seeking the best angle to strangle me to death.

I needed time. I had to stall him.

"You poisoned Sue. Was she planning to report you?"

Corporal Pinski's chin snapped up. "Nope. I feel bad about Sue. We're a lot alike. She figured it out, is what happened. Way faster than you did."

"She saw you go up the stairs."

"How do you know that? Doesn't matter, I guess. But yeah, she saw me. She tried to blackmail me to keep quiet. Which was clever. I'll give her that. She was a spitfire, but I can't afford that, Dottie."

"Why? What do you need so much money for?" It was the only question that came to mind. I wondered if Kirksey was on her way with Captain Devlin. Or maybe Wanda Wooten had discovered my absence and sent the MPs? Surely someone knew by now that I was missing. I'd left Kirksey a note, telling her I was going to the office. *Please, God, let her get here in time.*

"Before I got drafted, I worked as a clerk at a bank. Did I ever tell you that?"

"No, you didn't. Sounds like a good job."

Corporal Pinski dropped his hands, letting one end of the telephone wire drop. "It was! It was a great job. Just what we needed."

"We?" I swallowed hard and forced a smile that I hoped looked reassuring and not terrified.

"My mother. She got polio when I was in high school. I had to take care of her, Dottie. And to take care of a patient with polio—well, that costs a lot of money. The job paid for my mother's medical bills, and I was able to care for her. My boss was great. He let me off work whenever I needed. I was able to hire a nurse for her while I was at the office. The Army took all that away from us."

"I'm so sorry," I said, and I meant it.

Corporal Pinski sniffed. "You don't have to be sorry. The Army should be sorry. I did everything I could to get them to understand I couldn't leave my mother alone. But did they care? Hell no. If I don't send a hundred twenty dollars to mother, she's going to be left alone. She'll die. How come nobody cares about that?"

"I care. I'm really sorry, Pinski. That's not fair."

"Damn right, it's not fair." Corporal Pinski snapped the telephone cord in the air like a whip. "They draft me into the Army. They pay me half the salary I was getting at the accounting office.

*Half*, Dottie. I had to leave Mother alone, with no way to pay for the care she needs. What was I supposed to do?"

"You should have asked me, Corporal."

"What?"

"I would have helped you. Ruth would have helped. Kirksey. We all would have helped you."

"Oh, sure you would. But for how long?" Pinski sneered. "Forever?"

"Maybe. For the duration, anyway."

"What, you have money?"

"I have some."

"Wow, I never would have pegged you for a socialite."

"I worked hard for my money. I worked for Baker Hughes."

"Howard Hughes's company?"

I nodded, eyeing the door.

"Well, I'll be."

"I saved quite a bit. I would have given it to you, Corporal. I wouldn't even have thought twice about it."

"Bullshit."

"I mean it." And I did. If Corporal Pinski had told the girls about his predicament, I had no doubt Ruth and Kirksey would have helped out. Mary might have as well. But he'd never given us a chance.

"Well, I guess we'll never know, will we?" Pinski dropped the cord and looked furtively around the office. He went over to Ruth's desk and lifted the heavy metal typewriter, hefting it in his hands to test the weight. "I think this will be the quickest way. Sorry. I would strangle you, but I don't think I have the stomach for it. This will be quicker, I think."

Sweat coated my upper lip. My mind whirled. I had to think fast. I had to find a way out of this. Kirksey wasn't coming. Captain Devlin wasn't coming. I had to find a way to get myself out of this alive.

"Gotta be quick, gotta be quick," Pinski muttered to himself. He lifted the typewriter chest high, grunting with the effort. "Oh yeah, this will do it. It'll be quick, Dottie. Just sit still, and I'll hit you as hard as I can."

"Corporal, please, let's just talk about this." I dropped the carbon paper to the floor. I didn't want to crumple it up and put it in my pocket. It might become illegible. The floor seemed the safest place for the time being.

Pinski hefted the typewriter onto his right shoulder.

Maybe I could get him to miss. It might be my only chance. Physical training exercises flickered through my mind. Could I use one of those techniques to slip past Pinski? I'd have to be fast. Hopefully all the running, training, squats, and knee bends would power me through.

*Please legs, don't fail me now.*

*Get a grip, Dottie. You can do this. You can be strong. Save yourself. Nobody is coming to save you. You must save yourself.*

Corporal Pinski lifted the typewriter over his head.

Mustering every ounce of courage I'd tried to build since joining the Army, I thrust my right leg forward and fell to the ground, landing on the outside of my right knee and thigh to break the fall. Just like the Army taught me. I caught the rest of my weight on my hands and quickly rolled away from the file cabinet.

The typewriter crashed onto the wood file cabinet.

I fumbled for the knife in my stocking, struggling to get my skirt up high enough to reach the hilt.

Corporal Pinski roared in frustration.

Finally, I pulled the knife free.

Pinski bent over the typewriter, cursing. He struggled to get his hands around the chunky metal base again.

I swung my arm around and stabbed Corporal Pinski in the calf. A feeling of triumph rushed through me. For the first time in my life, I reveled in the attack. In the violence of it. And it frightened me. A gush of warm blood flowed over my hand.

Corporal Pinski shouted out in pain, shifted his feet, still struggling to lift the typewriter. To my utter shock, he managed to heave the thing to his shoulder again. He turned, his eyes blazing with hate and fury.

Before he had time to lift the typewriter and bring it down on my head, I sliced across the back of his ankle, hoping to hit the Achilles.

Pinski squealed like a hog. He threw the typewriter, his face twisted almost beyond recognition. I swung my feet wildly, spinning out of the way. The typewriter crashed down, pinning my right wrist. Pain shot up my arm. It felt like a grenade had gone off in my hand.

Corporal Pinski, hands on his knees, blood flowing from his legs, panted hard.

The knife gleamed in the lamplight. I grabbed for it with my left hand.

Pinski fell to one knee and reached for the blade. "Give it here, you bitch!"

Ignoring the pain in my wrist, I struggled to my knees and stabbed the knife in a quick jab, hitting Pinski in the abdomen. He blinked at me, surprise lighting his eyes.

He lunged for me one last time, but his strength failed him. He went down.

Panting heavily, right arm throbbing, I dropped the knife and lifted the typewriter off my injured hand. My physical training had not failed me. I still had the strength to move it, even with one hand. Or maybe it was the adrenaline. The power coursing through my body, equally thrilling and frightening.

I struggled to my feet, cradling my right hand. Tears flowed down my cheeks, but they were tears of anger.

Corporal Pinski stirred.

Ignoring the pain, I grabbed the nearest desk chair and brought it down on Corporal Pinski's head, letting out a long howl of pain, frustration, and fury.

# Chapter 38

Fighting against the throbbing building in my wrist, I used the telephone cord Corporal Pinski had pulled out of the wall to tie his hands behind his back.

My wrist thrummed, each movement an agony, but I couldn't risk him waking unrestrained. If I didn't subdue him now, he would easily overpower me, and God only knew what he'd try next. The fury that had fueled my fight had vanished like mortar smoke. My muscles trembled, and I knew I had only minutes before my body gave out on me.

Blood pooled underneath Corporal Pinski's prone body. He might die before help arrived, but I couldn't worry about that. Just staying upright was a struggle. My head swam, and I leaned against the desk, taking in deep breaths, forcing back the black spots popping up in my peripheral vision.

Footsteps pounded outside in the hall.

"Lincoln!"

My shoulders sagged with relief. He was here. Kirksey must have found the note and notified Captain Devlin.

The doorknob rattled. Fists pounded on the door. "Lincoln, are you all right?"

A single shot rang out and the office door burst open. Captain Devlin spilled into the room just as I pulled the cord with all my might, my knee on Pinski's lower back to gain some leverage.

"My God, Lincoln."

Kirksey entered, followed by Private Venturi and the guard from the gate.

"I'll be jiggered," Private Venturi said in his usual droll way. "What in creation is going on here?"

"Don't just stand there, Venturi," Captain Devlin barked. "Cuff him."

I swayed, the pain in my wrist making me dizzy.

Kirksey rushed to me. "Oh my God, Dottie. Are you okay? Let's sit you down." She led me to a nearby chair and took my hands to lower me to a seated position.

I sucked in a sharp breath.

Kirksey looked down at my hands hanging loosely in my lap. "Your wrist. Is it broken?"

I tried to smile, but thought it probably looked more like a grimace. "I think it might be."

"Oh, Dottie. We need to get you over to the clinic."

Devlin stood looking around the office. "You did this? You're here alone?"

"He was going to kill me. He said he was going to make it look like a rape." My voice broke on the last word, and I felt shame engulf me. I wanted so much to be strong. "I had Rivera's knife."

"My God, Rivera was right." Captain Devlin said, surveying the room. The typewriter on the floor. The cut telephone cord. The file cabinet with a gaping wound gouged into the top drawer. "Thank God you were armed."

"Yes."

Private Venturi lifted Corporal Pinski to his feet by the telephone cord, jerking Pinski out of his stupor. Pinski screamed, and if not for Venturi's strong arm, he would have crumpled back to the floor. As it was, Pinski lifted his injured leg and reached for the nearest chair to balance himself. Tears trailed down his cheeks. Despite all he'd done, I felt some sympathy for his pain.

"Suck it up, soldier," Venturi admonished. "Act like a man, for cripes sake."

"You bitch!" Corporal Pinski squealed, saliva spraying from his mouth. "You ruined everything."

"Damn, you're a crybaby," Venturi said, fairly dragging Pinski toward the office door.

"What's gonna happen to my mother now, you bitch?" Corporal Pinski gave a sharp cry, and I thought I heard the sound of bone crunching.

"Will you look at that, Corporal? Gotta watch out for those walls, buddy." We all heard Private Venturi grunt and his footsteps moving at a fast clip down the stairs. I suspected Corporal Pinski might take a tumble down those stairs before they were through. I hoped he made it back to the station in one piece. He needed to pay for his crimes.

"Don't worry about it, Lincoln," Captain Devlin said, quirking up one side of his mouth. "Private Venturi is a professional. He'll make sure our suspect gets safely back to the stockade."

"Good," I said, leaning back on the desk, cradling my injured hand.

"So that guy killed Auxiliary Wentz? That's kind of hard to believe."

I nodded. Bad idea. Nodding made my head swim faster. "It's kind of a long story." I lifted my chin toward the file cabinet. "On the floor over there, you'll find the proof of what Pinski was doing. His signature is on them. They might be a little smudged," I said apologetically.

Captain Devlin reached down and retrieved the single sheet of carbon paper from the floor. It was such a flimsy thing, but I knew it was the only proof we had of Corporal Pinski's crimes.

"He was selling orders, Captain. Taking bribes to transfer men from combat units to desk jobs here at Allied Force Headquarters."

"My God." Captain Devlin studied the sheet of carbon paper. "Private Tommy Wainwright."

I nodded, swallowing the pain that radiated up my arm. My stomach rocked like a ship at sea. "Ruth found out about it. She was always such a stickler for the rules. Corporal Pinski was signing orders, falsifying Sergeant Gilmore's signature. Ruth noticed. I don't know if any other soldier would've thought twice about it, but Ruth always followed regulations so carefully. She wouldn't have accepted shortcuts."

"There's enough here," Devlin said, holding a sheet of carbon up to the light. "It should be pretty easy to track down this Private Wainwright. Find out what his original orders were."

"The master copy is on top of the file cabinet." I clutched at the desk I was leaning on, steadying myself. The room tilted to one side, then another. "He was slated for transfer to the 133rd Infantry."

Captain Devlin frowned and moved to my side. "There's a blanket in my jeep, Auxiliary Kirksey. Would you get it for me? I don't want Auxiliary Lincoln here to go into shock."

Kirksey's eyes snapped to me, concern furrowing her brow. "Of course. Yes, sir." Kirksey walked out, leaving us alone.

Captain Devlin put his arm around me. "You look like you're about to fall over, Lincoln."

"Yes." Physically, I was a spent shell. I'd solved Ruth's murder, but instead of feeling satisfied with the result, I felt angry and depressed. Corporal Pinski had killed Ruth for money. Money I would have gladly given him if he'd only asked. It seemed like such a senseless crime. But then I supposed most crimes felt that way. Ruth had been killed for being a good soldier, the one thing in the world she really cared about. I supposed there was some comfort in that thought.

Utterly exhausted and pulsing with pain, I fell against Captain Devlin and let it all go. I cried so hard, I lost my breath. For the first time since joining the Army, I allowed my feelings to overcome me.

Captain Devlin held me. He let me cry without a single word or joke. When I was done, he handed me an olive green, Army-issue handkerchief. I wiped my eyes.

"I'm sorry. You must think I'm just another damsel in distress. A worthless, weak girl who doesn't belong in this man's Army."

"Are you kidding? It's not weakness, Dottie, what's happening to you. The tears are a release of tension more than anything. The aftereffects of an adrenaline rush, like any good soldier after combat."

I coughed out a laugh.

"No one is going to think of you, or any other WAAC in your outfit, as a damsel in distress after this. You hogtied him, for Christ's sake."

"Well, I am from Texas."

"Damn right you are. And what with your French and your German. And your fancy *merci* and *monsieur*? You're a lot of things, Lincoln. But weak isn't one of them."

"People can be more than one thing. I guess Corporal Pinski was more than one thing."

"He was a killer."

"He was also afraid."

"And a coward," Devlin added, but there was no venom in the words.

"Yes. I'm suppose he was. A brave man would have found another way. He told himself he was saving Private Wainwright. Maybe he was also afraid to fight. Maybe he tried to save those he believed were like him, the ones who couldn't fight."

"The ones that *wouldn't* fight, Lincoln. We can all fight. From the looks of this office, you fought like hell, and you're just a dame."

"I'm a soldier—"

"I know, I know. Just trying to keep you awake, soldier."

He smiled down at me, and for the first time in a long time, I felt a connection. Pushing away the unwelcome feeling, I rubbed at my scar, reminding myself of the dangers down that particular road. "Do you think we'll be able to stay? The WAACs?"

"Of course you'll stay. I'm going to talk to Cantry. Let him know what happened here. He'll talk to General Eisenhower. Nobody can deny you girls are serving a vital service for the war effort. Especially after this. Don't worry about all that now. What you need to do now is get back to barracks and get some much-needed rest."

"Captain," Kirksey said, returning with a wool, Army-issue blanket. "She needs medical attention, sir."

"Right. Of course."

But I didn't catch those last words. Blackness folded in on me. Pain jogged up and down my arm. I let the blackness come, falling willingly into Captain Devlin's open arms.

# CHAPTER 39

I woke up in the Church Villa hospital.

My tongue felt like a dried-up old fig. I blinked at the bright light streaming in from the window across the room. My eyeballs felt like they were retreating into my brain, like a mole crawling into a darkened burrow.

Captain Devlin stood leaning against the wall, an unlit cigarette hanging out of his mouth. He looked down, as if sensing my eyes on him, pulled the Lucky out of his mouth, and tucked it into his front pocket. "You're up. Good." He smiled, and I thought I saw relief in his eyes. "How are you feeling?"

"Groggy."

Devlin nodded. "The doc gave you a syrette."

"Morphine? Why?"

"Your wrist. He had to set it."

I looked down and saw my arm in a bulky plaster cast. "Oh, wonderful."

Devlin laughed. "He had to set the bones. Lots of bones in the wrist apparently. It was doc's first time giving a female soldier an ampule of morphine. I think he was pretty excited. He'll be bragging about it all over HQ."

I laughed, then coughed against the rawness in my throat. "Can I get a drink of water?"

Captain Devlin held a paper cup to my lips. I lifted my uninjured arm to take it, but he swatted it away. I took a swallow, then leaned back. "Thank you."

"You're welcome. Do you feel up to talking?"

"About what?"

"About what happened. About how you figured out Corporal Pinski was selling fake orders."

"Didn't I tell you? Is he okay?"

"He'll be walking with a limp for what's left of his life. Which won't be long, I'm guessing."

I closed my eyes against a wave of nausea. I wondered if it was the morphine. "Will they hang him?"

"I doubt it. The Army doesn't need a scandal, and it definitely doesn't want the American public to know that there are soldiers looking for a way out of combat. The War Department needs civilians to believe in this war, and that starts with believing in our soldiers. I'm guessing Corporal Pinski will find himself the head of a patrol in every battle from now until a German sniper picks him off."

"His poor mother." I licked my lips and took another sip of water.

"You did a good thing, Dottie. Do you want to tell me what happened?"

I recounted my discovery of the carbons in Ruth's utility bag and what happened when I got to the office. "At first I didn't know what it meant, but then I saw they were all signed by Corporal Pinski. I saw him at the Red Cross Club with Tommy Wainwright. That's where he must have been making contact with GIs."

"Cheese and crackers. He's not talking. I think he was hoping you would die. I told him no chance you were going to die with a broken wrist."

"It'll take more than that to kill me."

Devlin laughed.

"I guess Ruth's family won't get any death benefits."

"No, I guess not. Although I wonder if this will change things. You girls are at risk here in a combat theater. The WAACs deserve the same benefits as every other soldier stationed in Algiers, such as they are."

"Agreed," I said, shifting to sit up. Captain Devlin readjusted my pillow to rest vertically. "It's not fair. About Ruth. She died for this war."

"No, it's not. But I'll write to her family and offer my condolences."

"She should have had a full military funeral. She gave her life for her country. What she did, she helped the war effort more than any woman I know. God knows how many men Pinski would have been able to keep from the front if he'd continued unchecked. She stopped him. And nobody will know about it."

"We know, Lincoln. The Army will know. And the country will be grateful."

"Will they? I've never heard you sounding so optimistic before, Captain Devlin."

Devlin shrugged. "War changes a man."

"Yes. Yes, it does."

He shifted his feet. "I don't know if you're interested in this, Lincoln, but I spoke to Cantry about having you transferred to my office. Permanently."

"As an investigator?"

"No." Captain Devlin honked a laugh. "Army won't allow that. But I could use a secretary."

I tried to hide my disappointment.

"That's what I'd have to call it. Officially you'd be my secretary. But unofficially . . ."

"Unofficially?"

"Well, you'd still have to do the typing, but you'd also have to help me with investigations."

I looked down at my arm encased in plaster of Paris. "I don't think I'll be able to type for a few weeks."

"That's okay. Venturi can take up the slack until you're better. I need your eyes and ears on the job, Lincoln. And your mind."

"I bet Venturi would love that."

"He'd get used to it. I did."

"Fitzy won't be pleased either."

Devlin cracked a smile. "No, I don't imagine she will be. But will you be pleased? Would you like to continue working this part of the war? Do you want to come over to the silly side of the war?"

"You don't really believe that, Captain."

"I'm afraid most of it *is* silly, Lincoln. We spend as much time directing traffic and scooping up drunks as we do anything else. This murder was unusual. And the Army still won't allow women. So officially you'll be my secretary."

"Well, I have experience there. But that would be just on paper?" I left the question hanging in the air between us.

Devlin met my gaze. No trace of a smile. "It is."

"Then I accept. Thank you."

"It'll be good to have someone who speaks French here in Algiers. And it looks like we're staying for the time being. But someday we'll need your German language abilities when we march into Berlin."

"Yes," I said, my heartbeat quickening at the prospect. "Yes, you will."

Captain Devlin glanced at the doorway and lowered his voice. "I have something for you." He reached into his inside pocket and pulled out a crumpled letter.

My breath caught in my throat. "My letter."

He pulled out the two sheets of paper inside. He handed me the drawing, then scanned the words on the second page. For a moment, I thought perhaps the captain had been holding out on me and could read German, because he scanned the lines as if they made sense to him. "What does it say?" he asked without looking up.

I held out my still-working hand. I hoped the longing didn't show on my face, but I wanted the letter back. It felt wrong to see it in someone else's hands. The letter was mine. I had earned that letter. I'd paid for it with my own foolishness and naivete. The piece of paper with Konrad's sure and confident hand was proof of my stupidity, and I clung to it as a reminder to be wary. Wary of people. Wary of trusting too much. To trust was to lose everything. The letter was my constant reminder that I must always be on my guard. Corporal Pinski had only reinforced that belief. Anyone could turn on me at any time.

Captain Devlin handed over the letter, and I smoothed it against the hospital sheets. Tears stung my eyes as I looked down at my husband's words. The man I'd once trusted. The man I'd once loved. I cleared my throat and read the words to Captain Devlin.

*Dear Dorothea,*

*I hope this letter finds you well. Sadie and I have arrived! I know you will understand, once you give it some serious thought, my darling. I simply could not miss this glorious time in our nation's history. To be German and to miss such glory—well, it is unthinkable. We have received such a welcome as you cannot imagine, and I am certain to achieve great heights in this regeneration. Our darling girl will be a part of it all. Though you are not Volksdeutscher, you are her mother and will always have a place with us. We await your imminent arrival when circumstances allow. Despite your fears, I know you will come to the correct conclusion and join us as soon as you are able.*

*With love and affection, Heil Hitler, Konrad von Raven*

"Jesus." Captain Devlin rubbed at his chin. "He took her without telling you?"

I nodded.

"Is that how you got that scar?"

I shifted my position, wincing at the pain in my wrist.

"Never mind," Captain Devlin said. "That's none of my business."

I didn't tell him Konrad left me in a pool of my own blood. It seemed I didn't have to.

"How old was she?"

"Three."

"My god. You haven't seen or heard from your daughter in two years?"

"She'll be five now. Almost six."

"I'm so sorry, Lincoln."

"I can't divorce him. The law won't approve a divorce without his signature. By the time I received this letter and knew where they were, the Japanese had bombed Pearl Harbor, and we were at war."

"So you joined up, hoping to get to Germany?"

"No. I joined up to win it. The sooner we win, the sooner Germany is defeated. Then maybe I can get to this town, Minden, and find Sadie."

"Yeah, about that. I have a friend over in Recon. I asked him to check for me. There's no record of any bombs, British or American, being dropped on that town or anywhere near there. Yet."

"Minden? How did you know?"

Devlin shrugged, looking embarrassed. "I may not speak German, but I can read a postmark. I'm not completely thick, you know."

I swallowed back tears. "Thank you, Captain Devlin. That means more than I can say."

"No big deal. I need you focused."

"You need me?" I teased, wiping away tears. I would think about Sadie later. I would imagine my beautiful girl playing in a green field in Germany. But if I thought about it now, I'd break down, and I wanted to be strong. It wouldn't do to fall apart every time I was in Captain Devlin's presence. My new boss. I would be working for the Military Police. I would miss the Adjutant General's office, but with Ruth gone, I welcomed the change. Maybe I'd be able to contribute more directly to the war effort in the MPs, despite Captain Devlin's jokes about the silly side of the war.

"Hell, Lincoln, you know I need you. You're observant. You're smart. And you're tough to beat in a fight. Nobody could argue that after what happened to Pinski. I couldn't ask for a better sergeant. Did I mention that the transfer comes with a promotion? Fancy being a Junior Leader or whatever the WAACs call it?"

"I should hope so, sir. Working for you will be a hell of a lot more difficult than typing orders in the Adjutant General's office."

"Yes, it will, Lincoln. Yes, it will."

I looked around the ward. There were no other patients in the room. "Is Sue awake?"

"She is. She'll be sent home as soon as she's well enough."

"Will she face charges?"

"No. The Army decided it wouldn't be worth the public relations nightmare to prosecute a WAAC. Turns out they need you girls. Can't run a war without you."

"What about Captain Haywynn?"

Devlin shrugged. "That's out of our jurisdiction. The British will handle it however they see fit, I guess."

I wondered if Mary had told Captain Haywynn about her possible pregnancy yet.

"I'm guessing the Brits will keep him on. The battle in Kasserine was an utter defeat, though we're not supposed to say it.

The Allies can't afford to lose too many people. The Army needs WAACs now more than ever. You saved the Army's ass. That's for sure."

"How do you figure that?"

"They need men at the front."

"Right. So I just made sure that happens."

"It's going to happen anyway, Lincoln. Men are going to die. Hell, *we* might die. But it's not up to us. And I think we do have to defeat the Axis, right?"

"We do."

"Well, that makes you just like every other volunteer."

"Like you?"

"Maybe."

That was the best I was going to get at the moment. It might have been the morphine or the lack of food, but I had one more question. "Do you think maybe one day, when the Army's ready, I could become a military police officer?"

Captain Devlin cocked his head. "It could happen. Honestly, it probably will. This war's gonna change things."

"Hopefully for the better," I said, almost to myself.

But Devlin heard. "I'll drink to that. Speaking of drinking . . ." Captain Devlin reached under the bed and pulled out a WAAC utility bag.

"New briefcase, Captain?"

Devlin grinned. He was handsome when he smiled. I had no right to notice this, but I couldn't help it.

His eyes danced. "This is your utility bag, Lincoln. Doc Edwards returned it."

I'd never seen Captain Devlin so cheerful without a trace of sarcasm or irritation in his face. I looked away, embarrassed by my sudden attraction to him. He was my boss now. Feelings of attraction were out of bounds, even if I weren't a married woman.

"Oh, you're gonna want to see this, Lincoln," he admonished.

When I turned back to him, chin raised, shrugging off my schoolgirl flutterings, and saw what he held in his hands, Captain Devlin went from handsome to breathtakingly attractive. In his hands he held a single glass bottle of Coca-Cola.

"Captain! Where on earth did you get that?"

Devlin grinned and handed me the bottle. It was warm, but I didn't care. "An AAF buddy of mine nabbed one in Casablanca. When General Eisenhower went to the conference to meet Churchill, they had them shipped in, and my buddy was able to find one for me."

I blinked, fearing more tears. "It must have cost a fortune."

Devlin waved a hand. "Naw, he owed me. Do you want it now?"

Swallowing back a lump in my throat, I nodded. "Let's share."

Captain Devlin reached into his pocket and pulled out a bottle opener. The pop and fizz was like coming home. I raised the bottle. "To Ruth," I said, "and to us, the Military Police."

Devlin cracked a smile, blue eyes dancing. "To the silly side of the war."

# Epilogue

The wind came in off the sea, whipping my skirt around my legs and threatening to take my cap sailing over the terraces of Algiers. Kirksey stood beside me. The rest of the women of the 22nd Post Headquarters Company lined up on the rooftop of the St. George Hotel in marching formation behind us.

First Officer Fitzgerald was there. She'd ordered every woman in the company to attend the ceremony.

The general was shorter than I'd expected. I'd never met him before, though I'd seen him around the St. George Hotel. And of course I'd caught a glimpse of him on our trip to Constantine.

"Auxiliary Lincoln," General Eisenhower called.

When I stepped forward, he flashed his famous grin. I reciprocated without even thinking about it. I could see why the men loved him.

First Officer Fitzgerald read from a sheet of onionskin. "Attention, company. I present this award, the Soldier's Medal, to Auxiliary Lincoln for service beyond ordinary duty. Auxiliary Lincoln's dedication and fearlessness in uncovering dereliction of duty in her section should be an example to you all of what it means to be a soldier in the Women's Army Auxiliary Corps. Her actions, in keeping with the finest military traditions, reflect great credit on herself, her company, and the United States Army."

General Eisenhower pinned the medal to my lapel and flashed another grin. He leaned close. "Good work, Auxiliary Lincoln. Your country owes you a debt of gratitude for ensuring we have the soldiers in the field that we need. Can't fight a war without soldiers."

"No, sir," I replied, my voice louder than I'd anticipated. I glanced down at the starburst medal with a dark red ribbon, hanging on my chest.

He shook my hand and saluted. I returned the salute. I'd never felt prouder in my life. I thought of Ruth and felt a pang of sadness. Ruth was the real hero. She was the one who'd sniffed out Corporal Pinski's crime. She'd lost her life, but I had done my best to give Ruth justice. I would keep fighting.

The United States Army were beaten down after the "disaster in the desert." That's what the Brits were calling it. American forces had been beaten and bruised by the crack German troops at Kasserine Pass, but they weren't going to give up. Ruth and the men who'd lost their lives to this war would only truly be honored when victory was declared.

I suspected that this little ceremony was meant as a morale booster. But I was happy to do my duty as an American soldier. I'd joined the Army to help in any way I could, and I had found something like a family.

Kirksey smiled up at me. I smiled back. I'd found a place where people accepted me. I had a new job in a new career field that felt right. I couldn't wait to get started. The cast would come off in a couple of weeks, but Devlin wanted me to start right away. And I was ready to go.

I gazed out at the Mediterranean Sea below. Across the water, over the hills of Italy and into the Alps of Austria, north to a small town in Germany somewhere near the Dutch border was Sadie. All I had to do was fight. Win the war.

And bring my darling daughter home.

# AUTHOR'S NOTES

I based the Double Deuces on the 149th Post Headquarters Company. These brave women volunteered to serve overseas despite being denied full military protections at the time.

The roughly one hundred and fifty women who served in North Africa with the 149th worked as drivers, typists, translators, switchboard operators, and more. They worked in almost all major sections of Allied Force Headquarters and were an integral part of the successful North African campaign. When they first arrived in late January 1943, there was much skepticism and criticism of the WAACs. Many Americans believed a woman's place was at home. But throughout the campaign, they proved themselves to be capable soldiers, and as the war progressed, the demand for women soldiers only grew.

It would be several months before the Women's Army Auxiliary Corps became the Women's Army Corps, transitioning from an auxiliary organization to a full-fledged part of the United States Army. During their first six months of service in Algiers, the 149th Post HQ Co. did not operate under regular army command structure. They were outside of it. Since the 149th was the first company posted to a combat theater, the commanding officers often had no official army regulations to follow, and so they were left to create their own rules and procedures. For example, if one of the women went AWOL, the army had no legal jurisdiction to do anything about it. Because of this unusual arrangement, some details in *Murder in the Ranks* might puzzle readers familiar with regular army command structure.

Dottie's squad B is reflective of the WAAC officers' attempts to organize women for specific tasks. Traditionally, squads are numbered and related to an enlisted man's job. He is assigned to a company and a squad within that company, related to the work it's doing.

This was not the case for the WAACs. They were attached, but not actual members, of that company.

WAAC squads were groups formed by the WAAC commanding officers to manage the unusual aspects of keeping an auxiliary force together and safe in a combat theater. Small squads were formed to ensure women returned safely back to barracks from dances, arrived to do Kitchen Police (KP) and Physical Training (PT), and for other situations. These squads were created, disbanded, and reassembled as needs arose. They were a form of organization created by the WAACs themselves, to self-govern their company. I chose to designate these squads with letters as opposed to the usual numbered system, to signal the difference between regular army and WAAC squads.

These women were pioneers. They paved the way for women to serve in all areas of the military. Sadly, for the most part, their stories have been forgotten. I hope Dottie's story will illuminate their sacrifices, courage, and the critical role women played in combat theaters during World War II.

# Acknowledgments

Most of the Allied Force Headquarters documents were destroyed immediately after the war. Research for this book required a lengthy treasure hunt for information on AFHQ and the Women's Army Auxiliary Corps. I would like to thank Alexandra Kolleda and Francoise Bonnell of the US Army Women's Museum for granting me access to their archives. I would also like to thank the staff at the Eisenhower Presidential Library. I am also grateful for the documents sent to me during the Covid-19 pandemic by the US and UK National Archives.

Thank you to my sister Leah for reading so many drafts of this book. Your feedback and support was invaluable. Thanks also to my sister Ginger for being my final beta reader and my most enthusiastic reader to date. Lance Charnes, thank you for your detailed critiques, support, and encouragement.

To my husband and children, all things are possible with you guys! You inspire me every day. Chloe, thank you for your secret notes. Collin, I love our history talks and the way neither of us ever gets bored. Bryan, none of this is possible without you and your unwavering support of my impossible dreams.